hashtag magic
Open Source

HASHTAG MAGIC SERIES

BLUE SCREEN OF DEATH
CONTROL ALT DELETE
WEB OF TROLLS
OPEN SOURCE
SELFIE SACRIFICE (2021)

Hashtag Magic
Open Source

BY

J. STEVEN YOUNG

Copyright © 2020 J. Steven Young

ISBN 13 paperback: 978-1-943924-48-6
ISBN 13 hardcover: 978-1-943924-49-3
ISBN 13 EPUB: 978-1-943924-50-9

All rights reserved. No part of this book may be reproduced or transmitted in any form or by any means, electronic or mechanical, including photocopying, recording, or by any information storage and retrieval system, without written permission from the author.

This is a work of fiction, any similarities to any persons or places, is limited to city, places, and neighborhood names. Any description or references to locations are entirely fictional in nature and not intended to represent truth.

Chapter 1	1
Chapter 2	15
Chapter 3	29
Chapter 4	43
Chapter 5	57
Chapter 6	71
Chapter 7	85
Chapter 8	97
Chapter 9	111
Chapter 10	127
Chapter 11	139
Chapter 12	151
Chapter 13	163
Chapter 14	177
Chapter 15	189
Chapter 16	201
Chapter 17	213
Chapter 18	225
Chapter 19	237
Chapter 20	249
Chapter 21	259
Chapter 22	271
Chapter 23	283
Chapter 24	295
Chapter 25	305
Chapter 26	317
Chapter 27	327
Chapter 28	337
Chapter 29	347
Chapter 30	359
Chapter 31	369

Chapter 32 379
Chapter 33 389
Chapter 34 399
Chapter 35 409
   Author 417

CHAPTER 1

Colby landed on his ass again. This was the third consecutive time he attempted opening a portal, expecting travel to Stonehenge. Gathering his wits and rubbing his backside, Colby reached out with his time and space magic to make another adjustment before typing in the hashtag spell. Perhaps the fourth time is the charm he must have thought as he prepared to yet again attempt transporting to Salisbury Plains. **#PortalToStonehenge.** He began to step toward the vortex when a hand on his arm stopped him.

"As much as I enjoy watching as your cocky little ass gets thrown into the wall," Shelly said, "I think I should clue you into the definition of insanity."

Colby was her brother and, until recently, the biggest thorn in Shelly's side. Over the past two years, however, their bond grew closer as their magic blossomed. They needed one another more than they once ever imagined.

Looking defeated by repeated failure, Colby relented and closed the portal that refused to transport him. He shuddered as the magic winked from existence as though it pulled more energy upon extinguishing. As Colby turned to the wall where his body left visible dents, he raised his device to cast a hashtag spell. **#RepairWall**. Colby shook again as this simple spell drew the requisite energy from his reserve.

Noticing and feeling his best friend Colby's exhaustion, Jasper moved to push Emassa into him. Jasper knew it was unnecessary to offer, seeing as how Colby could take what he needed at any time from all of his friends. Jasper knew his friend as he knew himself. Colby would not accept what wasn't openly offered unless absolutely necessary.

"I'll be fine, but thank you," Colby said. "It's just whatever has the portal at Stonehenge blocked, must have drained me more than I expected."

"It shouldn't have drained you at all, Colby." Nana's concern carried on the voice of Bellatrix. Though his grandmother had regained the knowledge and life of her true past selves, Nana remained as the predominant personality even when Bellatrix asserted herself. "From my recovered memories and knowing your connection to the Emassa, you should be a magical proxy, not the source."

Colby shook his head in agreement but held a trepidatious frown. "True, but something feels wonky, and I have the taste of a dirty penny on my tongue."

Deciding to refuel himself and fill the magical storehouse in his core, Colby reached out mentally for the Emassa. He found it a strain to grab hold. He frowned deeper and grabbed again, this time getting a firm connection and pulling hard. The power surged into him and knocked Colby on his ass. The link stayed open, however.

Shelly smirked yet helped Colby from the floor, again. "You really need to practice staying on your feet, little brother."

Dusting himself off, again, Colby stared at the swirling event horizon of his portal. It remained open, but he saw the difference.

"It's still open this time, but not by my doing."

"What's that supposed to mean?" Shelly asked.

Colby frowned as he approached. "It's my magic, but it's not."

"Again," Shelly huffed, "not very clear little brother."

Colby waved his hand around the perimeter, feeling the sparks that charged and crackled around his fingers, tasting the magical signature. His brow furrowed deeper at his confusion.

"This is my magical signature, but it's mixed wrong and feels old."

As he peered more in-depth still, a shadowed outline of a hooded figure took shape within the swirling mists. Glowing blue eyes began to shine brighter from beneath the hood, while the face remained obscured. Colby did not notice the blue mist-infused hand reaching toward his own while his eyes remained locked on the Druid's.

"You are not what I," the Druid started, "expected."

"Who are you?" Colby asked. "What do you want?" Colby could swear he saw a smile in those eyes.

The Druid did not respond until he saw Colby's attention begin to drift. "I am the future, at present, with a highly involved past."

"What the hell is that supposed to mean?"

The Druid continued to distract Colby's attention away from the spell, working its magic on the boy's hand. "That is to say, I have come a long journey to be where I am now. There is much work needed before I'm done, and then I will only just begin."

"Begin what? What has Rigel brought you here to do for him?"

Laughter. "Rigel? Why he believes he brought us here to destroy you."

Colby shivered, not at the words, but a feeling that swept over him. He did not notice the mark appear on his hand or the touch of magic, infusing it from the ghostly blue hand. It waved and floated above his outstretched arm, casting the spell-work instructed by the Druid.

"Are you here to use my magic, or harm me?" Colby asked.

"In a way."

Silence followed as Colby contemplated what next to say. What could he have done to this creature or person he did not know which. All he could make out was the blue, glowing eyes and bitter old taste of magic coming off the portal that he also realized was not of his own making. The Druid cast this portal somehow, using Colby's own magic to reverse the hashtag magic and make a one-way vortex through which the Druid now faced him.

This Druid was ancient it seemed, or at least came here from a long-ago time. The senses that existed beyond normal hearing, touch, sight, and scent were very acute for the magically endowed. Colby could feel more magic flowing off of this being, but could not sense intent. This fact told him there was something else going on besides what Rigel had planned. Colby did not pretend to know what Rigel and the Daphnes were trying to accomplish. Still, the magical senses he now muddled around his mind confused him. Then he felt it.

A burning itch drew his eyes to look at the now branded back of his hand. Just as he began to pull away, the shade's hand grasped his wrist and held firm while a final jolt of power tore through Colby.

A ribbon of magic ripped out of Colby's chest and flashed out into the vortex. Instantly he felt a nearly complete drain of his magic. It took several pounding heartbeats for Colby to realize that he could fight back if he could tap his friends for magic. Usually, he would ask permission as just taking magic powers seemed like an assault to Colby. But at this moment, Colby could not speak. He could only react.

Tugging on his magical bond, he reached out for as much Emassa as he could get to repel away from the vortex. It did not come. A trickle filtered into him, enough to slow the drain of his own magical core, but he couldn't reach his friends. The bond was gone.

"You'll have to learn to do things yourself, boy," The Druid laughed. Before he said another word, he felt the backlash as Colby broke free of the shade's grasp and away from the portal. **#Shield.**

A stream of hashtag magic emanated from Colby's watch as he cast a stored spell. How he managed it without touching the display, Colby didn't think about it. The spell did the trick and blasted Colby back to relative safety.

"Nice," The Druid complimented. "Keep that up, and there'll be hope for you yet."

"What do you want?" Shelly shouted. She rushed to Colby's side and helped him from the ground. "We'll come for you, whatever you are."

"No," laughed the Druid. "You aren't ready for that…yet."

With the wave of his hand, the Druid closed the portal and backed away. His robe fell back, exposing his pale-fleshed arm covered in tattoos.

"Did you see that?" Jasper said. "His arm was covered in runes."

The yard that once held only Colby and Shelly was full of his friends and family. They must have entered during the struggle, but Colby was too engaged to notice. He didn't sense them either, except Shelly.

"You mean like this," Shelly said, holding up Colby's hand. "What is this?"

Colby pulled his arm free and stared at the back of his hand. Burnt into his flesh was an intricate rune, unlike any he had ever seen. It was old and obscure. This Colby knew from the jagged line to the edges and hard, purposeful ways the paths intertwined. It was meant to sever something. As he looked around at his friends and searched for the magic bond he shared with them, he knew what the rune was for. It severed his link to his friends.

"It's a rune," Gary said.

"No, really?" Jasper said. "We can see that, shit for brains."

"It's a component to a splitting spell," Aria said. She held back from the rest but remained near enough to see the rune and recognize its use. "I used it once to split my Shi."

"What?" Fizzlewink said as he transformed from cat to little blue man. "Is that what it wanted, that thing in the vortex?"

"No," Colby admitted. "He severed my link to the others. I can no longer feel our connection." Colby spoke frankly and without emotion.

By now, the group had made its way into the house and into the living room. Colby sat back on a chair in the living room and pushed his hair back over his head.

"The Druid must want me to face him alone and weak."

"Who is this Druid, and what does he want with you?" Fizzlewink fussed over Colby and checked the rest of his exposed skin for more runes. "How did he get here?"

Colby waved Fizzlewink away. "He got here through a spell cast by Rigel and the Daphnes, but I don't think he's here for whatever they called him for."

"Called him?" Darla asked. "What like on the phone?"

"Sure," Colby said. "Rigel called an ancient Druid from the past using his time warp calling plan. He's ancient, or at least from a long-ago time and brought here for some purpose." Colby raced through his mind for answers but found it difficult for the critical part of his intention to focus. "I think he's here for me, but not for whatever Rigel expected."

"What did Rigel want from this Druid fellow?" Nana asked. She stood in the entry between the kitchen and living room. "Did he say anything about when he came from?"

Colby shook his head. "I don't know anything more, except I don't think he's alone."

Colby explained how the Druid's thoughts seemed to float into Colby's head. Images flashed in his mind during their conversation. He saw several other robbed figures and some bluish ghost-like apparition floating around. This was what placed the brand on Colby's hand.

"Shade," Nana gasped.

"Don't be ridiculous, you old bat," Fizzlewink said. "They were just a myth. A story told children to get them to behave and do as instructed."

"No, they were, are, not myth or tales told to scare children." Nana shivered as she sat down. "They are what remains of a Nefslama soul forcibly removed from its body. Similar to a Shizumu, a Shade is a disembodied force of magic. A shade, however, is not a slave to need or want. It is what is left when the two opposing forces of Shi are split."

"What does that mean?" Aria asked.

"It means that the Shade is either working with or possibly controlling the Druid." Nana got up and poured herself a drink from the side table. "There were many reasons the splitting of one's Shi was forbidden, my child. The possibility of producing a Shizumu notwithstanding, the rarer but more unpredictable creation of a Shade is much worse."

"How worse can it be? They come from the Nefslama, the good side, right?" Darla asked.

Nana tittered. "Being Nefslama does not make one good or bad any more than there is good or bad magic. And the Shade is much more powerful than a Shizumu because it does not bargain. It does not explain. It does everything purposefully and without emotion. A Shizumu half carries all the emotion which drives its need to anchor back into a living thing. A Shade contains all the cunning, the freedom, the purpose, and access to Emassa without a host."

"What purpose?" Shelly asked.

"It was once believed that the final desire felt when the Shade is set free is what gives it a life of its own."

"Is a Shade powerful enough to control this Druid? I thought they were among the most powerful of sorcerers of their time?" Fizzlewink sat twirling his eyebrow as he asked his questions.

"It seemed they worked together from what I felt," Colby said. "Unless the Druid is meant to think that."

"A case of the tail wagging the dog it would seem. If you pardon the disgusting metaphor," Fizzlewink said and shuddered.

Colby slumped over and groaned. He thrashed in pain as Rhea came to his side to try healing him of an unknown injury.

"What's happening?" Rhea asked. "I can't sense him or what's wrong."

"It's because we're no longer linked," Colby grunted. "Something is pulling magic from my core."

"Shit," Gary said.

As Gary put his phone down and looked at everyone, Colby relaxed and lifted himself up from the floor. All eyes were on Gary.

"I think I know."

Gary handed his phone to Colby and showed him what was on the screen. It was a game that Gary was checking out called Hashtag Magic.

"Remember I said the hashtag magic code made its way onto the internet? Well, someone used it to create a role-playing game."

"How's that related?" Jasper asked. "It's just a game."

"Apparently not. When I cast a couple spells in the game, Colby felt the effects. It would seem that somehow the code is still attached to him and if people start playing this game…"

"I'm not a flipping game console," Colby said.

"You are until we figure out how to delete it or something." Gary picked his phone back up.

Colby sighed. "Can this day get any worse?"

Jasper exhaled and turned to Colby as he turned his phone around. "It's been downloaded by every kid in town and is spreading."

"Great."

"Oh, it gets better…or worse really," Jasper added. "Guess who the author is?" Jasper handed the phone to Shelly.

"Bruce?" Shelly said. "He hasn't the sense given a goldfish, never mind program a game."

"It's magical code, Shelly," Colby said. "The AI was designed to recognize the intent and adapt. Hashtag Magic is on the web, at least we can root out evil."

"Oh my dear," Nana said. "The interwebs are rife with the ugliness of people. Your magic app is nothing compared to the free flow of ignorance coming even from those you might call friends."

"Leave it to a wiseass old woman to point out the truth of human —or inhuman—nature," Fizzlewink said.

"One thing is for certain," Colby said. "I may not have my connection to my friends, but I can see the trail of magic tugging on me through the app."

"So, let's follow it," Gary said. "Lead the way."

CHAPTER 2

The kids all ran to the park following the trail of magical drain tugging on Colby's core. They all had this power center where they could gather and store magical Emassa for later use. Still, Colby's core was the proxy to all others since magic reawakened.

Magic flowed into, then out of Colby's magical center faster than any time in the past. Used to only a handful of his friends and family using him as a proxy for a short time was bearable. He managed to provide them all with direct links to Emassa, but somehow that did not work with the hashtag magic code out in the wild. This game that Shelly's jilted ex-boyfriend managed to create was plugged directly into Colby's chest. He felt tethered with an extension cord powering up every device playing the RPG.

Blue and red flashes or energy flashed, strobed, and swirled between the many personal devices in the park as people played. Blissfully unaware of the real magic behind this latest craze, the players dashed about the park locating new runes and engaging in wars of sorcery. The real magic-powered the intent of the code behind the scenes. Only a magically endowed being would see the truth behind the game.

"Quite the fireworks display, wouldn't ya say, son," Betelgeuse said from his bench. "Seems that even my regular runes playing pals are caught up in this new…mod version."

"Grandpa?" Colby said. "How long have you been here watching this go on?"

"Long enough, my boy. I could sense the flow of Emassa from quite a distance." Betelgeuse lifted an arm and pointed to the perimeter of the park. "And I'm not the only one that noticed."

Surrounding the park, a diverse collection of magical creatures began to congregate. There were Dreggs, which is expected as they have been around since this all started. But now there were other beings previously unknown to the kids.

Some of the beasts were identifiable as possible fairies or wisps of some sort. Then there were a few squatty toad-looking animals with long lower fangs protruding up. They were accompanied by some scrawny things with patchy fur, big round eyes, and double rows of saliva dripping pointy teeth.

"What are those things?" Darla asked.

"Pixies, Trolls, and Grimalts," Betelgeuse answered. "The Dreggs, I imagine, need no explaining, but the others are drawn to the collision of magic at play here."

"Why would that matter to them?" Colby asked.

Betelgeuse grunted a sort of half-laugh. The other half seemed to be laced with disdain. "They feed off the cast-offs. The residue that remains when two opposing magical forces cancel each other out. It is like drugs to these little-"

"Bottom-feeders," Fizzlewink hissed. He transformed into a cat state and began racing around the park, chasing off the smaller of their unseen audience. Unseen because they remained obscured to the non-magical or mundanes.

Darla shuddered. "Sometimes, I wish I remained unaware of this side of reality. Those little Grimalts are nasty-looking."

Betelgeuse laughed. "My dear, they are the least problematic. They usually just follow behind sorcerers and lap up their spent magic, sort of like a stray cat that you make the mistake of feeding."

"I know what that's like," Shelly said, looking at Fizzlewink chasing off a troll.

Betelgeuse agreed. "The ones to watch out for are those pixies. They'll provoke you just to get forced spells. They're like bees invading your picnic, and your magic is like honey-cakes."

Rhea noticed a nearby pixie and approached it slow and deliberate. Thinking about what Betelgeuse said, she wondered at how such a beautiful little creature could be so mean. Using the honey-cake description as inspiration, Rhea formed a hashtag spell and sent it to a nearby tree. **#HoneyHole**.

The spell hit the tree and formed a hole from which magical honey flowed free. The resulting residue drew in the pixies like a swarm. The pretty and unassuming faces widened with larger than seemed possible rows of greedily smiling teeth. They collected on the tree as a single unit and lapped up every drop of magic, leaving a sizable and real hole in the trunk of the tree.

"Be careful, dear, you feed them once, and you may never get rid of them." Betelgeuse winked at Rhea then at Colby.

Colby watched through the pain of magic still flowing in and out of him. The regular flow became bearable though he still needed to stem the tide if he were to have any chance at confronting this Druid.

Spells collided, fizzled out, and a cloud of smokey dust settled around the point of cancelation. Never noticing before, Colby saw how the magic never really stopped, it just transformed and flowed back through everything around it. It was recycled in a way, becoming something the real world could use as nourishment. He mentioned his observation to the others.

Betelgeuse sat next to Colby. "True, there is a sort of recycling, but this transformation has always existed. The Emassa is more than just magic, my boy. It is the lifeblood of the universe and flows through everything in one way or another."

Watching his grandson struggle with the flow of magic coursing through him, he breathed heavily and took the boy's hand. Turning it over, he looked at the rune now etched into his skin like a tattoo.

"This is new," Betelgeuse said. "It's severing your link to your friends, I expect."

Colby looked at his grandfather with restrained surprise. He knew there was a great deal his grandfather likely knew and had yet shared. There was a look of confusion there though that concerned Colby.

"Yes, but what else?" Colby asked. "You look like there is something you're not saying, gramps."

Betelgeuse laughed at being called gramps. "I haven't seen the use of these ancient marks in a few thousand years."

Colby told Betelgeuse about the encounter with the Druid and how he received the mark on his hand. The briefest of recognition crossed his grandfather's face, but most of the telling, Colby couldn't read Betelgeuse's reaction.

"What do you make of this Druid, my boy," Betelgeuse asked.

It was more a prompt to help Colby work through the situation, but he was unable to focus his mind. This was precisely the test Betelgeuse was applying and expected results.

"I can't seem to think straight. Normally I can sift through things easily, but I'm not processing information critically like Gary can."

"That's because you're disconnected from him," Betelgeuse said, pointing at the rune tattoo on Colby's hand. "You'll find it more difficult to do some things that you've accomplished relying on that connection."

"How do you know this?"

Betelgeuse just looked at Colby a few moments before answering. "It's what I would do to challenge you if I were the Druid."

"You speak as though you know this Druid guy."

"I have known a few, but only one that was covered in rune tattoos."

"So, what does he want?"

Betelgeuse stood and smiled at his grandson. "For you to work it out on your own. I mustn't interfere, I think."

"Seriously!" Colby said. "Rigel summons this guy from wherever to set against me, and that's all you can say?"

Betelgeuse tittered. "One thing I can tell you is that if the Druid is here, it wasn't by Rigel's design."

At his final words, Betelgeuse walked into the crowd of people playing the RPG.

Colby took a few steps to chase after the old man when he walked between two players. The magic from their spells raced through him and sent his mind reeling. As his nerves settled from the sudden charge of power, Colby heard the rumblings of people around him because the game stopped responding.

As he stood between the two linked players, he watched the tendrils of Emassa flow from their phones and into his chest. The magic continued to fill his core and energize him. Though his thinking was still muddled, along with the added prowess of strength, he usually felt from Jasper, he breathed easier. But when the complaining players began to move away, the flow of magic ended, and Colby started to feel the drain again.

The game resumed connection, and Colby fell to his knee, scrapping it deeply and cutting a hole in his pants. Rhea was the first to reach Colby's side and moved her hand to heal his wound. The cut would not mend.

As the others approached, Gary stepped beside Rhea.

"Try using a hashtag spell."

Rhea did as Gary suggested and watched as the spell left her phWatch and performed its intent on Colby's knee.

Before Colby could stand, a commotion in the distance sent everyone screaming and running out of the park. As he looked around, Colby saw that even the magical creatures hid from the approaching red glowing beast. Only the Dreggs remained.

The Shizumu closed in on Colby, sensing his weakening state.

"Time to play little poof."

The voice that came out of the Shizumu was not the raspy disconnected tenor expected. This was a recognizable voice filled with directed hate and recognition. Bruce.

The Shizumu was a visible construct of the game that Bruce was able to create and set after Colby. It wasn't Colby alone that recognized Bruce's voice.

"Come out here and face me, you spineless sorry excuse for a-" Shelly started but was cut off by Darla.

"Not helping the situation by antagonizing him, Shells."

"Whatever," Shelly said. "And stop calling me Shells. I'm not a freaking mermaid."

Shelly looked around at the others and made hand gestures that indicated directions for all to go. Divide, search, and find; they were going to flush out the operator of this phantom creature, Bruce.

The artificial Shizumu split twice, making a trio of floating red vapor menace closing in on Colby. The park emptied of everyone except Colby and his friends. The drain on his magic increased by a factor of three. The Shizumu, Colby realized, came from the game and was manifested outside the computer somehow. Colby squinted as he looked closer at the approaching energy-sapping wraith. It flickered.

"Look for projection devices," Colby said. "This is some sort of hologram magic connected to the game."

While Darla, Rhea, Fizz, and Jasper looked for the projectors, Shelly and Gary searched out Bruce.

Darla found the first device high up in a tree. Unfortunately, she could not reach the lowest branch to climb the tree, though as she thought about it, she wasn't dressed for climbing. Darla got Fizzlewink's attention and waved him over. When he came up, she pointed to the device.

"So, deactivate it," Fizzlewink said.

"I'm wearing a skirt Fizz, I can't climb in this without showing off my assets."

Fizzlewink grimaced. "Use magic, you dizzy human." Fizzlewink scampered away.

"Oh yeah," Darla whispered and smacked her own head.

#DestroyProjector.

The spell sailed from Darla's phWatch, the smartwatch specially built by Colby for himself and all his friends.

The Hashtag Magic Operating System, HMOS, controlling the device, gathered what is needed for power from the user. The AI interpreted and built a spell from the library of runes. The Emassa fueled the creation and sent the magic toward its target.

When the magic hit the projector, it fizzled and died. The remnants of the spell drifted down to the ground, where a grimalt happily lapped up the leftovers.

"Damn," Darla said. "Spells aren't gonna work on these things, they're just absorbing the Emassa."

Fizzlewink acknowledged Darla's assessment and looked up at the tree. As he leaped toward the trunk, Fizzlewink transformed into his favored cat persona and clawed his way up to the device. Claws and Fangs made quick work of the projector, and soon its constituent parts littered the ground beneath. The holographic Shizumu trio flickered and became less substantial.

"One down, three to go," Darla hooted. She pointed toward Rhea, who found another.

Soon they found the fourth and final projector. Hoping to take out the last of the magic draining his magic, Colby launched a large stone at the device. His aim was accurate, and the projectile bashed against the machinery, sending it down to the Earth and breaking into pieces. Colby breathed free for a second before the power-sucking feeling returned even stronger.

The Shizumu hologram surged back into full view and launched itself onto Colby. Though there was nothing corporeal about the beast, its Emassa draining effects were amplified by the number of projections feeding it. Colby could not pull on the source of magic, the Emassa, fast enough to refill his core as it was drained.

Not finding any more devices in the surrounding trees or lamp posts, Fizzlewink and the others scrambled to Colby's side. The kids surrounded him and helped him to his feet. The proximity of the others with the hologram slowed its effects on Colby. He began to understand the drain was increased by his being disconnected from the others, his golem.

As he contemplated the realization that not only Gary and Jasper were creations that connected to his magic, Colby heard a buzzing in the air around their group. He looked up to see several drones flying above, projections flashing from a device mounted on each. Colby pointed up.

"He's using drones to project the holograms. Those devices in the trees were decoys."

Fizzlewink growled and hissed at the nearest flying contraption. "We need to get somewhere they can't project."

Colby concurred, but he shook his head. "That may help, but it won't stop the drain of Emassa from me. At best, I can keep an even flow passing through me when we are all together, and I'm not in the center of a projection."

Shelly narrowed her eyes and looked at the drones. She had an idea of cooking as she looked at the gathering of pixies, trolls, and grimalts. It would need to wait. Right now, she needed her little brother safely away from here.

Meanwhile, Gary had a piece of the broken projectors in his hand. "I've been checking this thing out. It's got the instruction set inside they used to manipulate the Hashtag Magic Operating System."

"So?" Jasper said. "What good is that?"

Gary rolled his eyes. "I can limit the effect and use it to reduce the drain on Colby." Gary frowned.

"What's with the face?" Colby asked.

"Well," Gary started, "I can create the code block and store it in a spelled loop, but we'll need a device to put it in and a spell."

"Like a modern talisman," Rhea suggested. "Good thing we know someone who knows how to make talismans."

Everyone looked at Rhea with confused stares.

"Ugh, Bellatrix…Nana…her pendant." Rhea started walking toward the Stevens' home. "Really, sometimes I wonder if we all share a brain."

Colby wondered the same thing as he and the others caught up to Rhea and headed home.

CHAPTER 3

Nana was gathering her tarot cards from the table and reshuffling them when Colby and the others arrived back at the house. She barely registered their greeting as she shuffled and dealt a new series of cards.

"Order food," Nana said. "I'm not in the mood to cook."

"Oh, We're fine, thank you, Nana," Colby said. "Why yes, we did find the source of my ailment. We need to kill everyone and restart civilization."

"That's nice fart-blossom," Nana said. "Be careful and take extra underwear."

Nana stared down at her cards and stopped when she revealed the Hermit card again. She quickly gathered up the cards and immediately started shuffling again.

"Are you even listening Bellatrix," Fizzlewink said. He jumped up on the table and stood on the remaining cards before Nana. "We need your help with something."

Nana shooed Fizzlewink off the table as she reshuffled her tarot deck. After turning up the Hermit card repeatedly, Nana set the tarot deck down, and her manner turned to that of Bellatrix, the old witch's former incarnation of herself.

"What is it you want that you can't accomplish yourself?" Bellatrix asked.

Colby sat down and began laying out what happened in the park. As he spoke, he watched Nana's face remain the unaffected and inpatient facade of Bellatrix. Only when he got to the part about creating a device as a talisman did the old crone bat an eyelash and shrivel up her lips.

"No," Bellatrix said. She went back to shuffling her deck.

As Nana laid out her cards again, the Hermit came up again but reversed. She huffed and dropped her head.

"What do you mean, 'NO'?" Shelly demanded. "Listen, you tired-ass old bitch."

"Who do you think you're talking to?" Nana asked.

Shelly stood her ground with hands placed on hips and face pushed in toward her grandmother. "I'm talking to both of the nasty, cantankerous old witches inside your head. It's bad enough your estranged husband has decided to wash his hands of involvement, but now you too? What gives?"

That got Bellatrix's attention. "What did Betelgeuse say?"

"Work it out for yourself, basically. Gramps can't…or won't get involved," Colby interjected. "I don't understand what has you both so spooked about this Druid guy. What are you not telling us?"

Nana thought for a moment then pointed at the Hermit card turned over on the table. "This."

"I've repeated a reading over and over, this card always finds its way into the mix," Nana said. Bellatrix receded into the back of her mind. "It's the Hermit, but I fear it represents this Druid you have already met."

"What does it mean," Colby asked.

"I can't say?" Nana said.

"Can't or won't?" Fizzlewink hissed. "How typically useless. No different than helping me free my family from that spell in the Yucatan."

"She isn't sharing," Nana spat. "You think I'm useless? Well, I feel as much." Nana began to shake with pent up frustration and hurt. "As much as my past self shares, just as much is purposefully withheld. But I don't think it's done willingly. Believe me, if I could help, I would."

Silence hung in the kitchen like the smell of burnt popcorn. It left a feeling of disappointment at a spoiled treat and the knowledge that they would have to clean up a mess without supplies. When at last, they all began talking through the situation, one thing was clear. The Druid was known to the old Nefslama, and they were anxious about the day he'd return. It frightened Colby and the others that a being who came long after the original magic to Earth was powerful enough to instill fear in the last remaining ancients.

Food arrived, and the kids all dug into the various styrofoam containers eagerly. The situation hadn't deprived them of their appetite, Nana was glad to see. But she was not hungry in the least. She pouted over her latest tarot deal, perplexed and frustrated at the recurring theme. The Druid stepped in to alter anyway past whatever plan he laid. Nothing made sense until Nana saw something in the card she previously overlooked. The Hermit character held something in his hand at his side.

"Go get your father's journal," Nana said. Nana looked sideways at Fizzlewink. "You know, cat-man, you are far too cranky for someone who can lick his own balls."

Fizzlewink stopped what he was doing and retreated from the table.

When Colby returned, he set the large book down on the table. The mysterious book, with its set of sectioned off and separately locked pages, revealed its secrets as need warranted. There remained two sections closed, and Colby was anxious about what the pages held. With the thought of the previous section revealing the true nature of his friends being golems, there was no telling what next he might discover.

Colby looked at the golden symbol on the cover. The wheel of time was an artifact found in his father's study. When he first discovered that it fit in the indentation of the journal, his path was set as it opened to reveal his father's message. Now it was the first key to unlocking the tome but only from Colby's own touch. Relief settled in his tensed shoulders at finding the brush of his finger still enacted the magical lock.

Colby opened the book and proceeded to release the clasps of the sections currently open to him. On a whim, he tried to unlock the next two seals, but they were not ready for him yet. So he just turned the open book to his grandmother and sat across from her at the table.

"What are you looking for," Colby asked as Nana thumbed through the pages.

Nana grunted and pointed to the Hermit card, showing the book held in the character's hand. "I'll know it when I see it."

Colby saw the tome this character held, and instant recognition landed on his face. "That's my book."

"Yes," Nana muttered. "This Druid is playing a game with us."

"How did he have that journal, and how is he pictured in your cards?" Shelly asked.

"He screwed with my cards, girl," Nana said. "He's toying with me, with Bellatrix. And she's angrier than a wet cat up a tree."

Fizzlewink growled at the analogy. "Get to the point, batty old woman."

Nana began to look up as she turned the next page and stopped. "Get me some vellum and a quill," she said with Bellatrix's sharp-edged voice.

"Somewhat?" Shelly asked.

"Paper and pen," Nana said with her own voice.

Taking care to copy with as much precision her arthritic old hands could manage, Nana transcribed on two different sheets of paper. One she stuck in her pocket, the other she folded and cuffed in her hand. She snapped the book closed and pushed it back to Colby before closing her eyes and lobbing her head forward.

"Well?" Colby asked.

Nana's eyes cleared, and the facade of Bellatrix returned. "There is nothing in the pages I wrote for you, Colby." She looked at Fizzlewink before getting up from the table. "Come with me."

Fizzlewink shrugged at the others, but followed Bellatrix from the kitchen and outside.

Outside, Fizzlewink followed behind the old woman as she walked the perimeter of the garden. He zigged and zagged behind her, as though waiting for a treat. Each time he looked up at Nana, he watched as Bellatrix behind those eyes searched covertly for something. Fizzlewink scanned the area in hopes of discovering what she wanted of him but saw nothing but flowers, plants, and the odd weed pushing through the bedding.

When at last the old woman stopped, Fizzlewink ran into the back of her legs and fell on his ass.

"Get up," Bellatrix demanded. She held out the folded paper to him. "Take this and guard it until such time it's required of you to give it to me."

Fizzlewink took the paper and unfolded it. He glanced up to see that Bellatrix did not stop him from reading the contents. When he looked at the inscription, he realized why she let his curiosity win. He could not read the script.

Mages, sorcerers, witches, they all used their own shorthand or form of secret writing to guard their secrets. Bellatrix was no exception. Frustrated and perplexed, Fizzlewink refolded the message and stuffed it in his trousers.

"Why give this to me if only to return it back to you? And how shall I know the time?"

"I didn't say give it back."

Fizzlewink frowned and put his hands on his hips. "What in the seven hells are you playing at?"

Bellatrix pursed Nana's lips. "I don't want it in this time and place. I'll need it then, and you are to present it to me."

Fizzlewink pressed for clarity with his tilted head and glare.

Rolling eyes and huffing air, Bellatrix bent over to Fizzlewink. She noticed the sets of eyes watching from the kitchen window and didn't want to chance eavesdroppers.

"Time is a funny thing, little man." Bellatrix drew an infinity symbol in the dirt. "It is weighted just here." She pointed to the bottom of one loop and the top of the next. "No matter what happens, or how it loops, the course of time has a habit of righting itself."

"Riddles," Fizzlewink spat. "Why do you speak of time?"

"You will know when the time has come. Now go. I have other business." She bent over and began rummaging through the flowers.

Fizzlewink left Bellatrix, using Nana, to their fighting with the garden plants and headed back into the house. He thumbed the note in his pocket and was preoccupied when he brushed against something and fell. Looking up and around, all he saw was the old hag pulling weeds in the distance. He stood and brushed himself off, thinking he tripped over his own feet before heading back into the house. The kids were waiting.

"What did she want? What did she give you? What is she doing?" The questions came from all directions.

"Never mind," Fizzlewink answered. "It's between me and the old battle-ax."

Fizzlewink looked around at the unsatisfied faces. He told them as little as possible about his conversation with Bellatrix, assuring them it was nothing to do with the present situation. All he shared of intrigue was that Nana blathered on about time righting itself.

"That makes no sense," Gary said.

Fizzlewink watched Colby staring at his father's journal. The boy's face was blank, and his eyes locked on the cover. "What is it, Colby?"

Colby blinked and looked up at his little blue companion. "I was just thinking about this symbol of time."

"And? What about it?"

"Well, it doesn't make sense. You would think it would be something like an infinity character instead of a circle within a circle. And then these four sets of wavy lines radiating out from the center. It just seems like something more, and I'm missing the meaning."

Fizzlewink remembered what Bellatrix said and saw something within Colby's artifact on the journal cover. There were something like infinity symbols within two of them. But Colby was right, it seemed there was something more to this artifact, but he couldn't comprehend what either.

"I'm sure you'll figure it out when the time is right," Fizzlewink said.

Fizzlewink frowned as he realized he repeated what Bellatrix had moments ago said to him. From the look on Colby's face, Fizzlewink saw that it was as empty a statement to the boy as it was to himself.

"Sorry," Fizzlewink said. "It's the best I have to offer at the moment." Expecting a smart remark from Shelly, Fizzlewink turned to prepare a retort. She wasn't in the kitchen.

"Where's Shelly?" Fizzlewink asked.

Nobody seemed to notice when she left.

Shelly was outside. She dropped out of the visible plane while no one was looking in the kitchen. When she ran into Fizzlewink passing through the yard, she figured her secret was discovered. Since he hadn't noticed her and returned to his path for the back door, Shelly resumed her own march toward Nana.

Shelly stood as close as she dared in hopes the old woman remained distracted enough not to notice her presence. Having recently been instructed on how to slip into the void between the corporeal and spirit realms, she wasn't sure how easily she could be detected. Being as though it was Bellatrix by way of Nana's body that taught her, she needed to test how close she could get before her grandmother would sense the magic.

Nana was more in control than Bellatrix at the moment. Shelly became aware of the subtle change in the aura her grandmother gave off when the two personalities would switch. Perhaps her abilities with spirits were connected to this new acuity. She didn't care to ponder that at present. She needed to know what was going on.

Weeds and plants in equal share were flying out of the flowerbed. Half by magic, half by physically pulling, Nana ripped away the foliage to reveal the dirt below. With a full sweeping arm, magic flowed off of Nana and into the ground. The soil, pebbles, and clay all shifted to reveal a ring of bluish stone markers. They were each covered in runes.

The ring was ten feet in diameter. Shelly watched as Nana stepped inside and removed the other note from her housecoat pocket. As the words Nana spoke made the stones begin to glow, Shelly shifted and ran for the markers. She entered the ring just in time to be swept up in the spell.

"I wondered how long you were going to just stand there," Bellatrix said in unison with Nana. "Stay inside the ley-gate circle."

Shelly blinked at the sound of two distinct voices coming from her grandmother's mouth. "Where are we going?"

Nana shushed her. "Stay quiet and unseen. We're off to see the wizard." Nana laughed and began humming then singing. "Follow the yellow brick road. Oh, but the stones are blue. Follow the blue circle road. No, that doesn't work."

"I think you should shut up as well," Shelly whispered.

CHAPTER 4

The moment Shelly and Nana disappeared, they became swallowed by a swirling light. A moment of suspension in the glow was followed by a jolt, sending them plummeting through a ley line deep in the Earth.

Shelly wouldn't have been able to talk if she wanted as not even her screams could escape her chest while earth and stone passed by her on all sides. She felt as though her body was being stretched across the planet. However, she felt nothing aside from the power of Emassa buffeting her and pushing the two women toward the other side of the world.

Without slowing, Shelly and Nana were deposited on the grass outside Stonehenge. It was not a graceful landing for either as Nana stumbled, and Shelly landed on her ass. Somewhat expecting a different debarkation, Nana looked up at the purple glow surrounding the henge. The ley line magic sent them where it should, but they were thrown clear just shy of the expected location.

"This is-" Bellatrix started.

She was holding her hand to the magically charged force field around the stones. Of course, only those with magical blood would see or sense it. Still, it was generating enough magical residue that pixies and grimalts were skirting the perimeter, lapping up the cast-off magic.

"It's necessary," The Druid said as he approached. He remained inside the barrier, hooded and arms folded into opposing sleeves. Only his glowing eyes were visible beneath the robs.

"Necessary to allow you to remain, don't you mean?" Bellatrix asked.

"For the present," The Druid said. "Now down to business."

Nana glared with knowledge now released by Bellatrix. "You once said a time would come that our goals would cross. I did or will do as you instructed back in the Yucatan. I'll set Fizzlewink to task with a missive, now what?"

The Druid waved his hand and spoke a spell. "Ha'ashtagga runis brandii."

A swirl of fine blue Emassa formed at Nana's feet. As the power built, a metallic object took shape. When the power lapsed, Nana bent down and picked up the intricate device. It was an iridium laced silver rune or runes she noticed on closer inspection. Four runes in total lay across one another, fitting one into the next as they layered into one complete spell.

"What am I to do with this?"

"It's what you need to reconstitute your daughter."

Nana's eyes widened, and she looked back from the Druid to the enchanted rune brand in her hand. She knew at that moment what it was. This was a magic Bellatrix had never mastered. Enchanting was difficult enough for her, but to imbue a spell atop an enchanted object was far more complex.

"How? I mean, why would you do this for me?"

"It suits my plans, and a promise is a promise."

"Is this why you brought me here? To give me the means of eliminating the Daphnes and fixing my daughter's spirit once and for all?"

The Druid shrugged as he pulled on one ear beneath his hood. The runes that appeared on his exposed milky arm were ancient and powerful. The runes shifted and altered as each moved in concert with the rest across his skin. His posture changed when he heard Nana gasp.

Moving his arm back to his waist, covering his exposed skin, the Druid cleared his throat. "The top three runes must be branded into the Daphnes in reverse order of their creation. The last and anchoring brand goes on Aria. You must place Aria's brand first. The others only need the correct rune. You may brand them as opportunity presents."

Nana was set on edge. "You mean I have to go find those crazy bitches and brand them each?"

"They will come to you in short order, sooner than you might expect."

"And how do I apply the brand, burn it into them?"

The Druid laughed. "As you might like that, it is not necessary. Hold the rune and whisper your intent. Each rune will find its intended target. Look to the original to begin the chain. After she is branded, the others will come seeking the source of their itch."

"Just ducky," Nana groaned. "What do I need to do for this favor?"

"You have already done it. You may go."

Nana turned to leave and glanced at where Shelly was standing in the in-between. The in-between was what Shelly came to start calling the void between life and death. As Nana began to move toward the ley lines, she realized she was unable to travel back since the departure circle was within the boundary sealed off by the Druid's spell.

As though reading her thoughts, the Druid waved his hand, opening a tunnel to the center of the henge. "You may enter. I'll send along Shelly after I've spoken with her."

"How?" Shelly blurted out and revealed herself.

"It was you I wanted to speak with most, not the witch."

The druid released the spell, and the tunnel closed.

Shelly was trapped within as Nana was sent into the ley lines.

The Druid started toward her and adjusted his hood to better conceal himself.

"Hello, Shelly. I wish to present a bargain."

***

Nana exited the ley line with less grace than her departure in Salisbury Plains. Her legs fell from beneath her, and she landed on her sizable butt.

"Shelly," she shouted.

Turning to try and go back, Nana watched as the stones in the garden ley-gate locked. A purple hue coated them in Emassa magic. Pixies flitted out from behind rocks and flowers to dance about the stones. They bathed in the residue of powerful magic long-absent from the world.

"Shelly," Nana whispered.

"What about Shelly?" Aria said as she entered the garden.

Aria had only just returned from work to find the children in an uproar over Nana disappearing in the garden, and Shelly nowhere to be found.

"Mother? Where is my daughter?"

Before Nana could answer, a charge built in the ley-gate sending the pixies to scatter. As the power peaked, Shelly appeared and stubbled from the circle and into Aria's arms.

After being thoroughly spun around, checked, patted and poked, Shelly had enough. "Stop. I'm fine."

"What did he want?" Nana asked.

"It's not for you to know," Shelly said, half satisfied. The other half of her was terrified. More secrets and this time there was much more at stake. "I need something to eat."

Nana smiled to reassure herself. "Oh yeah, traveling those lines works up an appetite. I'll start dinner."

"No," came a multi-voice reply.

"Haven't we been through enough danger today," Shelly said. "There's take-out in the kitchen."

Nana stayed behind as Aria followed Shelly. She took out the rune brand and pulled the anchor piece apart from the rest. She whispered for it to find its mark.

"Traveling the lines?" Aria asked as she followed Shelly toward the house. She swatted her chest as she walked. A pixie swerved away from the magic that branded her chest. "Damn pixies. Little bitch bit me."

Nana smiled as she trailed behind. "Because you're so sweet."

Aria glared back at Nana. "I'm not finished with you, old woman. First, I want to know what the hell has been going on while I was at work."

Nana waved her off. "You'll forget about it soon enough, trust me."

Aria grunted. She followed Shelly into the house and waited after Nana came in before she demanded information. When the kids all started at once, Aria sat down and looked at the tarot cards.

Nana stepped up and took over the detailing of events. She repeated everything from that morning on. It began immediately after Aria left for work. She had forbidden them doing anything foolish without her home. Nana talked over Aria's argument for not listening to her. Things would happen anyway whether Aria was home or not, Nana explained to her daughter. Bellatrix was around and supervising in her own way.

"That somehow does nothing for my worry, mother," Aria explained. "Bellatrix may be back in your head, but she lacks the heart of a grandmother. She barely had one in her first body if you ask me."

Bellatrix used Nana's hand to slap Aria. "How dare you, insulant child. You know nothing of my sacrifices now, past, or future."

"I remember well, number one mother," Aria hissed as she rubbed her cheek. "All too well."

Bellatrix fumed for a few seconds before slamming back into the recesses of Nana's mind. "Ouch. You hit a nerve my dear. She just crammed herself so far in the back of my head it gave me a wedgie."

Aria looked sorry for a second, but it passed. "Who is this Druid?" Aria looked at Nana.

Nana looked at Shelly.

Shelly looked at the floor. She wasn't saying anything for fear of the repercussions.

"What's that about," Colby asked Shelly. "What happened, and where were you?"

"I went with Nana to see the Druid. I sort of tagged along." Shelly added the second part when she saw the look her mother gave Nana. "Nana didn't know I was there, but Bellatrix did."

"How could Nana not know? That circle is only about ten feet across."

"I was in the in-between," Shelly explained what that meant. Only Nana and Colby held blank faces.

"Did you two know she could do this?" Aria asked.

"I figured she'd tell everyone when she was ready," Colby said. He told everyone he'd seen her do it when they were in the chamber below the school.

"So how come you couldn't see her when we looked for her earlier?" Gary asked. "If she was with Nana, you should have seen her."

Colby mustered no answer, and that disturbed him. He was feeling more detached from some of his magical gifts that did not require hashtag spells. Not seeing Shelly in the in-between—as she called it—was the latest development. He resided himself to worry about more important things, such as where all the food went.

The food that remained from take-out was soon a few crumbs and empty containers. Before he could order more food, Colby saw Nana waddle to the cabinets and begin rattling around the stove. She was going to cook. He motioned to his friends to follow him out of the kitchen. Aria followed them.

Once the kids and Aria left, Shelly and Nana were alone. The kitchen noise was a relief to Shelly until she felt the icy stare of Bellatrix on her back.

"Can I help you with something?" Shelly asked.

Bellatrix took over Nana's mouth, while the rest of her remained intent on cooking some slop. "What did the Druid want from you?"

"Why did he have to want something? Shelly said. "Maybe he just wanted to chat with someone less...bitter."

Bellatrix measured Shelly's words with care. "He revealed something to you, didn't he?"

Shelly didn't answer. She glared at her grandmother's alter-ego induced expression and read a volume of possible connections between this Druid and the ancient consciousness inhabiting Nana's mind.

"You mustn't say-"

"I'm not completely without a brain in my skull, you cantankerous old witch. I have my part to play. You play yours and leave it be."

Shelly realized that Bellatrix knew something more about the Druid's identity than she was sharing, even with Nana. It amazed her how two separate minds could fit in Nana's brain and manage to keep secrets from one another.

The kitchen door swung open, and Aria returned. "Leave what be?"

"Nothing mom." Shelly got up from the counter and headed out. "I'll be out for a while. I need to hunt down an ex-boyfriend to pummel."

Aria stopped Shelly. "Don't go off on a fool's errand unprepared."

Shelly hugged her mother and pushed past. "I know how to handle Bruce, mother. I have all the knowledge I need to put him down." She turned back to Aria when her mother started to object. "Look, mom, he is hiding behind a game. I know how to stop him using it and take away his fun. He's just a spoiled child who needs a good spanking."

"Why not let Colby and the boys handle this one?" Aria asked.

"Because Colby can't do everything and certainly not in his current state. He has other things to worry about." Shelly sighed and looked at Nana. "Beside, Bruce is my mess. I'll clean it up."

Shelly noticed Aria rubbing her chest. Remembering the branding runes, she looked at Nana, who was watching her. Nana winked at Shelly, eliciting an unexpected smile. Shelly's grin faltered though as she recalled what the Druid said. Once Aria was branded, the Daphnes would come. They were connected, and the first rune would send a spell through their link.

"Looks like Nana will have her own mess soon enough as well."

Nana and Shelly knew that meant the Daphnes would soon come calling. They let Aria assume Shelly suggested the kitchen mess after Nana finished cooking.

CHAPTER 5

Rigel and the three Daphnes had watched the interaction when the old woman showed up, was allowed within the circle, and was then sent away. While inside the ring, the four could not make out what was happening due to the energy field surrounding the henge. The Druid's manipulation of Rigel's plan was becoming troublesome.

The Druid owed Rigel a debt, from millennia past, that it seemed he was paying in his own time. Rigel wanted action immediately.

"Druid," Rigel shouted. "Come out here and explain yourself."

"That would not be wise," the Druid answered. "This time is not prepared for me yet."

Rigel chewed on the Druid's cryptic answer. When the spell that allowed the Druid to traverse to this plain enacted, the Druid immediately cast a spell that encased him within the confines of the henge. He had not stepped out of it and only allowed the old woman in. Not even a Daphne or Rigel were permitted within the circle.

The only thing that gave Rigel pause about storming the barrier was the blue Shade doing the Druid's bidding. How the Druid managed to enslave a wraith sent Rigel's bones to chill. A Shade was a creature of myth and little known about them. An imprisoned spirit with magical abilities. Rigel was unsettled deeper than he expected.

"What was the old woman doing here?" Rigel found his spine, though he kept several paces back from the barrier. "And why did you allow her into the circle?"

"Her purpose here is not your concern. As for here entry, it was required to send her away."

Rigel realized then what that meant. "leylines. They're open?"

"Of course," the Druid said. "They were never completely closed, simply congested."

The possibilities coalesced in Rigel's mind. With open travel through the lines restored, he could use his stunted abilities to go anywhere now. He could also tap into the magical flow within those same lines. Leylines were conduits of Emassa flowing like veins throughout the entire planet. This meant that the boy Colby might no longer be required to act as that conduit.

"This changes things," Rigel said.

Rigel looked at the more coherent Daphne, and they shared a look. She must have come to the same conclusion. But before they could act, Daphne one buckled over in pain, followed by the other two.

"What have you done, Druid?" Rigel went to the first Daphne's side.

"I have done nothing to them," the Druid said. "Bring her closer."

Rigel eyed the Druid through tight lids. Hesitation brought another heave of pain from the Daphne in his arms. Rigel acquiesced to the Druid's demand only for the sake of his companion.

"Bring the others as well."

One after the next, Rigel ushered the Daphne clones to the barrier where an opening appeared. He sent them each through before stopping at the entrance.

"Are you coming inside, Rigel?" the Druid asked.

His tone carried a hint of warning for Rigel, but he accepted the Druid's invite for his own reason. Once inside, he felt it, the unmistakable power of a ley-gate. Rigel set his plan in motion, slow and steady, he began siphoning energy from the lines.

The Druid walked up to the first Daphne and lay a hand upon her chest. With a movement of his fingers and chanting of a spell, he placed the rune. "Ha'ashtagga brandii." He stepped back as the construct took root in her body and left its mark upon her skin.

Daphne gasped for air and let out a releasing breath. As she stood up straight while her color returned, she watched as the Druid moved to her clones, repeating what he did to relieve the pain. As her head cleared, she was able to begin making sense of what happened. This was coming from their original, Aria.

"What has she done to us?" Daphne said. "This is Aria's doing."

The Druid stepped away from the last of the Daphnes and worked his way toward Rigel. When he began to chant a spell, Rigel backed away.

"What are you doing?"

"Hold still. This will protect you from whatever magic the Stevens are conjuring against us." The Druid moved closer as Rigel was backed against a glowing blue upright stone with no retreat. "Do you not feel it?"

Rigel had felt nothing before that moment. But as he explored his being, Rigel began to feel a stinging that crept along his back. As the pain intensified, Rigel leaped forward, and his shoulder fell against the Druid's open hand.

The burning across Rigel's back shifted to his arm and settled on the top forearm where the Druid's hand rested. He heard the spell but was unable to move before it took root. "Ha'ashtagga brandii."

Rigel yanked free of the Druid's touch and sidestepped the robbed man. He lifted his arm to cast a spell but was prevented from enacting it. Rigel pulled his shirt aside to look at the rune he knew was now burnt into his skin.

There, overtop the pre-existing tattoo from his borrowed skin of Jarrod Stevens, Rigel found the mark the Druid placed. He didn't recognize the rune, so he knew not what its purpose was. His suspicions included the inability to act against the Druid was one purpose for this mark.

"What have you done?" Rigel demanded.

"It is for your own protection," the Druid explained. "These marks will prevent the use of the Stevens' family magic from harming each of us."

Rigel thought for a moment about the ramifications but did not understand. "I was unable to enact a spell against you. What else is this mark for?"

The Druid laughed. "Have you forgotten from where your borrowed skin comes?" The Druid waiting for Rigel's face to crease then expand with his widening eyes. "You see, you have the skin of Jarrod Stevens, and thus any magic you attempt will be tainted by a Stevens. You can not act against me. None of you can."

Rigel looked at the Daphne clones. They, too, were unable to cast against the Druid. This he ascertained from the frustration in their movements and rebounding spells thrown at the Druid. The Daphnes were magical clones of Aria. Aria Stevens.

"Did you think I would trust you without condition?" the Druid said. "You who stole the skin of your own brother that sought your help and promised your freedom."

Rigel had no argument to stand against the Druid's words. The truth was there before him. Rigel double-crossed Jarrod when first this path was lain. Rigel tricked his brother into thinking he would help protect Jarrod's son from the magical world. When in fact, he has done nothing but manipulate everyone and everything for his own ends.

Rigel stole Jarrod's skin, sending his spirit into the void. Rigel then worked his way into the lives of the Stevens family. He pushed along events to reach some goal where he could enact his revenge for being imprisoned long ago. It mattered little that his millennia of entrapment was of his own doing. He failed to admit that one always ends up where they lead themselves.

The Druid watched Rigel. His glowing blue eyes narrowed on the man, reading the comprehension and consequent formulating of a way out. Before Rigel could say or do anything, the Druid cast another spell. "Ha'ashtagga castori awas."

Rigel and the Daphnes became engulfed in blue mist and energy crossed from the ley lines to the spells around them. Within seconds, the four hobbled mages were cast away from the Druid's circular stronghold and out beyond the barrier. As the tunnel through the magical shield closed, the Druid stepped up to the energy separating him from the others.

"You changed the rules of our bargain set millennia ago, Rigel. As I knew you would. You no longer have my protection, but I will not stand in your way of removing the Stevens boy from our time as agreed. This part of our deal must remain in place, or you will not care for the consequences."

Rigel could not see the face beneath the hood, but the warning was understandable in the Druid's eyes. The pain in his arm flared to reinforce the possibilities should Rigel or the Daphnes choose to stray from their agreement.

Days before Rigel was sentenced and sent to the void for acts against the magical and mundane world thousands of years ago, the Druid came to him. A bargain was struck.

The Druid assured Rigel he would be found guilty and his spirit torn from flesh to be cast into the void of nothingness for eternity. But there was a way out. Rigel would spend millennia in his prison until, at last, his own brother would offer him a way out of that inescapable fate. None could return from this prison, that is how it was designed. Until Rigel learned who the architect was. The Druid.

In return for being set free, Rigel was bound to the Druid's pact. His agreement was that one day the Druid would require Rigel to call him from the ages and help set a balance in magic. Rigel would help send a powerful boy into oblivion for the sake of maintaining the Emassa in this world. That boy turned out to be Colby Stevens, his own nephew. Rigel's feeling about this familial connection was yet uncertain.

"If it means regaining all use of magic to this body, I will stick to that single agreement."

The Druid nodded once and began to turn away. "I assure you that magic will flow again in that body."

"What do we get out of this agreement?" one of the Daphnes said.

The Druid turned back to face the Daphnes. "You will be freed from your curse."

"How?" The promise of freedom from Aria coursed into the runes on their chest, setting them on edge from the backlash of magic. They looked at one another, feeling their own prison. Connected to their original.

"You must face yourself and prevail." The Druid pointed to a formation outside the barrier. A single upright boulder.

The Daphnes took only one meaning from the Druid's words. They needed to go after Aria and destroy her. With a wave of their arms, they each cast a spell to travel the ley lines. Their direction was to the single stone from the henge that remained outside the barrier to the north.

Rigel's eyes widened when he realized the heel stone was connected to the ley-gate. It hadn't occurred to him that he could connect to the power of ley magic from anything but a ley-gate itself. He looked at the Druid for a moment to gauge if he would be stopped. When the Druid turned away. Rigel took his leave.

They were going after the Stevens.

As Rigel and Daphne left, someone stepped from behind the heel stone. Shelly.

"You have what I asked for?" The Druid said.

"Yes, but I need to know why you want this old watch."

Shelly approached the henge, and the barrier opened for her to enter. She stepped up to the Druid and held out Jarrod Stevens' old watch for the man to take. When he took it, she shivered at the sight of runes swirling over the surface of his skin.

"What happened to you?" Shelly asked.

"A story for another time Shelly." The Druid rechecked the cowl of his robe. "Soon enough, this part of my journey will close, and the real struggle will begin."

"What the hell is that supposed to mean? And what's with my dad's old watch?"

The Druid put the watch on and relished the feel of the old timepiece on his wrist. "This is where the time loop began, with this old watch and the spell Jarrod cast for the child centuries ago under my instruction. But only a decade ago for your brother."

"But you're still going to help my brother, right?"

The Druid shrugged. "Help? Yes in some ways. It may not look as you expect, but you'll have to trust in my plans."

"Yeah well, I'm not sure I agree with all this. And where did Frick and the crazy Fracks just go?"

"Oh, they are running a little errand for me, only they don't know it."

Shelly glared at the Druid. There was something about this man that unsettled her. And the four other druids that just hovered in the distance as though waiting for orders to move.

"A straight answer would be helpful. Are they-"

"Go. They are at the house trying their best to fight your friends and family." The Druid raised his hand at Shelly's protest. "They can't hurt them. I've seen to that with a certain series of spells. Just keep our deal quiet, and everything will work out."

Shelly puckered her lips and huffed. "Fine. But don't think we're done with this conversation. There's something else cooking' here, and it ain't smelling good."

The Druid nodded and handed a scroll to Shelly before stepping back into the shadows. There would be much explaining, but not everything, and not yet.

"What's this?" Shelly asked.

"It is an added gift for bringing me what I asked. Read and perform the spell. I think you will find the expansion on your innate abilities, enlightening."

Shelly unrolled the scroll and immediately began chanting the spell. She had never seen anything like it. When a rush flooded over her skin, Shelly became dizzy for a moment before getting her footing. At first, she felt nothing different and began to frown.

"What gives?"

"Patience, dear Shelly. You will find that the gift is not obvious, or subtle, but something in-between." The Druid chuckled and dismissed Shelly by way of pushing her by magic into the lei-lines.

CHAPTER 6

Aria stood arm's length from the ley-gate uncovered in the backyard of her home. She could tell from the design and the ancient runes inlaid on the foreign stone, that it was not as old as it seemed. This construction was put here purposefully. Placement of the ring was likely near when the Stevens' purchased the property and after the children were born. More to the point, after Colby was born.

For the love of her husband, Aria accepted the secrecy as part of Jarrod's attempt to protect their son and family. Still, it fueled her agitation of being left out of the planning. This gate invited more attention than anything that had happened on the property prior. Emassa radiated off the stones, in spite of the locking spell currently covering them.

No sooner the thought entered her mind about the locked gate, the spell dropped, and sparks began to chase around the stones. Aria was thrown back when a bubble of energy erupted from the circle that expanded up and outward. Aria brushed the hair from her face and looked up from the ground to see three reflections of herself stepping out from the circle of stones. The Daphnes.

"Hello sister," the Daphnes said as one. "Glad to see you on the ground, groveling already."

Aria jumped to her feet and lifted her hands. She prepared a spell and shielded herself. She was confused when the spells thrown from her cloned lessors sputtered and fell short of reaching her. Not sure if they were playing games with her, Aria kept her shield in place with one hand, while she prepared an attack spell with the other.

Runes formed in the air as Aria drew them with her finger. When the last symbol was created, Aria launched it at her nearest assailant. The spell hit the Daphne squarely, yet nothing happened. The magical force dissolved upon impact, sending the residue cascading to the ground.

Aria was not solely surprised. Daphne, most lucid of the gradually degenerate clones, felt nothing of the impact from Aria's spell. She would have laughed had she not realized the implications. Aria could not more use magic against her clones as they could her. Daphne tried to stop her other sisters' futile attempts, but they were not as quick thinking. The problem with copies of copies, each is something less than its original.

"Stop," Daphne one shouted. "This will get us nowhere."

Her third clone took that to mean a physical assault and charged Aria.

Aria saw the crazed and violet-haired doppelgänger running for her. Without thinking, she turned to the closest thing she saw. A garbage can.

"Time to take out the trash."

Aria used her magic to levitate the trash can and sent it sailing through the air. It smashed into the oncoming halfwit, knocking her ten feet back and to the ground. Daphne number three was out cold.

"One down, two to go."

Aria scanned the yard. But she was not alone in her thinking. The remaining clones also found that they could use indirect magic against another.

Stones, dirt, garden statues, anything available was fair game as a weapon. The Stevens' backyard became an all-out frenzy of garden-gnome wars. With each object flying through the air at the combatants, the noise level grew with smashing into shields and other airborne missiles. All the residual magic drew a sizable audience of pixies, trolls, and grimalts. But they were not the only ones drawn to the ruckus.

Nana stood at the backdoor, stunned motionless at the scene. She watched for only a few moments before a cast aside garden spade flew a hairsbreadth away from her head and lodged into the side of the house.

"What the sam hell is going on out here?" Nana shouted. "Kids!"

Nana took a waddling run for the nearest Daphne and cast a bolt of energy at her. The magic scoured into the clone but only slowed her down. But it got her attention.

"The old wasp can sting," Daphne said. "You must not be entirely a Stevens' witch."

Nana lifted back her head on her necks and pulled up her lips. "What are you blathering on about? I'm not a Stevens. I'm the mother-in-law and not alone!"

The Daphnes understood that meant that whatever prevented the Stevens' magic from working on them only diluted the old witch's spell. Did that mean they could affect the witch as well? One of them decided to find out.

Middle Daphne, the one with dirty auburn hair, sent an energy blast directed at Nana. She was old and squatty, but the Daphne was surprised at how quick the old battle-ax could move. But then again, it wasn't just any old woman Daphne now faced. Bellatrix was inside the wiry-haired head, she could sense her presence.

"Come out and play Bellatrix," the Daphne taunted. "Why not try and finish what you started long ago?"

Of course, the Daphne spoke of the entrapment curse that Bellatrix used centuries past. But Bellatrix was reminded by her alter ego of the device she carried in her pocket. The rune brands.

As Daphne sent a spell at Nana's inhabited body, Bellatrix fumbled for the device and managed to separate the runes. Not knowing which she grabbed, she whispered her intent and cast the rune free.

The rune glowed and raced through the air between the two adversaries, but it sailed by the intended target and landed on the unconscious one. It found purchase on her chest and buried its mark into Daphne three, waking her from unintended respite.

When Daphne two saw that her clone sister was rising without apparent harm, she took this to mean the spell had not worked. Renewed in her intent, the Daphne launched another attack on Nana. But it never landed as another body leaped before the spell and took the hit.

Colby charged between Nana and the crazed copy of his mother. When the bolt of Emassa-fueled energy hit, it burst apart and dissipated. Colby landed hard on his side in the grass but was otherwise unharmed. Not taking time to check for injury, Colby launched a barrage of attacks on his grandmother's attacker.

Hashtag spell after another, raised from his phWatch. Colby used stored offensive spells because they were easiest to conjure. One after the next, the spells hit the Daphnes without effect. Somehow they were immune to Colby's magic. Not just Colby's magic was impotent against these intruders, none of his friends could manage any lasting repellent against the Daphnes except Nana to a certain degree.

Colby saw his mother, she used objects around the yard to direct an offensive. Locating a cement statue of some woodland animal, Colby sent it hurtling toward a Daphne. He hadn't realized it was a garden troll until it met with Daphne's body, an actual troll, not a statue.

The troll called out in anger at being launched like a stone. It cared nothing for the fact it was not Daphne who had disturbed its feeding on magical residue. The troll sunk his teeth into Daphne's leg and lock on.

As Daphne screamed, Colby used her distracted state to locate another troll. What he found as he turned was Nana fighting with another Daphne. He watched as his grandmother launched a metal object at the woman and how it burned into Daphne's chest. The spell didn't seem to do anything but annoy the already agitated clone.

As his grandmother fumbled in her pocket and ran toward the last Daphne, Colby realized Nana was up to something. She had already used this strange spell, and it seemingly failed. Why would she do so again? After it failed a second time, his grandmother was heading for the last Daphne. She had some plans.

Colby ran interference and signaled the others to help. They needed to keep the first two Daphnes busy and away from Nana.

"Help me keep these crazy bitches busy," Colby said.

"No problemo, dude." Jasper pushed out with his might and sent a wall of power at the closest clone.

While the kids kept the others busy, Colby glanced over his shoulder to check on Nana's progress with the last Daphne. She had something in her hand and whispered to it. As he watched it fly from her hand, a garden hoe raised up and intercepted. The piece of metal stopped glowing and ricocheted off to the side of the garage. Colby ran for the magical device.

Assuming his grandmother had planned for this attack with

Bellatrix's help, Colby figured this was some enchanted device. He reached the projectile and picked it up. It was a rune. It had the sweeping curves of part of a rune he saw in his journal. He rolled it in his hand a moment before hearing Nana's voice.

"Throw it at the crazy bitch."

Colby smirked and pulled back to throw the spelled object. Something grabbed his hand and pulled the rune away. Colby turned his head and swung around with his other arm when he saw Rigel.

Rigel smiled, showing his misleading perfect teeth. His guile and devious nature shone in his eyes, however. As Colby raised his arm to hit him, Rigel grabbed ahold of Colby's other wrist and chanted a spell.

While in Stonehenge, Rigel collected ley line energy for more than one reason. The least of which was to bolster his personal defense. This meant the rune the Druid placed on him was not permanent. At the very least, Rigel knew he could copy it to Colby and put the same limitations on his magic. He would be helpless against the Druid.

As Rigel spoke the last rune name, it focused a ball of energy over the mark on his shoulder. The ball reformed into a duplicate of the rune placed on him by the Druid. Rigel watched as the glowing form sunk into Colby's skin and burnt his flesh.

Colby screamed out from the pain. He fell from Rigel's grasp as the man laughed.

Rigel watched as Colby struggled but then noticed the rune changing shape on Colby's skin. It no longer had the sharp angles as it bent into what looked like a backward, tremble clef symbol from the musical annotation. His eyes hardened as he felt the duplicitous nature of the Druid behind this, and Rigel allowed himself to be used again.

Rigel turned to the kids fighting and went to the aid of the Daphnes. He could not affect harm against Colby, the Druid saw to that. Rigel also feared what would happen should he not follow through with his bargain with the hooded man. It was time to leave.

Rigel drove the kids back toward Colby and away from his companions, but one of the Daphnes was not behind him. Rigel scanned the yard to find her reaching down where the metal object had fallen from Colby's hand.

"No!" Rigel cried, but his warning went unheard.

Daphne ran for Aria with the metal in her hand, hoping to drive it into her heart. Aria's back was to the oncoming threat until Daphne screamed.

Aria spun around in time to feel the small metal rune hit her above the heart. A sharp twinge was all she felt as the device revolted from the glowing on Aria's chest.

The rune resumed glowing and burned free of Daphne, who let go due to the pain. She was looking at her hand when the rune blasted her back twenty feet and fell to the ground. The Daphne was down as well but began to stagger to her feet.

Two of the three Daphne began to yowl and hiss as the runes started to do their work. The last created Daphne stumbled and began to disintegrate. Her essence swirled and dove into the chest of the one she was copied from.

Aria yelped as her mind cleared, and her magical energy spiked. Her eyes widened when she looked up to see only two Daphnes left. The glow on her chest, she realized, was familiar. It was from a series of runes used in the spell that split her ages ago. Someone had set a reversal enchantment on her and her clones.

Nana stepped up next to Aria. "Breath easy, my child. This will be done soon."

Aria watched as her second clone dissolved like the first. Only one clone remained, her original twin. Aria prepared herself for the reconstitution wearing a trepidatious smile. Aria took a step toward Daphne.

Daphne screamed. "How have you done this?" She turned in a circle, looking for help when she spotted Rigel. "Help me."

Rigel was shocked into inaction from the sight of such magic in use. The power used to split Daphne from Aria and then create her clones was nothing compared to this. The fact something as simple as a metal rune, obviously enchanted, could accomplish such magic…he didn't know Bellatrix had it in her. When he looked at the old witch, he realized she didn't.

Nana stood next to Aria with the same awe in her eyes that Rigel held. One could not help but be impressed by such power, even from an adversary. That look told Rigel she only enacted something she received from someone else. The Druid.

Anger washed the awe off Rigel's face as he reddened. With a running leap, Rigel dashed for Daphne and wrapped his arms around her. They disappeared into the ley lines.

"Go after them," Colby shouted.

"No," Shelly said from the back steps.

Colby turned and only then realized she had been absent from the fight. "Where have you been?"

"I was out looking for Bruce," Shelly lied.

She had actually been on-line checking the web and social media for any indication on where he might be. In typical Bruce ignorance, he had checked-in a few times on his Blabber app, so it wasn't a complete lie. She knew where to find him now.

"What's been happening here?" Shelly asked.

Colby began the story and relayed what happened from his point of view, but differed to Aria to start at the beginning. After she retold how the arrival of the Daphnes began the battle, Colby turned to Nana to explain the runes.

"That was from that Druid fellow. He made a deal with Bellatrix long ago, and it was time to pay the piper."

"So he what, gave you these enchanted runes to do what exactly?" Colby asked. He still hadn't pieced it together.

"Were you not paying attention, boy?" Bellatrix's voice took control of Nana's mouth. "It is the means to fix your mother. But that little upstart Rigel has interrupted the process."

"That's not all he did," Colby said, rubbing his arm. "He branded me with something, and I have no idea what it's for."

Colby showed his arm to Bellatrix and the others. No one had a clue what it meant. It was unlike any rune ever used by any of them. Even Fizzlewink hadn't seen it.

"Couple more of those fancy tattoos, and you'll be joining a biker gang and hanging out with carnival folk," Fizzlewink said.

"That's stereotyping cat-man. Shut up, or we'll send you to the circus." Shelly scowled at the little man. "And what were you doing during the fighting?"

Fizzlewink straightened up and took offense. "I was busy chasing off the pixies. They were everywhere lapping up magical residue."

"I think the pixies were the least of our worries," Jasper said. "Though they were annoying."

"Ah yeah. And the pixies would have swarmed without my having run them off. A pixie swarm is nothing to be in the center of."

As they all walked back to the house and entered, Fizzlewink spat out some wings from his teeth.

"OMG Fizz," Darla said, "Did you eat a pixie?"

Fizzlewink smiled. "Several. I love pixies. They taste like chicken."

Darla gaged.

"What? They aren't all cute like Tinker-bell."

Everyone was still grossed out.

"Better on toast with a little butter."

"Shut up, Fizz," Shelly said.

"Fizzlewink's noshing needs notwithstanding, we should eat and decide what's next," Nana said.

Colby turned to the others. "Next? Forget eating again, let's take the fight to them. The ley-gate is still unlocked."

CHAPTER 7

The Heel Stone at Stonehenge began to glow as the energy burst forth, throwing Rigel and Daphne from the ley line. They landed with as much grace as a pelican landing in tar.

Rigel untangled himself from Daphne and charged the barrier, separating him from the Druid.

"What have you done?"

The Druid stood opposite the energy wall and stared back. He said nothing. He did, however, shift his eyes to Daphne and lowered his eyelids enough to speak volumes.

Rigel glanced back at Daphne and returned his glare to the Druid.

"You weren't expecting her back, were you?" Rigel said and began to pace before the shield. "You were reconstituting Aria. That was what your tête-à-tête with the old hag was about."

"My dealings with Bellatrix are my own concern. For that matter, that creature and her copies should be as little concern for you as your care for anything but yourself."

Rigel wasn't sure how to react. Whereas in previous dealings with the Druid, the man remained level and without emotion. Now it would seem a nerve had been struck.

"What is she to you?" Rigel asked. "There is a connection here that I'm missing."

The Druid laughed without mirth. "The great professor has been left in the dark. You've been used and manipulated. How violated that must make you feel."

"What is that supposed to imply?"

"I've implied nothing interloper. You'd be advised to steady the course and stay out of my way."

Rigel threw a punch at the barrier. His reward was a static charge that sent him head over feet back where Daphne was just finding her feet. Rigel took her back down to the dirt when they collided. Daphne was in too much internal turmoil to struggle with Rigel.

She remained limp on the ground as Rigel stood.

"Get up and fight," Rigel commanded.

"I'm overwhelmed," Daphne admitted. "This is too much."

Rigel looked at Daphne with a mixture of contempt and disgust. "Shut up and stay there then."

Rigel turned away from Daphne and left her behind. He walked with heavy steps back to the barrier, sparks flying from his outstretched hands. When he was a foot away from the shield, Rigel pushed his arms forward and released the magic he was siphoning from the leylines. The barrier began to waver.

The Druid stepped back from the energy wall keeping him within and safe from the paradox that threatened to undo his progress. He turned to the Shade hovering nearby. Then motioned for two of his companion druids to take position behind him.

The Druid looked at the Shade. "Stop him." He turned to his companions as the Shade moved outside the barrier. "Lend me your strength and cunning."

Power surged between the three robed figures inside the henge. The energy of the Emassa flowed between them and mixed with bolts of power coursing from the ley lines beneath the blue stones surrounding them. Each druid spread his arms and sent magic into the shield, keeping it from failing under Rigel's attack.

Before the Shade made it to Rigel, it noticed two new arrivals to the plains. Colby and Rhea stepped free of the ley line and walked away from the Heel stone. Upon seeing them, it moved back into the circle and whispered a raspy message into its master's ear.

"Shift your magic to the Heel. It's time to break the link."

As one, the druids turned to face the Heel stone and focused their combined might at the large unworked boulder. With a single show of force, magic slammed into the conduit of the ley line below ground. The rebounding power split the stone down the center. The way was closed from outside the henge. With the breaking of the rock, so ended Rigel's source of extra power.

The assault on the Druids barrier ended. And Rigel fell to his knees.

"No!" Rigel cried out. "I will not-"

Rigel's words cut short by a spray of dirt as a blast of Emassa landed inches from him. He turned to see Colby running toward him and Rhea toward Daphne. Rigel jumped to his feet and stood firm.

"You can't hurt me, nephew. That mark prevents it." Rigel pointed to the rune exposed on his arm through burnt away fabric. "I think we are at an impasse."

Colby paused when Rigel called him nephew. "What?"

"It's a shame, really. I was beginning to like you, despite your parentage." Rigel shifted his appearance to that of Jarrod Stevens. "Recognize this skin?"

The energy inside the barrier stopped. The Druid moved closer to the edge of his shield to listen. This was the moment he was waiting for.

Colby stumbled to the side as his eyes refused to focus, and his brain reeled from the sight before him. The truth stood there before him, and yet he refused to accept it.

"You lie," Colby said. "No."

"Yes, boy," Rigel said. "I stole his skin the night he tried to release me thinking I would grant him a favor. I granted him oblivion for his part in my imprisonment."

"No." Colby charged Rigel.

When Colby reached Rigel, He was unprepared for the shifting movement of his target. As he lurched forward, Rigel spun and pushed Colby into the magically charged barrier around the henge. Colby was held fast by the power coursing through him. He did not feel the Druid's hand push against his back from within the shield.

The Druid pushed his hand further toward Colby's back, using the arm that held Jarrod's watch. Emassa sparked between the watch face and Colby, fixing itself onto something within his body. The Druid pulled his hand back, making a fist and yanking something free. It was energy, red and pulsing. Colby's Shizumu magic.

With a final tugging effort, the Druid yanked his prize free and let Colby fall to the earth. The red magical energy of Shizumu that was part of Colby was now seeping into the Druid. It found a welcome return as though returning home. It was back where it belonged, from the Druid's point of view. It was his once and is again.

Colby hardly noticed the change inside him. His mind was racing with what Rigel revealed. His father was gone, and Rigel now wore his skin like a second-hand suit. Vomit and bile-filled Colby's mouth. The force of his expulsion from his innards entered his nasal cavity and shot from his nose. Stinging, burning, noxious smelling remnants of his last meal piled on the ground before him.

Colby's body revolted to the point of breathlessness. He gasped in hard.

Sensory overload took Colby away from the moment. He was unaware of anything around him. Colby didn't notice the barrier behind him fall as the Druid stepped free of the henge.

Instead of going for Colby, the Druid stepped aside and let the two other robed figures race out after Rigel.

"Take him," the Druid said. "He needs to be contained."

The four druid minions lumbered to life from positions within the circle. They moved past Colby with what he noticed as an almost artificial gate. It was as though they were being controlled as opposed to the natural, fluid movement of an individual.

Colby reached out toward one of the druids. His finger brushed its cold hand. As bumps rose on Colby's arm, he realized there was no life in that clammy appendage. The shiver raced down his spine at the thought of the Druid using corpses to do his bidding.

The first two lifeless things reached Rigel, but they were not fast enough. Rigel moved out of reach and headed for Daphne, who was not as fast.

Daphne struggled against the two creatures holding her. She felt the soulless nature of those restraining her. The hands, cold as stone, sapped the fight from Daphne. Her magic failing, mixed with the effects of her recombined constitution, prevented Daphne from rebelling. A charge of ley magic coursed through her just before she would have otherwise passed out.

The influx of power was just the boost required to send the druid captors flailing back from Daphne. Colby watched this taking place, the thoughts racing through his mind as what these creatures could be. As he stood, finally breathing freely and regaining some strength, He was forced back to the ground. He lay face to the sky as pressure from invisible forces held him to the dirt and pushed down on his chest.

The sun blinded Colby's vision until a shadowed head eclipsed the star. Rigel glared down at Colby.

"I may be unable to directly use magic against you," Rigel said. "But indirect magic is sufficiently capable."

"What do you want?" Colby squeezed the words from his burdened lungs.

Rigel laughed. He moved his head closer to Colby's face. "I would have thought that obvious by now. You are not as bright as I would have thought."

Colby found his words cut off by the increasing pressure. All he could do was turn his head aside and wait for the inevitable. Then he saw the blast of light that forced him to squint.

Energy from behind the Druid threatened to knock him to his knees as the ley line below the henge delivered its passengers. Nana, Aria, Shelly, and the remaining members of Colby's companions all entered the mix.

"Get away from my son," Aria shouted.

She ran toward the Druid, but pushed past him and headed for Rigel. Before Aria could reach her son and the monster hurting him, a familiar presence raked the edge of her awareness of the magical world. She slowed her pace just as something brushed past her.

The Shade, set forth by the Druid, sailed through the space between the mysterious figure and Rigel. The Druid ordered him to remove the threat on Colby. He needed the boy unharmed for the moment. It was not time to proceed to the next level.

The blue and misty specter reached Rigel and slammed directly into him. Where he passed through the side of Aria, his vapor form reacted as a solid mass when it met with its target. The reaction from Rigel was immediate.

Rigel's skin smoked from beneath his scorched shirt. The Shade knocked him away from Colby, releasing the spell holding the boy down. When Rigel attempted to gain his feet, the Shade renewed its attack.

The two foes wrestled in the dirty shadowed ground of Stonehenge. Rigel screamed without reserve each time the wraith made contact with his skin. Confused at how a non-corporeal form could have enough substance to harm him, Rigel was not prepared to fight back.

Colby, his feelings for Rigel set aside, could no longer witness what was happening to the man. The ghostly blue form pummeled Rigel into submission, but the screams made it sound as though Rigel was being torn apart. It was when Rigel lifted an arm in defense, making contact with the Shade, that Colby saw the truth. It was not only Rigel screaming. Somehow the connection between the two battling magics caused both parties intense pain.

Colby raised his arm without thinking. Calling up the hashtag magic app, Colby released a stored spell. The magic gathered and formed a sphere of blue light before him. Before the spell sped away from him, Colby's eyes widened at the blue hue his spell carried. It wasn't his signature purple brilliance.

The Shade lifted its head toward the oncoming magic. Just before it hit, the wispy spirit lifted free of Rigel and hovered just above.

The magic knocked Rigel ten feet from the torn grass and dirt pit created by the struggle. The Shade was unmoved by the result, Rigel was stunned.

Colby was able to use direct magic on him now.

Rigel began to gather himself and stand when the Shade reached down and grabbed him by the shirtsleeves. Lifting the man slightly above the ground, the Shade carried Rigel back to the Druid, depositing him into the waiting hands of the Druid's henchmen.

Colby, surrounded by his friends and family, tried to cast spells to halt the escaping mages, but their magic never reached the Druid and his crew. After watching his blue magic fade, Colby witnessed the Druid placing a collar on Rigel like he were a dog. They all disappeared into the ley lines as the Druid turned to look at Colby with glowering purple eyes.

Colby looked down at his hands, blue static bounced between his fingers. He sent a mental probe into his own core to verify his suspicions. His Shizumu magic was gone.

CHAPTER 8

Colby arrived back home, frustrated. He tried fruitlessly to track the destination of the Druid through the ley lines but came up blocked. He had a trail, a taste at the tip of his tongue, of where the Druid took his followers, but each time he neared a solution, something stopped him.

It wasn't until Jasper's constant prodding to go home sunk in, that Colby gave up and allowed Aria to lead the way back to the Stevens' house. When they did arrive back at the house, Colby's mood only darkened more. He was coming to grips with the fact something was taken from him. His Shizumu magic.

"Where are you going?" Fizzlewink demanded as Colby ran up the stairs.

"I have to be sure of something," Colby answered as he took two steps at a time. "Leave me alone for a minute for the love of… whatever."

Colby left the dumbfounded expressions and inaudible complaints behind him as he bounded up the stairs to his father's study. When at last he reached the door, he stood there with a hand over the door, waiting.

Colby felt no build-up of energy. He didn't gain the insight of time and space that accompanied the transition between the present from the protected time field that surrounded the room beyond this door. His magic was indeed hobbled again. Or it was taken.

Suspecting something amiss, Colby ran back down the stairs to his room. Reaching his shelves, he opened a small wooden box where he kept the key to the study. It was still there, but something else was gone. His father's watch. He remembered having it on that morning, he wore it regularly. He did not remember putting it back or taking it off.

Colby knew there was a connection between that watch and the time not long ago his magic resurfaced from his childhood. Over a decade ago now, his magic abilities were hobbled when his father enacted a spell to protect him. That same spell took his magic and bound it to the watch, he now realized. The watch was gone and along with it, his ability to warp time.

Colby still had the use of Emassa, just not everything he had only a day ago. How? Then he remembered something he saw before the Druid disappeared with Rigel, Daphne, and his robed minions. Colby focused on that single moment and vision. His father's watch, there on the Druid's wrist as the sleeve fell back.

"Shit!"

Colby ran back up the stairs with the key and opened the way to his father's undisturbed study. He called for his father's journal, half expecting it not to obey. The book appeared before him on the desk. Colby exhaled and rubbed his hands through his hair.

He opened the book expecting to find some insight on the Druid. He found no reference to the Druid, but he paused when reaching a passage on the formation of the golem.

Creatures, created from the earth, golem were servants to the will of their master. This was accomplished through hand molding the clay heart of their servants, then imbuing the center with a piece of their own will. A whisper of intent and sharing of their own soul was the life force behind something more than clay and mud.

While a mindless obeyer of commands could be easily formed, a more advanced creature could be made with something more added to the mix, a piece of one's soul. Colby shuddered.

He realized that the tether between him and his four friends was a piece of his own spirit. But he did not create them. Though now that he thought about it harder, flashes of their creation came to his mind.

Colby fell back and out of the chair. His nose bled, and head ached as he lay on the study floor. Colby could not complete the vision, it would not obey his recall as it seemed out of sync with his time. Colby was unsure how he realized this distortion of reality, but he felt it as truth.

There was more going on than Colby realized. The Druid was connecting to this in some way, but Colby had no way to determine how. Or did he?

Realization formed in Colby's mind as he remembered Bellatrix's connection to this new player in the game his life was becoming. Then there was the actual game being made of his magic. His temper flared.

Emassa flowed through to Colby from the ley line in the back yard. It pierced through the time field, protecting Jarrod's study and flowed into Colby's rage-filled hunger for answers. In a single moment of clarity, Colby saw the answers to his questions. Still, they were jumbled and set on a random and slightly changing repeat in his vision.

As his frustration built, the images raced faster and faster through his minds-eye. Colby began to convulse when an image of the Druid stood next to his father. They smiled and embraced. Colby's head hit the floor with force enough to crack the wood floor.

Magic spread across the floor, spiderwebbing around the room until it encompassed the entire time field surrounding the study. Before Colby lost consciousness, he witnessed his surroundings moving through time. Objects that once protected by the time field now aged as though it never had the protection the room once afforded. The field collapsed.

Fizzlewink and Bellatrix were first to arrive after feeling the disturbance when it first started. They charged up the stairs to the dismay of the others, until the house began to shake.

Colby lay there on the floor, shaking in a magically charged seizure. The Emassa folded in around Colby as his body shook, each contact with the floor sending an out-of-time ripple through the entire house. The barrier of time and space around the room was folding in on itself, and Colby was at the epicenter.

Fizzlewink tried to run into the room to help his charge, but the shockwaves coming off Colby sent the cat-man flailing back the way he came. Only Bellatrix's age-defying reflexes kept Fizzlewink from an awkward introduction to the walls outside the room.

Bellatrix lowered Fizzlewink to the floor before reaching out and grabbing hold of the doorframe to the study. The veil of time was shattered and they could see into the room's non-present state, but could not enter. As the other's closed in from the floor below, Nana turned her Bellatrix guided head and ordered everyone to get down.

Magic flowed from the frail appearing arms of Nana and into the wooden supports around the doorframe. Bellatrix used her borrowed body's voice to speak ancient words that did not register recognition in any ear beside one person who just appeared.

"Step aside," Betelgeuse said. "I've been waiting for this."

Betelgeuse pushed past everyone except Bellatrix's host, Nana. "Excuse me, but I think I can be of help."

Nana looked with frustrated anger at Betelgeuse before Bellatrix took over and realized that her estranged husband's dealings with the Druid might help.

"Be my guest." Bellatrix released the magic she was channeling and stepped aside.

The house began to shake more violently after Bellatrix stopped intervening. "I hope you know what you're doing this time."

Betelgeuse turned his head fast enough for the joints to crack. "Shut up, woman."

Bellatrix immediately realized and regretted her comment at once. She lowered her eyes and stepped back, leaving her husband to perform his appointed task.

Betelgeuse reached into his pocket and retrieved a package. The wrapping was an old withering cotton cloth tied with a vine. The fabric crumbled as Betelgeuse opened it to reveal a worm-eaten and crumbling block of wood. When he held it against the barrier, a flash of magic imbued light returned the object to its time-lost shape. A wooden windup train car.

As the few eyes that recognized the little train, it burst apart and evaporated in the time stream. When it was gone, so was the protection once afforded the old study and its content. Colby lay motionless on the cracked floor.

"Get the boy out of here," Betelgeuse said as he collected the journal and key to the room. "Now!"

"What's the hurry," Sheila said. She tried to help Jasper carry Colby, but he pushed away all offers of help.

"We need to get out of this room before the magic rebounds."

Nobody but Bellatrix seemed to understand the meaning of Betelgeuse's words. She ushered everyone out of the room before turning to pull her husband free and erect a shield in time to buffer the backlash. Energy slammed against her barrier of protection as the years of power from the room's spell rebounded along the strings of the continuum.

"Sloppy," Betelgeuse said. "Good thing this isn't a common ability."

Bellatrix motioned everyone downstairs after they laid Colby down in his bed. She stayed behind with Rhea, who insisted on staying to heal him.

"I can't heal his split skin," Rhea said. "His bleeding stopped, but I don't think I had anything to do with that."

Bellatrix turned as she heard someone at the door.

Betelgeuse looked at her only a moment before leaving her and Rhea alone.

Bellatrix retreated, allowing Nana to turned back to Rhea and patted her hand.

"It's not your fault, dear. Your connection to Colby is…let's just bandage him up as best we can."

Colby stirred as Nana wrapped his scalp with bandages and gauze.

"Stop it!"

"You stop it," Rhea said. "You've got a nasty bump, and you aren't healing under my touch."

Colby waved her off. As he rushed to sit up, the room swayed, and he caught himself falling back. "Whoa."

"Take it easy, Fart-blossom," Nana said. "You've had quite an episode."

Colby waved off Nana's hand. "It was more like four episodes on random repeat."

"What?"

"It's all fading faster than waking from a vivid dream." Colby shook his head. "Damnit."

"What is it, Colby?" Rhea asked.

Colby just looked at Rhea with glazing eyes. He felt dread when he looked at her, but he couldn't remember why.

"Rhea, can you leave us alone for a minute, please. I need to talk to Bellatrix."

Rhea left, though she hovered by the door before leaving. A pleading look from Colby sent her down the stairs, leaving him a private moment with the old witch inside his grandmother's head.

"Look into me, old woman."

Nana looked over Colby with Bellatrix's eyes. "What is it you want to know, grandson?"

"What don't you see?"

Bellatrix looked deeper until she realized what Colby was referencing. "It's gone."

"How much?"

"Just the magic," Bellatrix said with consolation. "Your spirit remains intact."

Colby slumped, defeated. "How am I gonna do this with only half of what I can barely even understand how to use?"

Bellatrix stood Nana's hunched body up straight. "Suck it up, boy," she said. "Or whatever they say these days. You aren't alone in this fight, you do realize that?"

"Yeah, well…" Colby started. "I can't very well help much when I'm half of what I could barely control. And now with Hashtag Magic in the wild…" Colby jumped when something appeared next to him at the table.

"I warned you that gizmo magic was a crutch," Fizzlewink said as he jumped up next to Colby.

"What the little obstinate blueberry means is that you have to adapt." Nana's voice returned as Bellatrix retreated. "You aren't alone. We'll all help you know."

As they all gathered around Colby to show support, he felt comfortable and less burdened. Perhaps it was the lessening of stress or the combined magical network around him, but his four-point vision returned.

"Hold on," Colby said. "I see those visions again. I see the Druid."

Colby focused on the thoughts that were floating in his mind as the visions returned. The unmistakeable golem nature of the Druid's followers. As he focused on their empty, cold, soulless existence, his tether jumped from the golem to their master. The Druid's mind now connected to Colby. Apter was the slamming together of consciences within Colby's minds-eye.

Pain and agony first spread through Colby as he delved into the memory of the Druid. Feelings of isolation and memories of hard lessons. He felt the branding of every rune that raced across the Druid's skin. He felt connected to him in every effort to create magic. This man endured much before he rose to whatever place among his people he now held.

But Colby felt nothing negative like a need for vengeance. He could find no motive whatsoever as he probed the Druid's thoughts. He dove deeper, trying to see further into the Druid's past but found the way blocked by a set of purple eyes staring at him in the darkest recesses of the shared vision.

"Not for you to see, but a valiant and unexpected effort."

The Druid threw Colby from his memories and pushed him from his mind.

But Colby resisted. With a final push, Colby was sent reeling from the place the Druid was, but not without a last visual reference.

Colby's body spasmed and lurched back in his bed. The

convulsions did not happen as they did the first time as he was more mentally prepared for the backlash this time.

"What did you see?" Nana asked as she offered a glass of water.

Fizzlewink handed Colby some licorice. "Eat this."

Colby took the water and chewed on the candy. "I saw a lot of things, nothing that tells me who this guy is or why he's here."

Colby noticed a look pass between Nana and Shelly but decided to file it away for a later explanation. He pulled over his tablet and brought up a search for images and googled Chinese man heads in a circle. He scrolled through many pages before Darla stopped him.

Darla pushed her phone in front of Colby. "Did you see these?"

Colby smiled at the photo. A large circle arrangement of white stone half-headed men. The look was much like the unearthed terra-cotta Ming dynasty statues from China, only white and only part of their heads peeking through the ground.

"That's it," Colby said. "Where is that?"

Darla smiled, but with a tremble in her lip. "Close. Really close. The

Chicago lakefront within walking distance from here."

The room grew still and silent. The Druid traveled all the way to Chicago with his minions.

"Time to see what he's up to," Colby said. "But we have to be careful with all the mundanes around."

Nana smiled. "Sounds like a good time to use some glamor magic."

CHAPTER 9

One thing that Nana and Bellatrix both excelled in was putting on a disguised face. This extended into the ability to glamour themselves into not only appearing as someone else but to become indistinguishable from another person. Bellatrix already turned down Colby's general spells he and Gary used at Halloween for costuming. Those Hashtag Magic guises would not fool the Druid.

"Why do you think the Druid would see through our guise spells?" Colby asked.

Nana cocked her right brow and tilted her head. "Have you never noticed the buzz your magic gives off?"

"Huh?"

"It's rather annoying," Nana continued. "Your magic, everyone's magic, has a distinctive signature. Yours, when conjured through your gizmos, also has a low vibrating buzz."

Colby frowned and turned on his grandmother, whose voice was distinctly that of her secondary personality, Bellatrix.

"Why am I only hearing about this now?"

Bellatrix laughed. "You have eyes but are blind to the subtle world around you, boy. Open your mind and magic up to your surroundings. You must learn to see with your mind as well as your eyes."

"Riddles from the harpy," Fizzlewink hissed. "I hear no such buzz. Just add something to your spell to blend in and obscure your spell." Fizzlewink snapped his finger and transformed into a gull.

"Well, see the cat-man makes sense, though now his bird-form suits his bird-brain." Bellatrix laughed alone at her joke.

Colby wrinkled his brow thinking of how to accomplish the obscuring, but it was Gary who suggested a solution.

"Add some static to the mix," Gary said. "Like at the end of the spell, you could add something to scramble the signature."

"That will still give off a magical residue thought, won't it?" Rhea asked.

"Yes, but it will scatter the signal and make it difficult to identify the source." Gary smiled at his brilliance.

"But the Druid—even Rigel or Daphne—will be able to sense the magic," Rhea said.

"Sure," Gary admitted, "but they won't know where it's coming from in all the magical noise."

Bellatrix grunted her approval before settling back in the recesses of Nana's mind.

"Ok, everyone, disguises on, and let's get moving." Nana was excited as they all went outside. "I love a good masquerade."

Nana transformed into a slightly less aged woman with bedraggled clothes and an overflowing cart of junk. She headed down the street toward the lakefront pedestrian path.

Fizzlewink turned his beak up at Nana as she waddled off, pushing her cart. He turned to Colby and offered an aerial recon. "Do you remember the first time you had visions?"

Colby thought back to when he first found his magic. His first vision was of himself soaring through the skies and around the city. He then encountered a group of Shizumu infested people, and as yet a few unidentified individuals having a secret meeting about himself. Colby later found out he was inadvertently connected to Fizzlewink and seeing through the cat-man transformed to bird eyes.

"Yes," Colby answered. "What about it?"

"I can let you see through my eyes again as I fly around and spy on our adversaries."

Colby shrugged. "I don't know how to purposely do that, though."

A chirping laugh escaped Fizzlewink's beak as he smiled. "You don't do it, I do."

"Huh?"

Fizzlewink explained how he would initiate the shared vision. Colby only had to allow himself to open his mind and accept the connection. When they tried to connect, however, their shared vision was unsuccessful.

After a dozen failed tries, Fizzlewink relented to Colby's suggestion of a hashtag spell.

#SharedVision. Colby thought he only layered the spell over himself and Fizzlewink. The gasps from Colby's friends was unexpected.

"Whoa," Gary said. "It's making me dizzy."

Colby also realized that his spell covered his friends and allowed them access to Fizzlewink's senses as well.

"I'm gonna puke!" Rhea covered her mouth as she calmed her overloaded senses.

The rest of the kids were beginning to settle into the enhanced sense and binding to their blue little friend and teacher.

"What's that, stink?" Jasper asked as he wrinkled his nose and squinted. "I've left gym clothes in my locker for a week that smelled better."

Fizzlewink grunted and sniffed at Jasper. "Welcome to my world, boy. Try some soap and better deodorant."

Jasper sniffed his armpits and shrugged. "Not the same smell. This is more like fresh turned mud and clay mixed with swamp water."

"Let's just get moving," Fizzlewink huffed, ignoring the implication of a golem getting a whiff of itself. Only recently had Fizzlewink even realized what that smell indicated, and it was coming from four individuals. Fizzlewink squawked and pumped his wings, lifting him higher into the cloudless sky. His vision was clear and crisp in the kids' own minds.

Rhea hurled.

"Time to go," Colby said as he steadied his friend with the healing touch. "You'll be okay in a few moments. Imagine closing your eyes to the vision and focus on your own here and now."

Rhea relaxed and did as Colby instructed. She and the others all settled their nerves and minds.

Satisfied, Colby cast his hashtag spell of glamour on himself and began walking toward the lake. **#GlamourDisguiseAddScatterResidue.**

In small groups, the others glamoured themselves and scattered their departures and routes. They were setting their inconspicuous paths to converge on the eight-head ring sculpture installation along the lake path, south of Belmont Avenue. Here they hoped to find out what the Druid was planning.

Colby and the others arrived along the lakefront in three staggered groups. They spread apart and decided to approach from the East, North, and South. Because the destination was so close to Lake Shore Drive, it was impractical to approach from the West.

Magic was permitting the area as Colby, and his comrades closed in on the location where the Druid was enacting some spell. He was using more Emassa than Colby could sense. The energy was not passing through him as all other magic. This was due to the hashtag magic app, along with Colby's direct link to the force of spellcraft. How was this ancient mage using the Emassa directly?

Colby had no time to focus on ferreting out an answer to the how. He was more concerned with what. He allowed an overhead vision of the sculpture and the surrounding area to focus. Fizzlewink's birds-eye view allowed Colby to see a circling panorama of the activities taking place.

Sensing Colby's desire for a closer look, Fizzlewink allowed the air current to push him lower as he circled the stone heads from above. As he dropped twenty feet, Fizzlewink looked at the Druid to find him staring back. His wings were not fast enough to escape the buffeting stream of air that came from the Druid's outcast hand.

Fizzlewink tumbled on the wind as he righted himself well enough not to break anything as he landed hard. The mundanes walking by noticed a bird landing at an awkward angle and making a spectacle. Only a magically gifted being or creature would have heard the human sound that escaped his beak.

"Oof!" Fizzlewink landed with less grace than a blue-footed booby with two left feet and stunted wings. He wasted no time dusting himself off and transformed into his favored cat visage.

Sensing that his friend was unharmed, Colby quickened his pace toward the Druid. Whatever magic he threw at Fizzlewink, also broke the connection to his senses. What Colby was able to see was not encouraging.

The Druid was drawing the Emassa through the earth and into the eight carved heads. They were evenly spaced in a twenty-foot diameter circle and to the magically sensitive eye, glowing purple. Colby's magic was purple, that is until something was done to him by the Druid.

"He stole my magic."

As Colby signaled his friends to begin closing ranks, he felt the distinct ripple of Emassa over his skin as he walked through a magical barrier. Pausing to look behind himself, Colby watched as the world outside the circle faded and twisted. This was not something he was familiar with. This magic was unlike the time fields Colby created.

"It's an obscuring spell of some kind, but I'm not able to ascertain the other components at work." Fizzlewink transformed back into his Nefsmari form. "No use keeping up the illusion, he knows that at least the two of us are here."

"How do you know that," Colby asked. He did not drop his glamour.

"Because he has already taken your friends." Fizzlewink hissed and haunched his back, ready to fight. "There is something I don't see, though."

"What?"

"Rigel and Daphne are nowhere in sight. But that doesn't mean they aren't around somewhere." Fizzlewink jutted his chin out past Colby to where Nana was approaching. "Keep your wits about you, Colby."

Colby watched as Nana waddled toward him, seemingly clueless to the fact the Druid was on to their disguises. She barely winked as she passed him by and kept on her path back out into the unobscured world. She whispered something just before exiting.

"He has no idea who I am under these rags."

Understanding his grandmother to mean she would use surprise to advantage, Colby played along and continued toward the Druid. As he approached, he could see his four friends being bound by magic and spread out inside the stone ring. Scattered as they were, between each of the teens, a robed figure took position while the Druid's spell took form.

A cramp hit Colby deep in the center of his chest. A sudden emptiness of being drained of all feeling, not just senses, but emotions as well forced Colby to his knees. Head pounding, Colby pushed himself up under the sluggish force surrounding him. He was nowhere near the Druid, yet he felt an attack all the same. Then he saw Bruce.

"Not so strong now, are you little cheese-poof!" Bruce laughed.

Standing with his hand out waving a smartphone, Bruce continued his assault on Colby by using the Hashtag Magic app on his device. He wasn't even directly attacking Colby. Bruce was making creatures appear and fight each other. When he bored of each construct, he sent spells to obliterate them and created new ones.

Each command in Bruce's app drained more magic from Colby, sending him back to his knees. Being caught unprepared, Colby had no time to prepare a spell to funnel the required Emassa through himself. He was only able to draw in barely enough to keep from being burnt out and completely drained of magical power.

Colby watched through glassy eyes as the tears flowed from pain and helplessness. His friends were in some magical trap with the Druid's followers, and Colby could only watch what might come next. When he felt the effects of the Druid, it came with a slapping clap on his core as the link to them was severed and pulled back to him. A rubber band sliced and snapped back from being stretched beyond its limit.

Colby no longer drew energy to fight off Bruce's draining of Emassa. Crumpled in the fetal position, Colby muttered and stammered as he squeezed his knees tighter to his chest. Then he felt empty and still.

As Colby raised his head toward the sculpture, he witnessed a pulse of power. The energy ran through his friends and to each of the Druid's companions. As Colby's friends fell limp to the ground, Colby pulled in a gulp of air, suddenly realizing he could breathe. As the first rush of oxygen met his lungs, sparks of light flashed before his eyes. Vision swirling and head spinning, Colby fell back to the ground.

"Get up," Shelly screamed. She stood over Bruce's crumpled form and holding a magically formed club. "I've taken Bruce out of the equation, now go get your friends."

Colby registered his sister's words and couldn't help the smirk that formed as his eyes shifted to view Bruce cowering at Shelly's feet. His phone was smashed to bits.

A feeling of loss coated Colby's heart as he moved toward the circle of heads sculpture. His connection to his friends—his golem—returned, but that link was slippery and thin. He mentally reached for and grabbed hold of that delicate fabric of connectivity between himself and each of his friends. Still, his grip faltered as those bonds faded and moved away from him, the harder he tried.

Colby wiped his eyes as he approached the circle where his friends began to stir. The loss of bond between them was overpowering his senses. He was not asking how or why this was happening. Colby reached Jasper and helped him to his feet.

The Druid and his followers were retreating, slow, and deliberate steps, when Rigel and Daphne appeared.

"Have you got what you needed?" Rigel asked the Druid.

"Yes," the Druid said. "Remember the boy and his family are mine. You are only to attack his friends." The Druid turned to his robed friends and nodded, signaling their exit. Before he followed them into the forming portal, the Druid turned toward Rigel while pointing to Rhea. "Start by killing that one."

Rigel nodded though his eyes held a look of hesitant concern. He looked at the girl as she staggered to her feet. Why should this child mean anything to him, she was inconsequential to his ultimate goal. Rhea and the rest of these children stood in the way of him regaining his power.

"Why do you hesitate?" The Druid asked. "She isn't anything to you?"

Daphne stood by impatiently, waiting to enact her revenge on these children. When the Druid promised the destruction of the children, she went straight for Colby.

"This one is though," Daphne said and lunged for Colby as a dagger materialized in her hand. She may have been a part of Aria, but this reconstituted Daphne held no love for Colby and did not see him as her son.

Colby raised his arm to block Daphne. His instincts kicked in as a magical shield began to form, but not fast enough. Daphne's blade sunk into the weak barrier and sliced Colby's hand.

Rigel turned as the Druid shouted, or was it a scream, he couldn't tell. He watched as the Druid emitted a wave of Emassa at Daphne, sending her across the ring of stones toward Rhea. Rigel noticed a long pink scar on the Druid's hand as he pointed at Rhea.

The Druid glared at Daphne before leveling his eyes on Rhea. "Kill that one. I will not warn you again to stay away from the Stevens family and leave them to me."

Rigel realized at that moment of admission, the Druid was somehow connected to Colby. Thinking back to his arrival and the events at Stonehenge, Rigel surmised that the Druid was stealing Colby's magic. Moreover, the Druid was not yet finished based on the scar he now had in the same place Colby was just cut by Daphne.

"You are taking his magic," Rigel said. "Why?"

The Druid turned to Rigel and stared. The purple glow in his eyes grew more intense as sparks began to dance across his fingertips. "Mind your place, skin-walker."

Rigel, realizing he struck a nerve, pushed his luck. Having begun a spell shortly after arriving, Rigel released the magic into the stone ring. He watched as the Chinese heads started to push up from the soil while arms broke loose and pulled the attached bodies up and free of the ground. Rigel animated the statues that everyone assumed were only sculpted half heads.

As the giant stone monsters clawed and pulled their way free, Colby watched, shocked into inaction. While the Druid began his own spell, Daphne dove for the nearest target, Rhea. Colby reached out in slow motion as the Druid's spell began to take him away, while he witnessed Daphne's blade sink into Rhea's chest.

The last thing Colby saw as he and the rest of his friends and family were transported home by the Druid's spell-craft, was Rhea's wide eyes and silenced scream. Her body crumbled into a pile of dust and debris.

CHAPTER 10

The Stevens' family and all but one of Colby's friends were tossed from the Druid's hasty portal spell and into the back yard of Colby's home. Only in the back of Colby's thoughts was the question as to why the Druid sent them all away. Colby heard the robed mystery man give Rigel and Daphne permission to kill his friends, so why would he send them all home with his family. Not everyone was sent home, though, Colby remembered.

Darla rocked back and forth, her knees pulled to her chest as she sat in the middle of the Stevens' backyard. Her best friend was gone. Rhea was murdered in front of her with some horrible spell that reduced her to dust. All she managed to mutter.

"Why?" Darla said.

"This is all my fault," Colby muttered as he headed toward the house. "Someone grab Darla and bring her inside, please." Colby never bothered to look at anyone. He entered the house and headed to the cabinet below the sink and grabbed the first aid kit.

As he ran water over his bleeding hand, Colby stared out the back window. He watched through blurry vision as Gary and Jasper helped Darla to her feet, guiding her toward the back door. He stood there, not feeling the sting as water poured over his wound that continued to bleed. Colby blinked once as his vision cleared enough to see his mother pull his hand from the sink and wrap it in cloth.

"Colby?" Aria said. "Colby." She shook her son until he turned his head and their eyes locked. "Hold this rag on your cut and apply pressure while I prepare a stitching spell." She waited until Colby registered her instructions and complied before letting go.

While Aria cast her spell over Colby's hand, he turned his focus inside himself. Colby searched for a connection that he knew was gone. When he reached out to that place where Rhea's connection once resided, Colby stuttered his breath while inhaling as he felt a phantom connection. Colby would have gladly stayed in that moment, feeling Rhea still there. Even though Colby knew she was no more real than the distant bond, he believed it persisted with her. Only Darla's incessant chatter cast aside his distraction.

"Darla shut up already," Colby said. "Rhea is gone."

"I know you insensitive jerk," Darla said. "But someone needs to tell her family."

Colby snorted. "What family Darla? There is nobody to tell."

"Her parents?" Darla said. "They would probably like to know."

Colby sighed and looked at Darla, who clearly did not understand or realize what Gary knew, and Jasper probably did as well. Rhea was a golem, just like Darla and the boys.

"Darla, she has no parents," Colby said. "None of you four do." He looked at Darla, Gary, then Jasper. "You do realize that by now. You aren't real people."

Darla snorted and smirked at Colby. "Don't be stupid." Yet there was a hint in her voice that betrayed the conviction in her belief. "What are you talking about?"

Colby looked at his empathetic friend, knowing it was just an extension of himself. A piece split from him long ago to create a golem friend for some as yet unknown purpose. "Where do you go when you leave here?"

Darla was unprepared for the question. As she looked at Colby, without expression, the realization began to set in. Darla realized she did not go to a home or family she imagined for herself. She went to the same place to which the others went. They all returned to the site of their creation. The place they would be ready to play their part, fulfill the need of their master. Darla looked at Jasper.

"Why did you never return to the chamber in the school basement?"

Jasper thought for a moment before answering. "Because I was set on another task. I returned to the home of the human who fathered me."

Colby let his shoulders fall, realizing he was tensed up. "So you all know what you are? Golem?"

They each nodded, but it was Jasper that Colby focused on.

"When did you know," Colby asked Jasper. "You've known for some time, haven't you?"

Jasper shrugged. "Since after we returned from Chichén Itzá. Mr. Bodine told me what I was and what he felt my purpose was."

"And what is that purpose?" Colby asked.

"To serve my master as friend and protector," Jasper said,

confident in his purpose. "I am your strength."

Colby smiled, but his face carried little joy since the smile made a dry mixer to the pain he still felt over Rhea's destruction. At least he now thought of her demise in the proper context. She was a created extension of himself—a tool—and her utility was at an end. His acceptance of this fact caused a change in him.

The phantom connection he felt for Rhea sparked within him. A warmth spread across his skin from the center of his chest, spreading across his body, joining in a purposeful union at the site of his magically stitched wounded hand. The stitches dissolved as his skin mended under the unconscious direction of magical self-healing.

Colby's separated self was begging for conflation, and only now was he understanding the genuine connection he had with these four distinct extensions of himself. He moved from the counter where he stood before the others and joined them at the table. No longer needing the bloody rag to staunch the blood of his hand, Colby tossed it on the table where it landed on his father's journal. Emassa sparked and danced across the next lock on the tome and released the clasp, freeing the contents to Colby.

Colby looked at the large book and frowned. The previous section opened when he and Gary were holding it at the same time. This time it opened with contact to a rag soaked in his blood. With every section opened to him, it involved something personal to himself. This journal of his father's was becoming more his own than his father's. Colby pulled it near and opened the new section revealing only one page.

This single page made available held no text. On the center of the page was a drawing much akin to DaVinci's Vitruvian Man, only the circle was the wheel of time. The man held one with hands before his chest. He stood at the center of a much larger wheel of time. Colby shook his head, not knowing what to make of the drawing. He closed the book and pushed it away for the moment as he began to feel tired.

Colby held his hand to his head and squeezed his eyes shut. The ache started behind his eyes and shot directly to the back of his mind. Not physical in the headache sense, but this pain was metaphysical in that it was attached to his magic. But the magic that this connected to was the part of himself Colby felt was missing. The Shizumu part of him that carried with it a red power of Emassa.

How could he feel pain from something that was not there…unless it was being used and somehow still connected to him?

"What's wrong?" Aria asked. "I mean, besides the obvious. You look like you've got a headache."

"It's more complicated than that, I think. Something is draining my magic, something more than just that damn game." Colby turned then to Shelly, who had Bruce tied and gagged in the corner.

"Speaking of that game, what are we gonna do about that?"

"We could beat him," Shelly suggested.

Colby let out an unexpected giggle. It made him feel better, though he was conflicted about laughing in the face of tragedy. But was it tragic to lose a friend who was nothing more than a tool? Can a tool be a friend? Can a golem be more than a servant? Colby's head began to pound from physical pain, now joining that which was magically induced.

"As much as that might help you, Shelly," Colby started, "I don't think that will help me much."

"Kick him and find out if it helps," Shelly said. "You don't know until you try." She shrugged when Colby declined. Shelly scowled at Bruce then kicked him for good measure. "It certainly helps me feel better."

"If I might be the voice of strategy here," Gary said. "I've been thinking about a solution."

Gary pointed out the problem with the source code for Hashtag Magic being open and free on the web and how this could work for them. What he proposed was to commit a change to the code. The amendment would alter the interface in such a way to buffer it from the Emassa. Essentially making it just a game and not a way to create magic.

"Since only those with magic can actually see the effect or produce real constructs, it won't be a problem really," Gary said. "I mean, there aren't real magic users out there accessing the game for anything other than entertainment. Right?"

"That doesn't explain Bruce being able to affect reality by using it," Colby pointed out. "There is more to his involvement, and we need answers."

"Leave that to me," Shelly said. "He's a patsy for the Druid, and maybe that's how he was able to do magic with the app?"

Shelly turned toward Bruce, who remained bound and gagged in the corner.

Bruce sunk his head and looked away from her as Shelly approached him.

"Time for you to start talking, buddy." She twirled her fingers and conjured a little light show to her fingertips using the Hashtag Magic app on her phWatch. A wicked grin spread across her face.

Colby wanted to feel sorry for Bruce, but he found it difficult to feel anything for anyone else but Rhea. He still tossed around the conflicting feelings for a friend knowing she was nothing more than a golem, a tool made from part of himself. At some point, he knew he needed to investigate how the golem were created and by whom since they predated his return of magic. But not today.

"Back to this new commit of code to the open-source of Hashtag Magic," Colby said. "What are you thinking?"

"Have you heard of polymorphic code?" Gary asked.

Gary explained how he would build a subroutine into the code base that would continually alter the source code to prevent further use of the original. Additionally, it would continue to mask the buffer in place to block out the use of Emassa.

"Only your server Colby will retain the original source."

"What do we need to begin?" Colby asked.

Gary asked for little help, only a suggestion on a key. "We just need something to focus the polymorphic changes with. A key of sorts."

Colby pointed to the symbol set into the cover of his father's journal. "What about this? It shouldn't be likely to mean anything to anyone else."

Gary smiled. "Perfect. I'll get started on the code immediately. We should have something by late tonight."

"Good, then you have time to eat?" Nana said as she walked into the kitchen from outside. "I took the liberty of picking up some takeout on the walk home."

"Where did you go," Colby said. He realized his tone too late, but he was still upset that his grandmother never returned to the fray once she passed the Druid unnoticed.

"About that," Nana started pointing to her head. "It seems my squatter had other ideas about our involvement today."

"What ideas where those?" Aria accused.

"To not interfere." Nana shrugged. "The old witch just took over my body and made me sit and watch."

"At some point, this convenient excuse of yours will stop working," Shelly whispered to Nana. "We both know you are more in control of Bellatrix than you let on. She is you, after all."

"True," Nana admitted, though with a bitter taste on her tongue.

"However, in this case, I was bound by the bargain she made with the Druid ages ago."

"Any chance you know anything more about that bargain?" Shelly asked.

Nana smirked and winked at Shelly. She did so without mirth. "I'll tell my secret if you tell yours."

Shelly huffed and stepped back toward Bruce and kicked him to satiate her frustration. She continued questioning Bruce about his deal with the Druid and how to undo what he started. When she had what she needed, Shelly let the others know what she learned.

"Seems Bruce here has latent magic in his blood by birth, so that is why he was able to use the app with that particular phone I smashed up," Shelly explained. "It was enchanted by the Druid after the app was downloaded."

"Well, that's at least encouraging news," Gary said. "Wish I could say the same for getting this code changed."

"What's the problem?" Colby asked.

"I found the source code master branch to alter the app Bruce distributed, but I have no idea how to link the code to the key and start the polymorphic sub-routine."

Colby was the only one who could follow Gary's statement. He waved off the confused looks and pulled the journal closer, releasing the circular metallic symbol from its recess on the cover. Opening the book to the latest page revealed to him, Colby mimicked the image drawn and read the only line of text present.

"I think I know what to do," Colby said to Gary. "Transfer the code to my smartwatch."

Gary held out his tablet, allowing the modified code to wirelessly transfer to Colby's phWatch. Once the transfer completed, Colby mimicked the drawing on the page. A man figure stood, legs squared to his shoulders, arms outstretched, and holding the wheel of time out before his chest.

Colby looked down and phonetically read the words as he saw them. "Ha'ashtagga compilé morphica connectus." As soon as the last word was out, Colby immediately regretted his actions. Colby felt the magic coarse through his chest, then arms and into his hands before finally soaking into the object he held. The power rebounded and sunk deep into his core. As the wheel of time dissolved in his hands, a brand appeared on his chest. A new tattoo replica pulsed and turned in the form of the wheel.

Nana gasped and shook her head. "Crap on a cracker."

CHAPTER 11

Every muscle in Colby's body twitched as a spasm rippled across his body. He crumpled into a ball on the floor. Though his friends and family surrounded him, Colby was deep within a vision he was unable to navigate.

The visions of a distant past flashed before his eyes. As the images blurred and faded, each became indistinguishable from the others. When a few scenes began to clear, they would dissolve before Colby could grasp content or meaning. The only sense Colby gained was one of familiarity. A sense of grabbing onto the final moments of a dream as one wakes, but unable to grasp the edges of a fraying memory. One image burned into his mind and superimposed as a flash negative over each that followed. His father's face.

Colby couldn't understand why he was seeing his father. Why now? Though seeing and focusing on his father's image brought a dampening to the searing pain on his chest, Colby preferred it to the pain in his chest. His missing father's face burned into his thoughts but also tore into his heart. Just as he would squint his minds-eye tight against the ghostly sight, it shifted to that of a glowing blue being of power floating above the Druid.

The Druid was talking to his Shade servant, and Colby was thrust into a vision of observation. From what vantage point, Colby was a little concerned; he was getting his first glimpse into the dealings of this mysterious man from the past. This Druid has a history with the ancient magic users of this world. Colby wanted to understand why he was here in the present.

The Druid noticed his presence. "You shouldn't be here." His eyes began to glow, purple, Colby's color.

In an instant, blindness to his surroundings and such pain, it invoked ringing in Colby's ears and the feeling of nails piercing every inch of his skin. Colby gasped and awoke to the faces of his friends and family hovering above him.

When questioned about his experience, the only thing Colby clung to was a singular presence. A healing touch and calming though of Rhea. She was somehow still connected to him from wherever her artificial soul was taken. Her golem was no more, but the creature, the girl persisted.

"Rhea," Colby whispered.

Darla heard Colby and began sobbing. The recent loss of her best friend overrode the realization that Rhea, as well as the boys and herself, were nothing more than creatures created to serve Colby.

The feeling was shared as the grief of loss cascaded through all gathered. Even Nana, who knew best of all assembled the utility of magic and people as tools, was touched by the combined feeling of missing a comrade. A friend.

"STOP!" Colby cried. "She is not yours to feel such a loss." He wasn't sure where the desire came from, but Colby wanted this moment to himself. "She was a piece of me, but I still have her. Here." He pounded his chest.

The moment he accepted her presence within, Colby's body began to glow. Every wound on his body healed, and his aches and pains evaporated. The euphoric sensation that followed made him sway from dizziness. Colby gained Rhea's healing ability.

"What was that?" Jasper asked.

Colby shook his head in disbelief. "She is still here, within me somehow."

Nana let out a half-laugh, half snort. "She always was, boy. You simply didn't understand that before. Not entirely." She looked at his remaining friends. "They all are an extension of yourself."

Colby, who loved and respected his grandmother more than he could put to word, had enough. "Oh shut up, you old battle-ax. I want none of your split wisdom at the moment. Either you tell that self-serving incarnation of your former self inside your head to pony up some details, or keep your selective wisdom to yourselves." Colby stood with a single —magically driven— movement. Then he fell back to the ground.

Emassa pulled from him and spread out through the air and out of the house. He felt it coming from within him but did not feel magic being drawn from his core. As he focused on the invisible assault, Colby isolated it and pushed it aside. It was difficult, but it was attainable for the moment. He tracked it back to the source. The Druid.

"Double Shit!" Colby said.

"What?" Jasper asked. "I felt a rebound of energy from you just now."

"The Druid just tapped into Hashtag Magic."

"Why did it affect you so much?"

Colby looked down at the new tattoo brand on his chest. "Because of this."

Colby looked through the open pages of the journal and still found them empty. No answers. The only thing that stood out was the fact he knew without proof is that the spell to morph the Hashtag Magic code was somehow added to the book by the Druid.

Colby felt something, a memory, a singular moment of clarity that paused in his mind and then cleared faster than it started. Instantly he knew the Druid was there for Colby or something he was involved in. "He came here for me."

"What do you mean by that?" Nana said though something in her tone was telling. "Why should this Druid character be interested in you?"

Colby noticed that Nana's voice withheld knowledge that belied her question. "What does Bellatrix know about him, Nana? Is she sharing her secrets in your head, or are you just feeling an impression from her presence?" Colby held up his hand when Nana began to rebut. "No denial, I can hear in your voice that there is more to what she knows."

Nana shrugged and sank back as her failed denial flowed over her posture. "Only that she has some odd feeling of knowing he is here for some purpose that involves you. Nothing solid."

"Well, that's friggin' obvious," Shelly snorted. "How 'bout you and your mind squatting past self, just shut up until you have something useful to share."

Colby and Aria spoke as one. "Shelly, Shut-up."

The room sat silent for five minutes before anyone spoke. It was Gary who broke the silence as he spun around and lifted his table for Colby to see.

"The Hashtag Magic source code has been getting updated. It looks like whatever we did with that symbol has caused a new branch. Do you feel anything?"

Colby concentrated on feeling for the flow of Emassa. "I don't feel any-. Wait, I feel a slight pressure. Like something pushing against my chest, but meeting resistance."

"Then it's working," Gary said. "Try your own spells on your phWatch."

Colby raised his hand and called out a voice command into his smart-phone-watch. Nothing happened. Thinking his voice was not adequately recognized, Colby repeated his command. When again his spell passed without activation, Colby scrolled through his app and manually called upon the spell. And still, nothing occurred.

"Gary, what's going on?" Colby asked. "I can't do Hashtag Magic, either."

Gary shrugged and tried something from his phone. His spell formed and activated. "It's working for me."

Jasper, Darla, and Shelly all confirmed that Hashtag Magic was still working for them. Since it connected to a separate and secure server controlled by Colby, they were unaffected by the block put in place. Only those using the stolen and open-sourced code would be unable to effect magic. Except for Colby.

Theories abounded as to what was preventing Colby from actuating spells using his app. Ultimately it was decided that the magic block tattooed onto Colby was connected to his ability. This connection bridged real magic and that in the wild app.

"So, I can't do spells now?" Colby shouted. "Even in the virtual prison of the Shizumu, I could draw on spell runes."

"The Shiznet," Gary said while palming the side of his head. "Try drawing a rune," he told Colby.

Colby rolled his eyes but drew a rune in the air with his finger. The unexpected charge of Emassa hanging in the air before him left Colby confused since there was no rune image. There was just the static of magic. He tried drawing more runes without success.

"I can feel the Emassa, but it isn't fueling my rune drawings."

"What are you trying to spell cast?" Darla asked.

"Hashtag, find the druid," Colby said. As soon as the last syllable passed his lips, Colby jerked as Emassa wrapped around his body while escaping his core power reserve. It formed into a ball a foot before him then slammed into Colby's chest. "WTF-"

As Colby picked himself up from the floor, he tried another spell. "Hashtag, heal myself." It worked. Colby felt a soothing energy wash over himself and soak into his muscles. All of Colby's aches and pains faded away.

"I'm a self-serving magic app," Colby laughed. As he joked with his friends, Colby spoke mild and harmless spells aloud, watching as they sparked into existence. With each spell, the runes flashed into existence and faded toward Colby. Each one landing on him and fading past his clothing. "This is much more efficient than using a device."

"So long as you're able to speak," Fizzlewink grumbled. "You still rely on your devices too much and not knowledge and self-reliance."

"Well, I am self-serving now, so to speak," Colby admitted. "It's me saying my own spells and not using the app."

"Yet the fact remains," Fizz started as he got down from sitting on the back of the couch. "You are using Hashtag Magic. You are not using ancient runes."

"Fizz," Colby chided, "Magic is thought, desire, emotion…all put into action using some anchoring symbol or tool, right?" After Fizzlewink shrugged, Colby continued. "So my symbols, old runes, spoke words…it is all representational of my desire."

Fizzlewink huffed. "So why did you not find the Druid with your spoken spell?" His eyes remained fixed on Colby's wrist, where his sleeve moved and revealed something tattooed on his skin.

"Okay, so the Druid must have some sort of blocking spell surrounding him," Colby said. "We'll have to be more creative with that guy."

"I wouldn't be so certain of that," Fizzlewink snapped. Before the cat-man could grab Colby's wrist, Nana intercepted him, swatting the little blue man away with a broom.

"Fizzlewink," Nana said. "Come to the kitchen and help me make some food for everyone. I think the kids will all be staying here from now on?" Nana raised her brow to Fizzlewink, yet nodded to Aria.

"Oh yes," Aria agreed. "It's not safe for you all to be separated at the moment, I think."

"It's not like we have real homes or families," Darla pouted.

Shelly shoved a tissue toward Darla. "You have a family here." Shelly allowed a moment of softness to escape before she caught herself. "Now wipe your nose before you leak snotty clay on the carpet."

"I'll call Mr. Bodine and let him know what's going on," Jasper said.

Colby noticed this was not the first time Jasper called the man who fathered him, Mr. Bodine, instead of dad. When he asked Jasper why Colby was not prepared for the answer.

"He may have raised me, but he isn't really my dad," Jasper chuckled. "You are."

"Okay, that's just weird," Shelly said before turning away. Shelly's huff broke the awkward silence that followed Jasper's declaration of parentage. "Where's Bruce?"

"He was just here a few minutes ago, I remember because my foot still hurts from kicking him." Shelly began the search of the house.

They looked everywhere. Bruce was nowhere to be found.

"You don't think he used a spell to escape?" Shelly asked.

"I would have felt it," Colby said. "So either he is one foot, or he used the portal."

Shelly slammed her fist on the counter. "Can't we even keep a dim-witted line cook tied up?"

"I thought he was your responsibility?" Colby asked. He sighed and turned away. From Shelly's scowl. "What next?"

"Soup's on," Nana said. "Come and eat."

"Just when things couldn't get any worse," Colby said.

CHAPTER 12

Colby pushed his food around the plate, unable to settle his churning stomach. Jasper's pointing out that Colby was their father, of sorts, made him stare at his friends and wonder as to how they were made. A bit of himself was within each golem, this much he knew. The how, when, and where, were all cringe-worthy thoughts. Colby was not in the least hungry at present.

Pushing his plate away—more forcefully than he'd planned—Colby muttered his apologies and excused himself from the table. "I need some air." Colby left the others and headed out the back door.

Colby sat on the back step, dropping his over-weighted shoulders down as they pushed him forward, elbows on his knees. His mind stirred with thoughts of Rhea and his other friends, golem, he reminded himself. One of them was now destroyed, perhaps the best of them. He tried clearing his mind by looking out at the yard and sensing the magic surrounding the house.

The glow of Emassa over the portal stones nearly blinded him before Colby adjusted his level of sensitivity. Focusing on a much smaller source of magical energy, Colby found a clutch of pixies scavenging magical residue around the flower beds near the garage. Here and there, a grimalt would poke through the bushes before darting back into hiding. The more magic that Colby began to use, the more he attracted these creatures, bringing them out of long hibernation and seclusion. He wondered at what next he might draw out of hiding should he produce potent enough magic. Colby hadn't been strong enough for what mattered. He couldn't save Rhea.

Rhea was the healer, the compassionate part of Colby. He felt the loss but wondered at what happened to the spirit. It was a piece of him, and yet it did not seem to return to his soul. He felt more hate now than ever before. The hatred was directed at Rigel, the remaining Daphne duplicate of his mother, and most heavily distributed toward the Druid.

Simmering at first, his anger began to fester further when Colby redirected the blame upon himself. He felt taken in by Rigel. Colby's own ineptness at understanding the runes or magic when his life took this incredible turn allowed him to get played. Now, this Druid guy was pulling strings and perhaps even having done so long before the present.

"Manipulating me before I was born?" Colby asked himself.

"Who," Jasper asked as he sat next to Colby. "You thinking about that Druid guy again?"

Colby shrugged as he looked sideways at Jasper. "He knows too much like we're all just following some path, and this guy has written the map. It just doesn't make any sense."

This time it was Gary's voice that joined the mix. "So he knows stuff. Could be he uses some crystal ball, or tea leaves use to interpret prophecies."

It was a possibility, Colby admitted to himself. But then there were the runes, Colby thought as he looked at the new tattoos on his body. The Druid was most certainly behind Colby's latest body art, but to what end Colby couldn't ferret out.

"You boys mind some company," Darla asked. "I couldn't eat either. I can't stop wondering what happened to Rhea."

"She got killed, you ditz," Gary blurted before he could stop himself. Looking embarrassed, he turned away and mumble. "Sorry, I didn't think."

"It's a valid question, though," Colby said. "I mean, if you are all golem linked to me, is your life your own or a magical extension of myself?"

"What does your father's journal say? You found the spell in there, right?" Darla asked.

Colby stared at her with a blank stare for a moment. "Yes and no. The spell is in there, but it's not written in my father's hand. It also doesn't fully explain the energy of a golem. It seems purposefully left out of the entry."

"Entry?" Darla asked. "You make it sound more like a logbook than a journal." Darla slid herself up from the porch and began inching toward a couple grimalts sparring and chattering in the flowers. The furry little creatures—looking somewhat like miniature teddybears—stared at her with oversized round eyes before darting off around the house, daring her to follow.

Turning from Darla, it struck Colby that she was right. Thinking back on each section that opened, Colby could see where each entry logged and read like milestones or tasks completed. Sure there were spells and histories, but those histories read like first-hand accounts of things his father was not old enough to have witnessed. Then there were things not written by his father.

"Maybe," Colby said. "What matters is what comes next. We have to keep you all safe."

"We're safe here," Gary said.

Screaming erupted from the far side of the house.

"Where's Darla?" Colby shouted.

The boys ran to the side yard to find Darla surrounded by two dozen grimalts. They no longer appeared as the docile little creatures. These teddy bears were rapid, with rows upon rows of pointed teeth, red eyes, and Emassa laced saliva dripping from their mouths.

Colby broke into a sprint before Fizzlewink jumped in his path, stopping Colby.

"Don't agitate them more," Fizzlewink warned. "They aren't easily worked up like this. I suspect someone has set them to attack."

"Who?" Gary asked. "Why?"

Colby turned to Gary. "I think we can guess at least three people who would do this. And the why is probably to kill her." Colby reached out his right hand, "Not today!" **#DarlaToMe.**

The moment Colby finished speaking, his spell Darla disappeared, and Colby's arm burned from the inside out. He knew that meant another rune etched into his skin, but put the pain aside as Darla reappeared next to him. Colby allowed the momentary embrace of gratitude before pushing Darla away.

"Right then, Who's up for some target practice?" Colby pointed at the nearest grimalt and shouted. **#LightningBolt**.

Emassa fueled bolts of energy shot from Colby's outstretched hand, soaring directly toward his target. The moment the magical ball landed on the grimalt, its high-pitched screech forced the kids to cover their ears. The ear-piercing scream vibrated higher and louder until it ended in a sudden and unremarkable pop. The grimalt was gone.

Magical residue remained on the spot the creature was dispatched from, but the other grimalts were of a single mind. They ignored the invitation to feast on the leftover magic. The grimalts began a steady and stalking walk toward the kids and Fizzlewink.

Taking Colby's renewed assault as a cue, the kids began launching attacks at the encroaching fur-balls. Orbs of fire, lightning bolts, and energy streams cut through the air. Snapping, crackling, and booming echoed through the yard. A full-scale war was brewing in the yard as the kids attacked, but Fizzlewink glared and scanned the yard.

The wise old cat-man knew something was amiss. This behavior was unlike these creatures. It wasn't unnatural for these ordinarily docile creatures to protect themselves when cornered. They had to be externally influenced, however, to exhibit this aggressive behavior. As he examined the perimeter, Fizzlewink spotted more grimalts entering the yard.

Outside the yard, they appeared normal, sniffing out the remnants of used magic that they feed on. No sooner did the sickeningly adorable things cross the border into the yard, their features shifted. Teeth bared, and eyes glazing over, the grimalts became ferrel. Driven by an outside force, the grimalts joined the others in advancing on the kids.

"Something is controlling them," Fizzlewink shouted over the chaos of booming and explosions of fur. "Cover me while I locate the source."

Colby nodded his acknowledgment as Fizzlewink made a wide-angle off and around the grimalts. Bolstering his friends depleting energy reserves, Colby pulled in more Emassa to fuel the combined offense. His own magic reserve refilled as he used magic without his conscious effort. Not able to explore this change in his ability, Colby refocused on eliminating the threat before him.

"Keep these little bastards' attention off of Fizz," Colby directed the others. "More are coming in from outside the yard."

With each critter they destroyed, another two took its place. The kids were losing ground. It was slow due to the small stature of their attackers, but if the little buggers decided to take to sprint, they would be overrun. Looking across at his friends, Colby realized that the advance was directed most at Darla. She was overwhelmed.

"Get closer to Darla. The grimalts are targeting her."

The kids tightened their circle. The closer they grew to one another, the tighter the collective of grimalts became. A riling mass of fur and teeth descended upon the kids as they huddled and defended themselves. Panic began to affect Darla's aim as her strikes only grazed the creatures. The stench of singed and soiled fur wafted through the yard.

Fizzlewink caught wind of the smell and curled his nose. "As if they didn't smell bad enough."

Fizz noticed the kids drawing together, and the sight of their hastening loss renewed his search. He could feel the change in the magic surrounding the battle. Colby's magic was different yet familiar. Then Fizzlewink felt another source of strange magic coming from nearby. The portal stones were glowing.

Within the circle of stones connecting the backyard to Stonehenge via ley line, a purple glowing mist swirled. A hood-covered head was inside the fog that Fizzlewink recognized as the Druid. He was orchestrating the activity of the grimalts.

Fizzlewink reached within his limited core of power. Gathering all he could muster, Fizzlewink prepared a bombarding construct and released it on the closest stone in the ring. Energy Blasted into the rune-etched rock and crackled along the surface. Fizzlewink's spell soaked into the stone and pulsed, drawing the gaze of the Druid.

"And what do you think you're doing, little man?" The Druid asked. "You will not stop this happening."

Fizzlewink huffed from breathlessness and depletion of Emassa. His magic was too far spent to launch another volley of such strength. The fact his last attempt was fruitless confirmed Fizzlewink was no match for the magic this Druid wielded.

"I can slow you down if nothing else."

The Druid laughed. "You are welcome to try, old friend. Just don't hurt yourself."

"You are no friend to me," Fizzlewink fumed. "I would never consort with the likes of such repugnance."

Looking away, the Druid let a mirthless laugh escape his wispy image. "You'd be surprised what one is capable of when faced with far worse possibilities than what I propose. These incarnations of earthen-born must be destroyed."

The Druid dismissed Fizzlewink by way of a low charged energy blast off the rings. As Fizzlewink fell back and away from the stone ring, another energy fell over the Druid's projection.

Bellatrix stood at the back door, her spirit dominating the use of Nana's body. "This is not acceptable."

Squeezing her hands together and slamming them down, Bellatrix poured enough magic into her spell to dismiss the Druid. Dust and rock fragments pelted Fizzlewink as Bellatrix's magic also obliterated the stone circle.

As the Druid's connection was severed, the grimalts became more frenzied. The little monsters scattered and reformed as a circle around the kids. As the grimalts tightened rank around the kids, Colby reacted with a swift and whispered spell. **#AnnihilationRing.**

A purple fog coalesced around Colby before forming a ring around himself and his friends. As the grimalts attacked in force, they passed into the smoky barrier. Nothing reached the other side. After the last of the creatures were gone, the annihilation spell drifted down and into the ground. The grass withered away, leaving a circle of death around the kids.

Colby ran to help Fizzlewink to his feet while looking at what remained of the stone ring portal. "What the hell Nana? That was our only way to get back to Stonehenge quickly."

Nana shrugged as Bellatrix receded to the back of their shared mind. "I didn't have any control over that."

Colby huffed and looked back at the damage. "Could we rebuild the portal? I don't think I have the strength to spell myself there without it."

Nana waddled over. "There are ley lines all over."

"Except this portal was built on a direct path to Stonehenge," Gary pointed out. "Without knowledge of how to traverse the lines, Colby would get lost trying to blindly navigate our way."

Fizzlewink spoke between licking his wounds. "I wouldn't worry overmuch, there is another portal from the ancient gateways of the world."

"Where?" Colby asked, his spirit-lifting.

"It's not that far, but we'll need a boat." Colby began to press for more details when Fizzlewink lifted his head and sniffed the air. "We have more visitors."

From the perimeter of the yard, menacing red eyes broke the shadow's dominance. Grunting and snarling accompanied the disheveled Dreggs that wandered into the yard. They headed for the scorched ring in the yard where Colby performed his annihilation spell. They were drawn to the altered magic that Colby performed.

"What's wrong with them?" Darla asked. "Did the Druid cast a spell on them as well?"

"No, my dear," Nana said, using Bellatrix's demeanor. "That is how a Dregg behaves when on the hunt for the blood of a rogue mage."

"Then why are they here and not going after the Druid?" Gary asked.

Colby watched the Dregg sniff at the magic scorched earth and slowly turn their heads his direction. "They're here for me."

CHAPTER 13

"Run," Colby shouted. He sent a magical ball at the Dreggs and ran away from his friends and family. "This way, you ugly monkey-goblins."

Colby sprinted around the side of the house. The feral Dreggs followed on his heels without distraction. Colby recognized the determination in their bloodshot eyes. When he finally stopped to stand his ground, Colby squared off his posture and prepared a spell. **#FreezeInTime.** He waited to release the spell until his pursuers stopped and began to circle him. Whatever effect the new tattoo on his chest had allowed the return of this time manipulation ability.

Nana came around the side of the house, soon followed by the others. "Colby!"

"Stay back," Colby shouted. "I have to time-freeze them so you can all get to safety. It's the only thing that works on the Dregg."

"You can't stay in there with them," Jasper said.

"I don't plan on it."

Colby held his time magic ready in his right hand. Time magic was one of the few spells he could conjure without preparation or runes. Colby was grateful to have it back. Raising his left hand—palm down—Colby gave little consideration for the spell he decided to use before shouting the command. **#BlastOff**. As soon as the construct left his left hand, Colby released the Emassa fueled magic.

Colby flailed as his body launched into the sky. As he spun in the air, his satisfaction that the time spell encircled the Dreggs clouded the imminent collision with the ground he was falling toward. When Colby's body turned toward the earth, however, the grin of satisfaction was pushed away by the wind as he plummeted toward his family and friends.

"Move aside," Jasper said, pushing people away as he prepared a spell. **#AirCushion**. His spell took form only heartbeats before Colby slammed into it, breaking his fall. Jasper released the spell, and Colby fell two feet to the ground.

"Oof! That was a bit harsh," Colby said, laid out on the grass.

Jasper reached down and wretched Colby to his feet. "No time for pleasantries, dude. We need to haul ass before those things get free." Jasper pointed toward the Dregg frozen in the time bubble Colby erected. There were already micro-movements as the creatures began to absorb and negate the spell. "Time to go."

By the time they turned to flee, another group of Dregg had entered the yard. They were blocked from exiting the side yard. Colby reacted with another time spell on the new arrivals realizing too late his mistake. "Shit."

"What?" Darla asked. "You froze them. Let's go around them."

"Where Darla?" Colby responded. "The time bubbles are blocking our path. We can't enter them without being trapped inside with the Dregg."

Gary tapped Colby's shoulder. "We better do something fast, because the first group is breaking free."

No sooner did the last word escape Gary's lips, the first of the Dreggs freed itself from the trap. It, followed by another, then another, turned to the group and growled.

"They aren't charging us," Fizzlewink said. "Good, that means they're being cautious and won't make the first move."

"How is that good?" Colby asked, "We're still cornered."

"It buys us precious moments to think of something."

Shelly looked at the Dregg, then at Nana, and finally at Colby. "There's something I can do."

Colby looked at his sister, knowing what she had in mind. "Are you sure you want to use that gift?"

"I don't think we have a choice."

Looks of confusion passed between all but Nana, Shelly, and Colby. Once Colby nodded to Shelly, she and Darla disappeared.

"Where did they go?" Jasper said.

"The in-between," Nana answered. "Shelly has the gift to walk between the realms of the living and the dead, remember?."

"What?" Gary and Fizzlewink said in concert.

"There is a realm, a thin veil of space between-" Colby started.

"I know," Fizzlewink interrupted. "When did Shelly become a shadow-walker?"

Before anyone could voice their question of what a shadow-walker was, Shelly reappeared. "Who's next?"

Gary jumped at Shelly's reappearance. "Jeez-us! Could you warn us next time?"

"Sure, would you like heralds and trumpets sent ahead next time?" Sarcasm was Shelly's particular language. "Meanwhile, the rapid batmen are inching closer, and I think they can sense when I pass them."

Shelly explained how the veil or "shadow" between realms was thin and murky, like walking through a foggy black and white movie. Sound entered from either side of the veil in hushed and muffled tones while your feet felt as though you were stepping through warm jello.

"If the Dregg can sense you walking in the "shadows", why not go deeper in to avoid them?" Jasper asked.

"You mustn't fully emerge yourself into the realm of the dead," Nana warned, but with Bellatrix's formality and overbearing.

"Those who have ventured within rarely come back. And those who have returned are forever changed by whatever they encountered."

"Thanks 'B'," Shelly said after an ominous silence hung over them. "I'll keep that in mind. Care if I take Gary along now?" Shelly didn't wait for an answer, and the two disappeared.

"What did she mean with 'B'?" Nana asked, returning to her usual self.

"I think she was referring to Bellatrix, or worse," Colby grinned. "You can't be too certain with her."

Shelly heard Colby and smiled as she felt how well her little brother knew her. The moment passed when she felt a caress across her shoulder. Turning to usher Gary forward, careful to not let go of him too soon, Shelly caught a glimpse of an apparition reaching for her from the world of the dead.

"Looks like it isn't just the Dregg that have taken notice of me. Let's move."

Shelly pushed Gary toward the house and deposited him on the back porch. As soon as she let go of Gary's arm, he reappeared in the realm of the living, much to Darla's surprise.

"Go get your things packed," Darla said. "Fizzlewink's people, the Nefsmari, said this place won't be safe for long." Darla twisted her hands around her backpack straps while peering out into the yard. "I hope Shelly hurries."

Shelly moved as quickly as she could through the in-between. More lost souls gathered along the border between realms, watching her with longing for the life-force Shelly represented. More than once, she had to dodge reaching arms while skimming past the Dregg.

Shelly repeated her careful dance between the living and dead worlds. The last two awaiting her ferrying back to the house were Jasper and Colby. Jasper didn't leave without argument after Colby insisted Shelly grab him and go. Shelly was not pleased with leaving Colby alone with the Dregg again, but he insisted he would be fine.

Colby wasn't confident of his escape, being that all the Dregg were free of his time spell. If he used it again now, Colby feared it may not work in the future, as the Dregg could adapt. The Dreggs were created to negate magic and fight the enemies of the Nefslama millennia ago. These creatures—mutated from the original Nefsmari people, Fizzlewink's race—sensed the odd change to Colby's magic and considered it a threat. The Dreggs surrounded Colby.

Shelly was unable to squeeze past the Dreggs and reach her little brother. The single-minded creatures surrounded Colby. Dreggs were blocking her way past even in the in-between. Shelly looked for an opening, walking around the circle of Dregg. The bolts of energy Colby shot toward them made the Dregg waver, but not enough to make room. Shelly tried to be patient.

Colby sent one blast after another into his assailants. They barely had an effect. As Colby reached deeper into the power of magic, Emassa, he felt tingling across his skin. At this point, Colby knew this reaction meant that runes were forming on his skin, but he couldn't afford the distracting thoughts. Colby snatched at Emassa with a primal need fueled by fight or flight instincts. When his efforts brushed against the energy flow of the ley lines in the earth, he pulled hard. Energy surged and enveloped him. Colby shone with magic, that shocked the Dreggs. The creatures halted and began to withdraw.

Shelly took her opportunity and dashed between two Dregg. Not wanting to lose the moment, Shelly grabbed Colby's arm, intending to pull him into the between. The opposite happened. Shelly re-entered the living world and was knocked to her feet from contact with Colby's skin.

"What the-" Shelly started as she fell back.

"Sorry," Colby said. "I've sort of…well, I have no clue what I've done, but I feel like I have a battery on my tongue. Times a thousand."

"Well, let it go, dumbass. We need to get the hell outta here."

"I have no idea how to release this much magic," Colby admitted.

"Well, you better think of something and fast," Shelly said. "I can't pull you into the in-between like this."

Colby tried thinking of any spell that would help, but his mind was too clouded by the energy to consider more than a few words. Then he heard a voice shout from the porch. It was Darla.

"Honey," Darla shouted. "Remember the honey and pixies."

Colby smiled. He focused on one phrase and spoke the spell while funneling the magic to his hands. "Hashtag Honey!"

Colby spread his arms as the Emassa gathered in his center and blasted outward. A circle of gooey and golden magic expanded. It hit the Dreggs and covered them in spell created honey. At first, there was no reaction besides revolt. Then the pixies appeared.

Pixies descended upon the Dreggs, teeth extended, and saliva dripping from their razor-sharp fangs. The Dreggs began to scream and scatter under the aerial assault.

Shelly wasted little time as the energy enveloping Colby abated. She grabbed ahold of Colby's arm and yanked him into the in-between. They ran for the porch. As they stumbled through the yard, trying to dodge debris and holes left from the battle, the two siblings got too close to the boundary of the spirit realm. Something grabbed at Shelly and pulled her closer.

Had it not been for the arm of her brother wrapped around Shelly's waist, she would have been entirely surrounded by the dead. Colby's grip halted the transition into the spirit world. Shelly was halfway between life and death, feeling detached from reality and mind clouding over.

"Let me go," Shelly muttered. "They need me."

"Not a chance," Colby said. "I need you more."

As Shelly was pulled wholly into the nether, Colby's body collided with the boundary. He felt Emassa surge through him and push him back from the barrier between life and death. The familiar itching began to race over his skin. Colby was equally grateful for his affliction saving him and Shelly from inevitable demise. He revolted at the idea of more runes etching into his skin. What had the Druid done to him?

Colby wasn't confident whether it was his pulling on Shelly, the energy he gave off, or Shelly's shock at hearing his admitting he needed her. Still, his sister began to snap out of the trance.

"You need me?" Shelly said. "Is the great techno-wizard Colby Stevens admitting he needs help?"

Colby smirked, his mouth pulled into a mirthless smile. There was no joy in his eyes. Pulling back his sleeve as the pair exited the between, Colby revealed his rune-tattooed arm on the steps of the back porch. "They are forming all over my body."

Shelly reached out but stopped her fingers just shy of touching Colby's skin. "What are they? I mean, I know they're runes, but why are they on your skin?"

Colby shook his head. "I don't know, but I think it's something to do with why I can't use hashtag magic from my smart devices. The Druid did something to me."

"Why?"

"That's the question, isn't it. Why is the Druid doing any of the things he's doing? Why is he here?" Colby pulled his sleeve back down and motioned Shelly into the house. "Can we keep my new body art to ourselves for the moment?"

Shelly tilted her head and looked back at Colby, pausing at the open back door. She said nothing, only nodding before leading the way through to the kitchen.

"Ok, that's everyone back in the house," Shelly said. "Time to get the hell outta here."

"Let's all convene in the living room once we've gathered what we need of our personal effects," Aria said.

Colby sent his mother along to meet the others in the living room. "We'll be along shortly." He glanced over at his grandmother.

"I'll be ready in a jiffy, fart-blossom," Nana said. "I just need to get a bit more food items in my sack-"

"Nana, we can pop out for food as needed. There's no need for you to try and cook."

"Pish-tosh!"

Colby rolled his eyes and headed for the stairs. "Fine. I'll just run upstairs for something from dad's study."

Colby took the steps two at a time, racing against the inevitable invasion of the Dreggs from outside. Pausing to breathe, Colby slowed his intake of air, fighting against the pounding ache in his chest. As his pulse slowed and heart-rate dropped, Colby made his way toward the magically locked room at the end of the hall.

There was no longer a time bubble protecting the room, but with Betelgeuse's help, a magical lock was established. After casting the entry spell, Colby strode over to his father's desk and sifted through the books left scattered from past research.

Runes, never Colby's strength, he needed more information on what now covered his skin. He didn't recognize more than a few of the obscure symbols of magical intent now slithering along his epidermis. More would be joining these, he felt sure of it, so Colby needed a reference. And he found one.

Colby pulled the tome near and huffed a chest full of air at the cover. Dust billowed from the book and broke the light in tiny sparkles before the window. Colby pulled the book close before depositing it in his rucksack beside his father's journal. He looked at the books together for a moment before glancing at his watch.

"Time to go," Colby told himself.

Exiting the Room, Colby didn't hesitate before heading toward the stairs. The stairs were blocked. A Dregg stood barring Colby's escape down, so he turned to head toward the attic door. Two arms wrapped around him. Conrad.

"You going somewhere, sorcerer?" Conrad said. "You are tainted now and must be dealt with."

CHAPTER 14

Nana heard the yelling from upstairs and dropped her sack of food. Faster than her squatty and ancient frame should allow, Nana climbed the back stairs to reach the third floor. Her way was blocked. A Dregg stood to bar the path to Colby.

"That's far enough, ancient one," The Dregg said. "We have no dealings with the Great Witch unless you interfere."

"What is the meaning of this intrusion?" Bellatrix's voice blended with Nana's own before taking over. "This is not your charge, beast."

The Dregg snarled and starred his hatred into Bellatrix. "You're control over the dealings of the Dregg ended long ago, witch. We seek out corrupt magic and eliminate as we see fit."

Bellatrix became incensed for a moment, then calmed and straightened her housecoat. "Ha."

She laid only the tip of her finger on the creature's nose. Before the whispered spell carried its full intent in her breath, Bellatrix began pushing past the Dregg. She moved aside just as the Dregg fell to the floor.

"Dream well, pet."

More Dregg began to appear from the attic door and around the corner. The goblin-headed monsters blocked the old woman's path toward Jarrod's study and Colby's aid. Bellatrix and Nana, as a single mind for the first time, cinched her housecoat at the knee and squatted into a defensive posture.

"Bring it on."

Bellatrix used Nana's body to charge the Dregg that blocked her way. Waddling became a full gallop, and Bellatrix spun her spell for a shield and began knocking her human-sized goblin obstacles to the floor. She was in full defensive tackle mode. Though the Dreggs had more bulk and height than the body that Bellatrix was possessing, she used Nana's low center of gravity. She mixed this advantage with a magical shield and the shock factor to take down the Dreggs.

The Dregg figured the old woman an easy target. The fact they were going down like NFL rejects did not sink in as they continued to eat floorboards.

While Nana had her hands full in the hall, Colby stood against Conrad in the study.

"Conrad?" Colby said. "Is that you?"

A snarl sliced through the darkness, giving a location to Colby's search for the Dregg. As Colby turned to find his presumed ally, a cold rippling prickle raced down his spine, causing him to shudder. The turned-in brow and dagger-filled stare of the approaching Dregg spoke of the malice now filling the air between them. Conrad was no longer a neutral player in this fight with the Shizumu. The realization spread from Colby's thoughts to his face.

"I see you begin to understand your place in this war, young mage," Conrad said. "It is unfortunate your powers have turned into something unnatural."

Colby began to speak. Conrad lunged, wrapping his arms around Colby before he could react. The magical energy surged from Colby's core and started draining from him. Breath after heaving breath, Colby tried to speak. He attempted to move, struggling against his captor. As he reached for his fleeting power, Colby connected to something, a part of his magic, he always failed to acknowledge. No time to think, Colby pulled it back within himself.

Confident in his ability to neutralize a magic user, Conrad failed to sense the slow reversal of energy feeding back into Colby.

Finding his voice, Colby began to mutter the names of symbols that flashed before his inner thoughts. Runes, he did not recognize formed in Colby's mind and found purchase on his lips. Each utterance, caused a burning itch on his skin as the runes marked his body. More tattoos spread across his arms and shifted positions with those already present. As he stared at the new symbols, Colby pulled harder on the returning magic. A distant and clouded vision entered his thoughts. A memory he did not recognize but embraced as his own.

Colby stood in a room, surrounded by Nefsmari. Viles, beakers, enchanted objects, and an old crone faded in and out of his peripheral. Bellatrix was that woman, Colby realized, but it was him teaching her.

With a wave of his hand and a spoken phrase, Colby transformed the small-statured blue creatures around him into hulking beasts. The Dregg. Colby was seeing a memory of the Druid. His connection to this mystery man gave him insight. The Druid created the first Dregg, and now Colby knew how to undo the spell.

Reversing the symbols in his thoughts, Colby readied the casting of runes. He could not enter them into his smartwatch, he thought. As the singular wish crossed his mind, the runes on his skin lit-up and sent a shining duplicate into the device on his wrist. The spell was ready, but he could not manage physically using his hashtag magic app. But he could speak it.

Conrad realized his folly too late. As Colby ripped power back from the Emassa that Conrad drained, the spell left Colby's lips, and Conrad understood what changed in the young sorcerer. He was not tainted. He was using the purest form of Emassa.

"How?"

Colby's voice cracked and sounded out with a whispered authority, "Hashtag Return To Nefsmari."

Conrad's arms went limp, and his tight grasp on Colby waned. As he watched Colby step aside and take a replenishing gasp of air, Conrad began to weep. "It has begun."

"What has begun," Colby asked.

Conrad was unable to respond as his body rippled and shook in convulsions. The once towering tool of the Nefslama shrank, magical energy evaporating away the excess bulk, a blue-skinned little man took shape. Conrad returned to his original form.

Colby was wedged between disbelief at what he accomplished and the intrusion of a memory from the Druid. He sat back on the sofa in the study. The Nefsmari before him, squatted on the floor at his feet and uttered apologies and self-recriminations. Colby looked at Conrad, or what once was Conrad, and then the runes covering his skin that retreated beneath his sleeves.

Conrad, in all modesty, gathered the bundle of clothes now too large for his use. He covered his naked blue body as best he could.

Colby took pity on the little man that moments earlier would have squeezed the life right out of him. It was an odd sensation. From friend to enemy and now apparent sycophant, by the way, Conrad was behaving.

Pointing to the remains of Conrad's Dregg-sized pants and jacket, Colby enacted a spell to shrink the articles.

Conrad behaving awe-struck accepted the gift and donned the clothes. He kept his awe-filled stare locked with Colby as he slipped into the miniaturized pants and shirt. Once he finished, Conrad presented himself to Colby as aa soldier awaiting orders.

Colby had to choke down aa laugh as he examined this new shrunken version of the once mighty and imposing Conrad the Dregg. Standing before him was a more militant version of Fizzlewink. Colby's smile tightened as he imagined Fizzlewink's bossy and unwavering temperament combined with Conrad's hard and aggressive nature. Looking at the Nefsmari now before him, waiting patiently for direction, Colby wondered if a small platoon of these creatures would be an asset.

The study door burst open as Bellatrix—by way of Nana—broke the magical seal to enter.

"We have an incursion," Nana shouted. She half waddled, half ran to Colby's side. "Did you hear me?"

Colby looked at his possessed grandmother and then pointed to the Nefsmari at his feet. "I hadn't noticed."

"Not the Nefsmari," Nana said. "Where did this one come from? Never mind" Perturbed by the lack of urgency in her grandson, Nana looked at the Nefsmari and waved her hands, shooing the creature out. "Why are you up here? Go downstairs to the others."

"I will stay with the pure-born," Conrad said. "The end has begun."

"What are you twaddling on about? We are under attack from the Dregg."

Conrad snickered and looked with a knowing smile at Colby. "The Dregg have outlived their need."

Nana waved off the nonsensical ramblings of a lower being. This was the influence of Bellatrix resurfacing. She reached for Colby's arm. "We need to go." When her hand wrapped around Colby's arm, energy rebounded and shocked her hand away. "What on Earth?"

Colby mirrored the old woman's surprise. "Maybe a residual from doing that," he said, pointing to what remained of the Dregg Conrad.

"My name—the short version in the least—is still Conrad."

Nana's possessed eyes opened wide, and she looked closer at the blue man. The residual energy of a transformation spell surrounded him. Looking back at Colby, her eyes narrowed. "How did you do this?"

Colby wasn't prepared for long explanations to something he couldn't yet explain. "Short answer, I reversed the spell that made him Dregg." Before she could press for more, Colby pushed past his grandmother and headed toward the door. "We have to go, remember?"

Pausing at the doorframe, Colby ran a finger along the broken hinges. The spell that once locked his father's study was gone. He reached out with his magical senses to find any lasting energy from the last known spell his father cast. It was gone, and that wasn't all that evaporated. The spells around the house were falling.

First, the perimeter obscuring spell dropped. Before spell failure, the goings-on within the boundary of the Stevens' home was filtered from the eyes of anyone outside the yard. Now all activity was on public display. The added spells that afforded early warning of enemies, gone as well.

One-by-one, Colby watched as his family home became all the more vulnerable and unsafe. What once he saw as a safe haven, was now becoming another battlefield and place to flee. The house could be repaired, his friends and family could not. Colby wanted nothing more than to put a stop to this but wasn't in a position to stop and think things through. He still reeled from the spell he used to remove Conrad's curse.

"Come along, Conrad, let's get you some friends."

Bellatrix used Nana's hands to stop Colby in the hallway. "What did you see when the spell to reverse the Nefsmari curse was revealed?"

Colby looked at his grandmother. He stared into her eyes and past the facade of his Nana. He saw her, Bellatrix, just beneath the surface.

"I saw you. And I saw the Druid. He was teaching you the spell to create the Dregg. You were his student at some point."

Bellatrix tried to deny the allegation, but it was no use. She knew there was no point. "You will find there is no ancient mage left in this world who did not get through this life without some dealing with the Druid."

"How old is he? Where did he come from?"

Nana was granted the use of her body back as Bellatrix hid. "I'm afraid the witch has left the building," Nana said. "She's not saying anything more. I do think though that this Druid is someone to be wary of based on the fear I sense from my old self."

"That is painfully obvious," Colby said and waved his rune-covered arms at her. "I just wish I knew what the connection was."

Nana began to turn her head away, but her eyes remained locked on Colby. "The connection? Yes, that would be a good thing to know."

Sensing there was more she knew and wasn't saying, Colby began to stare back at Nana. As he began to question her, more noise from the yard reminded Colby of the urgency to leave. There wasn't much time, but he needed to know just how long they had before being overrun.

Colby reached out again with his sense of magic to see the

remaining spells around the yard, failing faster than moments before. They were under siege and needed to retreat. Colby sensed that he still had another task as he heard the beginnings of a melody playing in his head. Someone or something was coming.

"We really gotta go, Nana. The house's protections are lost."

Nana, with aid from Bellatrix's power, looked outside the confines of the yard outside the house using a wall-penetrating stare. "Crap on a cracker."

CHAPTER 15

The yard was surrounded on all sides by creatures, both enemy and curious onlooker. Many were there to attack the Stevens and friends, but half as many were magical beings long forgotten to time. They came out of hiding at the source of magical energy emanating from Colby.

Around the perimeter of the yard, Colby observed all manner of creature. Among the clutches of pixies, grimalts, and trolls, there were a series of new beings. Some of the gathered masses were human-looking save the odd set of fangs or features that made them known as supernatural. Most were small and easily hidden among the bushes.

There were seekers among the trees, hovering as though waiting for some instruction or order to attack. They moved around the branches in an agitated state, bumping into one another. Small skirmishes began to break out among the more gruesome-looking beasts.

A could grimalts began gnawing on the ankles of a large half-man half-pig creature. It bent over and grabbed one of the pests and ate it while stomping the other into the dirt. It snorted and began walking the perimeter, eating more grimalts, and chasing away pixies. While this little pig-man was offered a wide berth from some of the smaller among the gathering monsters, the larger ones were unfazed or even pushed the boar away.

A few of the more apparent beasts gathering was a Centaur and a silken-dressed, raven-haired woman. She moved with a light wave as though walking through water. While most of these new creatures remained quite in their cautious approach, this woman was humming a soft and oddly harmonic tune.

There was a definite hierarchy among these magical beings. Some were higher up in the ranks while others were maintaining understood place at the bottom.

Colby stepped back from the windows and motioned his companions closer. "The wards around this house and property are nearly spent. The magic has destabilized, and our enemies are gathering."

"What does that mean for us?" Shelly asked. "The remaining Dreggs are entering the house."

Conrad stepped in from the kitchen. "We need not worry about my brethren. They now understand our calling to the maker."

Shelly looked at the way Conrad revered her little brother. "Who is this little guy?"

When he caught Shelly's squinting glare, Colby winked at her before waving Conrad forward. "You remember Conrad, the Dregg. This is him returned to his normal Nefsmari state." Colby waved off questions. "I removed the curse. I'll explain later."

"Conrad," Colby said. "There was a particular creature out in the yard, a siren, I believe."

"Yes, maker, we call her Lady of the Lake."

Jasper laughed. "You mean like from King Arthur? Can you find us, Excalibur?"

Conrad was not moved by the attempt at humor. "Not exactly, but that was the inspiration for the name. She resides in the depths of Lake Michigan, living off the souls of those who have perished beneath the waves."

Casualties of boating accidents, lost in storms, drownings. Any life taken by the waters flows to the waiting embrace of the siren who protects the depths. This particular siren had been dormant for decades, awakened by the resurgence of Emassa.

Colby learned from Conrad's story that the siren had abilities to call unsuspecting sailors to their death, but long ago discovered that the stupidity and greed of man replaced that need. Over-shipping, drunken revelers, even the over-privileged thinking themselves accomplished sailors without training, they all found their end at the bottom of the lake.

"Could she be convinced to assist in a spell?" Colby asked. "I have an idea."

"For a price," Conrad said. "The siren are a tricky lot, sir. I would exercise caution in whatever bargain you might strike."

"Thanks, Conrad. I'll keep that in mind, but somehow I have a feeling she wants to help me."

"What are you planning, grandson?" Nana interrupted. "Sirens can not be trusted, they leech the very soul of men. How did you know what she is?"

"I don't know. I just have an awareness of things lately, but she just seems like a siren. And then there is that humming."

"I don't hear any humming," Shelly said.

"You wouldn't," Nana said. "You're not her type. Only men are fools enough to fall victim to the incessant song of a siren."

Colby told Nana not to be worried. With Conrad's assistance, Colby was able to lure the siren to the back porch. She approached with caution but eventually made it to within a whispering distance of Colby.

After a bit of head-shaking and passive agreement, the siren stepped back into a billowing wall of mist and evaporated.

Colby looked up, seeing the confusion in Conrad's eyes. As the new sigil burned into his skin, Colby moved the rune-marked hand into his pocket and strode past the uncertain Nefsmari.

"Something best saved for later," Colby said. "I got what I needed."

Colby walked to the base of the back steps and welcomed the cautious Dregg closer. While several near the back of the yard hesitated and looked behind them, they too moved closer to Colby and took to the knee. Heads down, the Dregg waited for what they had long-awaited.

Colby spoke the hashtag spell, the words of unmaking, and added one last rune to the mix. As the newest mark on his body glowed from within his pocketed hand, energy lifted from his center. It flowed from the body to watch and out into the surrounding yard.

The air shook from the unmaking magic that grew in amplification and power as it used the siren's charm to envelope every last Dregg.

As the magic did its work, the aching screams of reforming creatures accompanied the confusion of the other beings scattering from the yard. All that remained within the yard when the spell completed was the Nefsmari. Seekers still lingered in the shadows beyond.

"Conrad," Colby said as he squinted and saw the new threat. "Get the Nefsmari inside, we may be needing your special ability."

Conrad caught sight of what Colby saw along the parameter of the yard and hurried his brethren into the house after himself.

"Crap on a cracker," Nana said as she watched the movement of a glowing figure present in the distance. "The Dregg would have kept them away. What have you done, Colby?"

Colby paused before his grandmother but addressed the ancient witch hiding in the depths of the old woman's mind. "I have released them of their burden and curse. Something you should have done long ago, Bellatrix."

As Colby entered the house without awaiting a response, Bellatrix mumbled past Nana's unknowing lips. "It was not the will of he who made them that I should undo his work."

Colby paused, hearing her words, but did not turn. Without responding, he continued into the house. Colby knew precisely to whom she was referring. The Druid made the Dregg and used them as he did everyone else the robed man encountered over the centuries, no doubt.

"Everyone of human origins, please gather in the next room." Colby patted a groveling Nefsmari on the head as he moved from the kitchen to the living room.

Shelly glared at Nana as she passed. "That rules you out, old woman. Both voices in your head are not human and just a bit cra-cra."

In the living room, Aria finished shooing out the last of the Nefsmari so the rest of Colby's group could sit and hear what he had to say.

"It seems that the magical gathering outside has shifted unfavorably," Colby said. "We now have an emergence of seekers along the outer yard, and they-"

"Are here because you took away our only method of holding them off," Fizzlewink interrupted. "I know you had your reasons and whatever altruistic obligation your vision left you with, but we are now in a fight or flight situation."

"Thanks, Fizz," Colby said. "I wouldn't have put it quite so…well your way of putting things. Suffice it to say, we need to depart. The seekers were already here observing. My removal of the Dregg curse simply encouraged them into action."

Colby explained how the Dregg, before transformation back to their correct forms, destroyed all the protections around the house. Even the spells on Jarrod's study were gone. The only recourse was to leave.

"And where do we go and how do we fight our way out?" Gary asked, looking at Jasper. "Not all of us are that good with spells for defense."

"I can help you out," Jasper said. "We all can't be fighters." He flexed his muscles and grimaced at the responding groans.

Colby waved Jasper to stop flexing and looked at Gary before passing a glance at everyone in the room. "We all have our talents, and we can all help. The first issue of escape is the easiest. We use Nefsmari."

Explaining how the Nefsmari had an innate magical gift for teleportation was the easiest part of Colby's plan. The more difficult was yet to come. Colby had no idea what was next because he did not know his adversary or what he wanted. It was already clear the Druid had his own agenda and not under the control of Rigel. There were many pieces of this puzzle yet to gather, let alone fit them together.

Colby made sure all the Nefsmari retained their abilities and prior knowledge they gained as a Dregg. Colby instructed all but a few to see Nana before they would leave and remain at the retreat location to await everyone's arrival.

Nana already began gathering things from the pantry, cupboards, freezer, fridge, and anywhere else she could find items they might need. When a Nefsmari attempted to take a few items too many, Nana snarled and told him to wait.

Besides the customary junk drawer any midwest kitchen has, there is a cabinet, drawer, or another spot for storing the overflowing hoard of plastic grocery bags. Nana was a collector of all things useful and otherwise. Below her supply of scrap paper and wrinkled reusable wrapping paper was a thin cabinet door that barely stayed closed. When she opened it, wads of plastic bags spilled to the floor.

"Each of you take some bags and fill them with as much as you can carry."

One over-eager, Nefsmari tried to stuff pots and pans in a bag before Nana pushed him toward the food items. "I'll take care of the big stuff. Get the small things."

The Nefsmari headed toward the piles of food and gave a sideways squint at Fizzlewink, who sat huddled in the corner.

"What?" Fizzlewink said. "Is there something you need?"

The Nefsmari put his hands on his hips and stared Fizzlewink down. "You have some nerve even being here, let alone speaking to me with such superiority. I'm surprised you haven't run off to safety like the last time there was a fight for the source."

Nana stopped fighting over a tangled mess of plastic bags and set them on the counter before turning toward Fizzlewink and the other Nefsmari. The old witch Bellatrix, clouded over Nana's eyes as she took the driver's seat in their shared mind.

"What are you speaking about?" Bellatrix asked. "Do you recount the days of the first mage-wars?"

Fizzlewink turned a lighter Shade of blue as the color drained from his face, ushered away by the memories that returned at the mention of the Great Emassa War.

CHAPTER 16

The look that passed between Fizzlewink and Bellatrix spoke of a shared and unspoken experience. A shadowed memory that each was unable to hold tightly beneath the weight of scrutiny.

Bellatrix spoke aloud of how she remembered seeing Fizzlewink running frantically toward a Nefslama stronghold. She had thought he entered before its being sealed against the oncoming nullification of magic. She felt he was safe. The little blue man, first among the Nefsmari, created to stand vigil and serve the Nefslama until the return of Emassa's natural flow, Fizzlewink entered her witch's den. That is where the memory evaporated.

As her mind struggled, the images in her head began to fade. Bodies of those she last saw before enacting her splintering spell, broke into dust and drifted off on the winding stream of thought. Bellatrix was not one to become easily confused. The missing—or instead shifting—memories of the final moments before the binding of Emassa, soured her more than was usual.

"What, in the name of Emassa, is going on here?" Bellatrix pushed past the counter and squatted toward a quivering Nefsmari. "What is it that you recall?"

"Him," The little blue man said, pointing toward Fizzlewink. "He was leading us toward the enemy one minute, then ordered us to retreat the next. He said we would not win the day and must scatter to the far ends of the world and prepare for a resurgence. Fizzlewink knew, Great Witch."

"Stop calling me that. It makes me feel old."

"But you are-" the little man started to say.

Bellatrix leveled her eyes, "Be very careful how you finish that statement."

"Not inexperienced," he finished. "You must remember. He said he was going to see you."

As the restitching of her fragmented memory began, Bellatrix locked eyes with Fizzlewink. In an instant, resurgence washed over them both, and they exchanged knowledge of their individual agreements. They both partook in a game staged long ago but was beginning in the here and now.

"He did know," Bellatrix said after a minute of reflection. "He knew how to lead you then. Let him lead you once again."

Fizzlewink nodded at her words but appeared busy with his own thoughts. He stroked something hidden away in his pocket with one hand. His other hand gestured for the Nefsmari to continue taking supplies to their retreat location.

When Bellatrix moved toward Fizzlewink, he pushed her away with a glance. "Our time to discuss this conundrum of the continuum is in the past. I only now begin to understand my bargain, focus on your own."

Turning toward the first group of bag-laden Nefsmari, Fizzlewink gave them their orders. "Take what you have to the warehouse. Its protections remain intact, and we shall all retreat there once all we can take has been gathered."

One after the next, Nefsmari gathered supply-laden grocery bags and lined up for inspection before Fizzlewink. He checked their bags, making sure they each had enough to carry but were not overburdened. Though he relished the return of his kinsmen, Fizzlewink still longed for the company of only a few. His family.

Refocusing on the task at hand, Fizzlewink began ordering his people away with their supplies and to the safety of the warehouse. He recognized some as they saluted him and smiled, while others glared and only obeyed under threat of Bellatrix's wrath. He glanced ahead in the line and nodded they were all doing fine without his supervision.

Fizzlewink left the frantic scurrying of his kinsmen behind as he exited the kitchen in search of Colby. He continued to fidget with the note in his pocket, brow furrowed, and using his other hand to rub his temple. The old Nefsmari wore his worry like a mustard stain, exposing his inner turmoil to any who would bother to see.

"What troubles you, teacher," Colby said, trying his best to lighten the old blue cat-man's burdened mind. "You walk as though you are heading toward your own execution."

Fizzlewink stopped short of running directly into Colby. He looked up at the young mage and searched his eyes for answers, knowing they would not be there yet.

"I have sent the others of my kind to the warehouse to transfer what we can from the house. The rest of us should be ready to leave soon."

"We have less time than we hoped," Colby said and looked out the window. "There are more seekers arriving, and they have become more…eager."

Along the perimeter of the yard, seekers hovered and drifted on the wind, edging closer to the yard. They exhibited a cautious staggering of their movements, as would the pieces of a chessboard making methodical and strategic alterations in their game of conquest.

"What are they doing?" Fizzlewink asked.

"Whatever it is, it can't be good. I'm more concerned about their numbers."

Fizzlewink pulled on his eyebrow. "There seems to be more than I would have thought were still in existence. I wonder where they've been hiding?"

Colby shook his head. "I fear they are not a pre-existing group. I sense some familiarity among their ranks."

"What do you mean?"

"I feel at least a few souls among them that I felt among the Shizumu with which I previously bargained."

"They've betrayed your deal?"

"Perhaps," Colby said. "Whatever the reasons, we need to leave now."

Fizzlewink did not wait for instructions. He ran back into the house and began sending his comrades off with the remaining supplies, a few of them reminded to return for a passenger.

As each Nefsmari blinked out of existence, another stepped in to grab remaining supplies to transport off to the warehouse. Once all that could be managed was away to their place of retreat, most of their party was gone. Those that remained were only enough Nefsmari to accompany each human unable to perform the teleportation magic.

Usually, Colby would be able to manage a larger group than four people when traveling through the Emassa. Still, with the increasing drain on his magic, Colby was not willing to risk the effort. As his friends joined him on the back porch, Colby began to assign Nefsmari to take his friends to safety.

"We should stay together," Jasper said. "I'm sure if you use my strength and Gary's sense of GPS, we could manage ok."

"I'm not interested in just managing ok, Jasper. We've lost one of you already, I won't be responsible for another."

Darla smacked Colby. "One of us? Her name was Rhea. We didn't lose her, she was murdered."

As much as Rhea's loss pained Colby, he maintained a stoic face. "She was as much a part of me as the rest of you, and I feel her loss more than you understand. Right now isn't the time for acting out of anger or fear."

Before Darla could argue more, Colby nodded toward a little blue man to take her away. Each, in turn, his friends and family were spirited away to the warehouse, leaving Colby, Fizzlewink, and Bellatrix alone on the back steps.

As two more Nefsmari returned short of the back porch, seekers began to close in.

"Get out of there," Colby said. He turned to Fizzlewink. "What are they back here for?"

"I instructed them to return for the old bat and you."

"I can transport myself."

"You are underplaying the effect this open-source of your hashtag magic is having on you."

Colby halted himself from arguing further as he watched the

confused Nefsmari become frightened to inaction as Seekers surrounded them.

"Leave now!"

Colby's command did not reach them before each Nefsmari was taken away by a Seeker. The remaining mass of red-glowing entities swarmed toward the back porch.

Colby began to enact his hashtag spell to transport to the warehouse when he heard the wailing sound of disharmonious singing from the back of the yard.

The Siren stepped out of the shadows and increased the volume of her powerful and command-filled song.

Fizzlewink hissed at the onslaught of discomfort to his cat-like hearing. He looked over at Bellatrix, who began to fall under the spell of the Siren. Colby seemed unaffected. In an instant of action, Fizzlewink grabbed Bellatrix and blinked away with a muffled pop.

Colby stood alone on the back porch as the Seekers spun around the yard and began retreating.

One, then three, then entire groups of Seekers evaporated as they soared past the boundaries of the Stevens' property. Their screeching faded along with the mesmerizing song of the Siren.

Colby felt relief from the departure of his adversaries. He still agonized with the increasing tug on his Emassa-filled core that was caused by his magical translation application being loose on the internet. Trying his best to show a strong face and stance, Colby leveled his gaze on the Siren as she approached.

"You are indeed an interesting and powerful creature," the Siren said. "My lure seems to have no effect on you. Why do you suppose that is?" She looked Colby over from head to toe as she drew nearer.

Colby lifted his hand to halt the Siren's approach when she was several feet from his position on the back steps of the house.

"That is close enough." Colby's sleeve fell back as he lifted his arm, revealing the swirling of ancient runes on the surface of his skin. One rune stood out as it glowed brighter than the others.

The Siren's eyes grew wide as she recognized the marking upon Colby's skin. "That can not be."

"What?" Colby pulled down his sleeve but glanced at the bright symbol on his arm before looking back at the Siren. He did not recognize the mark, it only formed when first he made a deal with the Siren. "What is this symbol?"

The Siren looked skeptically at Colby before making a movement toward him. She stopped at Colby's clearing of his throat. He didn't want her getting too close.

"That symbol is why my song does not work on you. It also explains why I was drawn back ashore from the depths of the lake and to your doorstep. You carry the mark of our master, and our bargain is null." The anger at being tricked sizzled on her words.

Colby looked again at the symbol and began to run his finger along the lines. Following the outside left line from its triangular tip to a sharp right angle and back up again, Colby saw the beginnings of understanding for the rune. Once he lifted his finger and ran down the line that intercepted the center of the elongated and stiffly constructed "U" shape, he comprehended the trident and its power over the creatures of the seas.

"Our bargain stands. I do not pretend to understand why this mark is now upon my skin, but I will honor my debt to you for helping to send the seekers away."

The Siren looked up at Colby. Though doubt circled her eyes, she nodded and backed away into a mist just as Fizzlewink returned.

"What are you waiting for?" Fizzlewink asked. He looked around and noticed a yard empty of anything magical except a few pixies and grimalts that lapped up residual Emassa. "I see our friends have gone, along with that tone-deaf water witch."

Colby explained his original bargain with the Siren and that he would owe her a favor if she assisted in ridding the property of seekers. Once the revelation of his latest skin art nulled their first pact, Colby mentioned his promise to still honor the deal. Fizzlewink wasn't happy about the situation, but he was less concerned about the extent to which the Siren would push being as though Colby had a hold over her.

"As much as these runes on your body are perplexing and worrying, at least they are serving a purpose."

"To what ends?" Colby asked. "I haven't a clue what they all mean, and my journal is less than useless on the topic."

"Once we get to the warehouse," Fizzlewink said ass he looked closer at the runes tattoos. "Perhaps we will have a moment to breathe and think this through."

"Perhaps," Colby said. "Let's go."

Colby grabbed Fizzlewink's hand and allowed himself to be taken passenger to the. Perceived protection of the warehouse on Goose

Island."

CHAPTER 17

Colby and Fizzlewink appeared in the center of the warehouse, surrounded by a blur of blue. It took Colby a moment to realize it was the frantic scurrying of Nefsmari. They wandered about blinking in and out of existence.

Jasper and Gary moved things around, trying to organize all the items brought from the house. At the same time, Darla sat on a makeshift cot.

Colby smiled when he looked at Darla, to spite the hurt he felt radiating from her. She still felt the pain of Rhea's loss and found comfort in a small furry bundle she held on her lap. At first, Colby thought it to be one fo the Nefsmari in cat form, but then he saw the jagged teeth and glowing eyes. She was petting a grimalt.

"Darla, do you think that's a good idea?" Colby walked toward her. "Those things are...well, we don't know anything about them."

"Fluffy, he is harmless," Darla said. As she caressed the creature, it made a sniffing and snorting sound that might have been some sort of purring. "He likes me."

Colby looked at her with a mix of pity and skepticism. "Well, just don't let it near Fizz. He'll probably pass a fur-ball over having that creature in here."

Darla patted the puffy bundle of fur and teeth before tucking it away inside her backpack. She put the bag over her shoulder and got up to help settle everyone in.

Colby looked around at the rest of the activity within the warehouse. Over the shouting of Nana and the hissing calls from Fizzlewink, things were not settling down much.

There were cots all over the place. Bags of supplies lay in scattered bundles and half-spilled. While there was a kitchen area that once served as a break room, it was a flurry of blue and banging as Nana tried to waddle through the Nefsmari and piles of pots and pans. Nana would be looking to start cooking, so Colby silently wished for the kitchen to remain out of order.

As he refocused on the center of the living area, Colby noticed Shelly pulling the hair atop her head and shouting at a mass of Nefsmari. They ran circles around Shelly, dropping and picking up the same items. Feeling sorry for his sister, Colby decided to provide a supporting shoulder.

As he tried to push his way toward Shelly, Colby grimaced at the expression on his sister's face.

"Welcome to my hell," Shelly said. "Surrounded by dozens of Fizzlewinks. What level of the inferno is this?"

Fizzlewink leaped from head to blue head as he made his way from the other end of madness. "This would be the hidden level of hell. The devil himself would avoid a frenzy of Nefsmari with no direction. This is why my people never gathered in groups."

"Is that because one of you is annoying, but dozens are head-exploding?" Shelly said.

Fizzlewink blinked slowly at Shelly and clicked his tongue in his lips. "Haven't you tried to stop them and calm things down?" Fizzlewink asked. "They just returned to their natural form and immediately got thrown into service. Add to that, two of their friends being taken away by seekers."

Shelly raised her hands to her hips and locked eyes with Fizzlewink. "Do you take me for an idiot? Wait, don't answer that. Look around at this madness. It's like watching some demented game of whack-a-mole from inside the console. Only this game is beginning to smell like a cat shelter."

"I take insult to that, Shelly. Lest you forget my kind has much better noses than the likes of you and believe me, what we smell coming off of you-"

"Enough," Bellatrix said. She walked up beside Colby and pulled back one of his sleeves. "We need to talk."

"There are more pressing matters," Colby said and pointed at the flurry of blue cat-people. "Things need to be settled and plans made."

Bellatrix cleared her throat and used magic to amplify her voice. "Everyone calm down."

"There, the rest can be managed by Fizzlewink. They already look to him for guidance." Bellatrix turned Nana's body toward Fizzlewink. "See after calming your people and situating this place for an extended stay."

Taking Colby by the arm, Bellatrix led him toward the only area empty of activity. She pulled back both of his sleeves and examined the now stationary runes marking him. More images existed than even Colby recalled the last time he looked. Before Bellatrix could pull open his shirt, Colby unbuttoned it to reveal those symbols as well.

"This is not good, my boy," Nana's voice overtook the use of her own body.

"Nana?"

"The battle-ax has retreated into her own counsel. All I can understand is the worry she feels or rather remembers of seeing this once before on a pure-blood."

"What does that mean, pure-blood?"

Bellatrix returned. "A pure-blood is the parentage of the Nefslama, the first of our people to arrive on this Earth. They have not been around for thousands of years. Even my first body was of mixed lineage."

Bellatrix recalled how the original split of Shi that the Nefslama experimented with decimated the ranks of the elders. They began repopulating through mixed breeding among humans. After the wars with the Shizumu, the elders were nearly eradicated. Only one original Nefslama was known to survive, Betelgeuse.

Colby's grandfather was still around, but he did not mate with a pure-blood. Even though Colby came from a potent family, he would not be considered pure-blood. That is unless particular magical transformational magic was enacted on him at an early age.

Aria joined them, scratching the center of her chest that bore the mark of Bellatrix's spell from the Druid.

"There were no spells or incantations performed on you as a child. That kind of working would require a shi crystal from an original descendant."

Colby turned to his mother. "What is that?"

"The magic of a Nefslama," Aria said. "The shi is a sort of cage for both sides of the soul. It is extremely small and even more difficult to isolate. That kind of magic it risky, to say the least, and isn't even written in the oldest of texts."

"Then how do you know of it?" Nana asked Colby. "You haven't studied the texts of old."

"I just know things now. I can't explain it, but there are flashes. It's like long-forgotten memories are surfacing."

"What memory is bringing about the images of a shi crystal."

"The night my magic was hobbled. I think there was a crystal involved," Colby said. As the thoughts raced around his mind, a shout came from the other side of the warehouse. "You said dad pricked my foot with something, drawing blood. What else happened that night you haven't said?"

"I really can't remember," Aria admitted. "It did involve blood, though, and some text from your father's journal. I don't remember more."

Colby discussed what this might mean with the others. Only if his father performed some ritual that not only hobbled his magic but also transformed him in some way would things make sense. This might explain much of why he was at the center of the resurgence of Emassa. Maybe he used the shi crystal of another to bind Colby's magic, and there was a side effect.

"Perhaps Jarrod's magical workings that evening were not meant to take your magic, but transform it, make you more than intended," Fizzlewink said. "The loss of your abilities might have been an adjustment period."

"So what am I, my father's attempt to bring back the purity of the elders' blood?"

Bellatrix took full control of Nana's body. "I believe it is more than that based on the appearance of the Druid. I can say very little more, but he is connected to this in some way. Many have made a bargain with that creature, and payment has come due. Who's to say

Jarrod did not make such a deal when the time came to protect you from those who would have seen you neutralized for even being conceived?"

"You speak of that stupid prophecy linked to my son?" Aria said. "Bullshit. I didn't believe it then and sure as hell not shopping the idea now. Where did that prophecy even come from? I never met with an oracle. About my future children."

Colby took all that was being said to heart. He felt, more than knew, that bits of all that was being told were actual as parts of the whole. He pondered what might have happened.

During that night, as a child, something happened that changed him in some way. When he thought about the shi crystal, and being pricked for blood, it made more sense. When the watch his father left behind began to burn his wrist, Colby became confident the crystal hidden within was not a normal part of its operation. That crystal somehow held the wake-up call to his magic. He was a pure-blood now, or at least it appeared that way.

"Colby," Gary said. "The final section of your book just unlocked."

Gary handed the journal to Colby as he reached out his hand. The pages were blank. Colby was confused as he flipped through the pages. His frustration and rough handling of the journal resulted in a deep and stinging paper-cut. As Colby pulled his finger back and pushed it into his mouth to staunch the bleeding and pain, he watched the tiny remnant of his blood on a page as it was absorbed.

The page began to reveal runes, many Colby recognized as part of his new skin art. The page started to fade, so Colby squeezed another drop of blood from his finger on another page. The next page was also filled with runes that required his blood to be read.

Colby wanted to read through the pages more but was stopped by a static charge. Then the appearance of Rigel with the last of the Daphnes made him stop. They carried the two abducted Nefsmari, bleeding, and limp as they were discarded to the dusty floor.

"How the hell did they get in here?" Fizzlewink said. Though he did none know them personally, Fizzlewink began to weep for his fallen Nefsmari kinsmen. "You've killed them."

"Essence draining magic," Bellatrix said, looking at the dead bodies of two Nefsmari at the feet of their adversaries. "Monsters."

"You took my sisters from us," said Daphne, "Who are the true monsters."

"You were not sisters," Aria said. "You were copies, and poor ones at that. You would have never been more than a second rate version of the original."

"A monster would better describe the one who wanted your creation. I'm only correcting that poorly conceived mistake." Bellatrix fumbled through the folds of Nana's petticoats for the remaining piece of the Druids enchanted device. "One, I am nearly finished rectifying."

A rumble rolled on an ill wind through the warehouse. A flash of blinding light filled the room. Before anyone could move, a volley of magical energy was sent around the warehouse, immobilizing the Nefsmari, including Fizzlewink.

"Can't have any pesky cats taking the fun away before we can get to business," Daphne said. "You've dispatched my sisters, but that just made me stronger." She waved her arm and opened a portal to allow seekers into the warehouse. "You have your orders."

The seekers, three of them, went off in opposing directions, each with resolute intention. They headed toward Colby's friends, Jasper, Gary, and Darla.

"Leave my friends alone," Colby said.

He aimed his hand toward the first seeker without casting a hashtag spell. Energy poured forth from Colby's hand, purple and brighter than midday sun on a blanket of snow. The light of his instinctual magic filled the warehouse with blinding light.

Before the light faded, an echoing crack rebounded around the interior of the warehouse. A skin rippling curdle followed as one of the seekers was blasted from existence.

As the magic faded, all in the space uncovered their eyes to readjust to normal light levels. The two remaining seekers hesitated for a moment before changing tactics. One went for Darla, while the other headed for Colby.

Under normal circumstances, Colby would have been ready for the attack. The outburst of magic he had let out, however, drained what little remained in his core of stored Emassa. He could not resist the seeker when it reached out and took him from the warehouse. In an instant, Colby was gone alone with Rigel, Daphne, and Darla.

CHAPTER 18

Colby used what little strength he had to fight the energy-sapping grip of his captor. His body convulsed as the seeker leeched out the last of Colby's stored Emassa. Once the creature was finished, it let Colby fall to the ground, limp and drained.

Rigel stood near Colby's unresponsive body. He tittered as he looked down, kicking Colby in the side for a reaction. When Colby groaned, Rigel laughed.

"I just don't see the use of him," Rigel said. "He hasn't the talent or fortitude to manage his abilities."

"Why have you brought him here," the Druid said. He moved from the shadow of a monolith inside the barrier around Stonehenge. "I gave specific instructions to bring me the three remaining friends and not to touch Colby."

Rigel narrowed his gaze on the Druid without lifting his head.

"Why? I fail to see the need to prolong this boy's existence. He's been a boil on my ass for the last decade."

The breeze over the plains pulled into a tight swirl toward the Druid before stopping. Stillness hung over the henge as the robed figure loomed toward Rigel.

Rigel hesitated, a moment of visible worry rippled over his face and body until he stood his ground.

The Druid's voice was carried along with a buffeting wind directly toward Rigel. "Because I said the boy was mine to deal with."

Rigel could not remain standing against the force of the Druid's magically enhanced words. He fell back on one knee before reaching for a hold on Colby's restless form. As he struggled to regain his feet, Rigel's fingers gripped hard on Colby's wrist. As he lost his hold, Rigel scratched Colby with his nails. A hissing sound drew his focus upward.

The Druid stepped back, holding his wrist as scars formed in the same spot as Colby's.

A smile began to creep along Rigel's face. There was a connection between the boy and this Druid. Rigel wanted to know what was the extent and reason for this bond.

Rigel ordered the seekers to head for Colby, to drain him completely. They did not make the distance to their quarry.

The Druid lifted his arms to the sky and called forth several bolts of energy from storm clouds that formed from nothing. Each strike of energy extinguished its target. The echoing of thunder drowned out the wailing screeches of each fallen seeker.

"How dare you destroy my servants," Rigel said.

"You forget yourself, skin-walker. The seekers were never yours to command. It wasn't even your spell that first created them."

As Rigel and the Druid continued to argue for dominance, Darla tried to move toward Colby. She didn't get more than a few feet when she was yanked back, flying through the air to fall hard upon the ground near Daphne.

"And where do you think you are going, little girly?" Daphne said. "Plans for you remain the same."

Daphne stretched out her arms on each side of Darla and began to draw upon the Emassa. The crackling of energy echoed and reverberated around the uprights around the henge. Static built up around the huddled girl in the center of the magical construct.

Darla huddled down, whimpering into her backpack as another set of eyes from within met hers. The grimalt rattled its discomforting purr as Darla scratched its head. Residing to her fate, and knowing it was coming eventually settled upon her being as Darla began to look up with defiance. Before she could muster a syllable of a final statement, a set of hard and bone-chilling hands settled upon her shoulder, hoisting her up and away from Daphne's spell.

Anger filled the air around the magical clone of Aria. Daphne screamed her displeasure of being robbed from her willful act of hate for all things Stevens. Darla was a part of Colby's circle of friends, and he was their progenitor and anchor to life. They couldn't destroy Aria, but they could anyone else they chose. Darla was the current target of Daphne's hatred, and she was snatched away by one of the Druid's priests.

"What do you think you are doing?" Daphne said.

"She is to die," said Daphne. She chased after the mysterious and silent druid priest. "Come back here."

Energy encircled Darla and then transferred to her handler. The Emassa entered the priest before traveling along its raised hand, sending a bolt toward the oncoming Daphne.

It said nothing as the magic left Daphne on the ground. The priest continued to move away and toward the opposite end of the stone circle, where it deposited Darla.

Darla curled up with her grimalt pet. She squeezed her eyes shut, expecting an immediate deathblow, but it didn't come. Relief allowed Darla's shoulders to relax, though she remained guarded. Being an adept empath, Darla was concerned that she felt nothing from the robed being that stood near, both motionless and emotionless.

Before Darla began to reach out with her powers to probe the priest, it turned to her. Its face was hidden in the shadow of the hooded robe. Darla discovered there was no face at all when a bright flash of light chased away the shadow. An accompanying clap of energy pulled Darla's attention back to Colby and the two men fighting over him.

"Why should we not kill him now, Druid?" Rigel asked. He bent at the knees to squat down next to the now stirring Colby. "How easily I could reach down and slit his scrawny little neck."

A red shaft of light appeared in Rigel's hand, transforming into a nearly translucent red crystal dagger. He reached down and pulled Colby's head back by the hair atop his head. As he eased the blade near Colby's throat, the dagger dissipated into particles that drifted away on a sudden breeze. The breeze began to pick up speed.

"When I tell you not to harm him, I speak not for the pleasure of hearing my own voice." The Druid lifted his arms toward the moon that hung its full bottom from a bed of clouds as it rose in the night sky. "Ha'ashtagga Shadda," the Druid said.

The winds abated as the Druid lowered his arms. Nothing happened.

Rigel laughed. "Seems the link between you and the Stevens boy has weakened you, Druid."

The Druid said nothing, his cold and penetrating stare leveled at Rigel.

Unmoved by the locking of eyes, Rigel created another magical dagger and plunged it toward Colby.

Too quick for the Druid to react, it was Colby who turned in time to raise a hand toward the oncoming assault from above. His open palm began to glow a rich purple just as the pointed tip of the red dagger penetrated his skin. Colby screamed as the dagger—slowed by his instinctive reaction—stopped a half inch through the back of his hand. The echo Colby heard was strange. It was his scream but from a voice more mature than his own.

The Druid pulled his hand to his chest and swore a spell over it. As the magic healed his wound, so did it affect Colby.

Rigel bared his teeth as a realization lifted a fog from his eyes. "You are linked to the boy. You are trying to take his magic, is that it Druid?"

"Don't be so sophomoric in your assumptions Rigel, it belies your level of intellect."

"Then what? If I kill him now, will that reveal your double-dealing?" Rigel pulled Colby back up from the ground. "Perhaps I end this now. You've failed to deliver on your promise in any case."

The Druid stopped forward. "And what was the bargain we made skin-walker."

Rigel's defiance wavered. "You said that one day I could call on you to give me what I truly desired."

"And what do you desire?"

"I want the Emassa back, all of it. And that means this boy has to open it or that power taken from him."

The Druid bowed his robed head a moment then looked back at

Rigel. "The deal does not stipulate how I do this?"

Rigel tilted his head and looked at the Druid, narrowing his eyes. "So you are taking the necessary power to open the full flow of Emassa from Colby? Is that it?"

"In a manner of speaking, yes."

"Then get on with it. What are we playing with the boy then? Rip the magic from him and discard the rest or let a Shizumu take his body for a new home."

Tittering preceded the Druid's answer. "I will conduct my end of the deal in the manner in which it best serves. And what was the price of this bargain?"

Rigel loosened his grip on Colby before reenforcing a firm hold. "It cost me dearly. And this inept Nefsla-freak is a constant reminder." Rigel created another dagger and meant to push it through Colby's heart.

Icy breath escaped Rigel's mouth as the Shade's hand reached through him from behind and knocked the dagger from his hand. The spectral creature pushed itself through Rigel to float away toward the Druid. Rigel dropped Colby.

Colby turned to see the color begin returning to Rigel's face. As he scooted away, Colby turned to the sound of Darla's whimpering and decided to go work his way toward his golem friend.

"How soon you forget the sensations of a disconnected Shi," the Druid said. "Perhaps you need a reminder of who is truly in command."

The Druid waved over one of his followers. "Take the boy through the lines back to his home."

Colby started to correct the Druid on his desired destination but thought better of allowing another intrusion on his friends and family. His hope was the warehouse was already refortified against unwelcome guests by then.

"You can't take me home, the stone ring is destroyed," Colby said.

The Druid laughed. "You will find it restored upon your return. Go."

Colby was pulled into the ley line without ceremony. His last vision of Stonehenge was that of the Shade hovering between the Druid and Colby's point of departure. It reached out for him.

The speed and force at which Colby traveled the ley lines around the planet prevented him from seeing anything as the light was more intense than staring directly at the sun through squinted eyes. Colby tried to close his eyes before remembering that he was not in a solid form while traversing the magical lines of power that webbed the globe. Only the hard slam of the ground brought Colby back to the corporeal realm.

His vision cleared as he focused on the departure of the druid priest through the stone ring of his backyard. Scrambling on hands and knees, Colby reached the circle to confirm it had reformed. Remembering Darla, Colby stepped into the ring and cast a spell to travel back to Salisbury Plains. As he began to enter a state of physical transformation, he snapped back to solidity and was thrown from the portal.

The way was blocked by a spell. Colby crawled back to the ring and placed his hand on it to probe the portal's enchantment. He could sense connections to other portals around the world, but that of Stonehenge was absent. The Druid must have done something to prevent travelers.

As he traced a finger around the reformed lei-gate, Colby failed to sense the arrival of Jasper and Fizzlewink.

"What are you doing here?" Jasper said. "And where's Darla?"

Colby turned from the mixture of amazement, envy, and worry he had at the Druid's abilities. The man somehow rebuilt a ley-gate from the opposite side of the planet. He then removed access to Stonehenge, like putting it on Do Not Disturb.

"I was sent back here from Stonehenge. The Druid rebuilt this portal, and he has Darla."

Fizzlewink jumped over Colby to grab a fist-sized rock from the garden and enchanted it with a spell. The stone transformed into an oblong crystal. Pushing Colby out of the way, Fizzlewink drove the crystal into the ground, centered in the ley-gate ring.

"That'll keep them from coming back through here," Fizzlewink said, grabbing Colby and Jasper. "Let's go."

CHAPTER 19

"How do we get to Darla," Gary said. "If the ley-gate has been disabled, we can't get there in time to save her."

"I think I can get there, and take a few with me," Colby said. "I've been there so I can use my own ability to transport back."

Shelly hissed. "If you had the strength. You are spent and need time to recharge your core. Darla doesn't have that kind of time."

Jasper—who had been sitting back and appeared to be sleeping—got up and moved to take Colby in a bear hug.

"What are you doing?" Colby said but didn't back away. Then he felt the power surging into him. "Oh."

Colby started to giggle, and Jasper joined him as they maintained the awkward embrace that produced a glowing bubble around their midsections.

"You're like an extra power bank," Colby said and laughed again when Jasper snorted.

"Boys," Shelly huffed.

Fizzlewink pulled Gary then asked Nana and Shelly to join them. "While Jasper and Colby do…that, we need to figure out how to get the gate open from the other end."

"How do you propose we do that?" Gary asked.

Fizzlewink explained how he used a crystal to interrupt the use of the Stevens' gate. It was an old tactic used in the Shizumu wars eons ago. He figured that Gary might figure out a way to bypass the block in Stonehenge using Hashtag Magic.

"How can Colby's app work against the Druid's spell?" Gary asked.

"Call it a hunch, but there is also precedence for repurposing someone else's spells."

They argued and bantered for several minutes before Colby joined the discussion. He looked refreshed and back to his usual self, while Jasper needed to recharge his core. Colby maintained a connection to the Emassa and continued to pull hard to fill himself with as much energy as possible. The trickle effect of Hashtag Magic on the web was still siphoning off magic, but it was slow.

"Just keep drawing in some Emassa," Fizzlewink said. "We need you once we figure out how to get all of us there as quick as possible."

Colby looked at the scribblings that Gary and Fizzlewink were calling a plan. Then it dawned on him.

"The Crystal."

Fizzlewink looked at Colby and began to sense the direction he was going. "Perhaps."

"What about the crystal?" Nana asked.

Colby began to explain. Crystals are useful for many things, including storing data and acting as a conduit. His plan was simple, but implementing it would be difficult on the other end. First, Gary and Colby would devise a subroutine for Hashtag Magic that would be stored in the crystal in his backyard, currently blocking the gate. A new crystal would be used to store the same code and be used at the other gate in Stonehenge.

"So, what happens?" Shelly asked. "How will this help break the Druid's spell?"

"We don't need to break it," Colby explained. "We are going to bypass it. The Crystals will similarly connect to each other using a virtual private network works on the internet. We will be building a private gate along the ley line."

"I still don't get how it will work," Aria said. "I understand how a VPN works, but if this Druid has blocked the gate-"

"That's just it," Gary said. "He's only blocked the gate. He can't block the ley lines…can he?"

"No," Bellatrix said, using Nana's mouth. "Not unless he wanted to destroy the flow of Emassa."

"That's impossible," Fizzlewink said.

"No, it is not," Bellatrix said. "Have you never wondered why there are dead zones around the globe. What of the spots where vortexes of power exist that even humans can sense? These are all the results of accidents in the past with dangerous and overpowered spells failing.

"Those spells destroyed the veins of ley lines they tapped into to draw Emassa. The result is a zone too far from other lines to draw energy from. That rerouting or backing up of the flow has caused vortexes."

"Can we get on with it?" Shelly said. "Tick-Tock."

Colby agreed and worked with Fizzlewink to create a crystal from what stones they found around the exterior of the warehouse. When they could not find one, a Nefslama appeared with a stone from the Stevens' backyard. Being helpful, the creature figured the best stone would be one from the same location as the one already being used.

"That was very dangerous, and brave," Colby said. "Thank you."

Wasting no more time, the crystal was formed and encoded with Hashtag Magic and the subroutine they coined 'Hashtag Private Gateway'.

Gary went with that same Nefslama to the Stevens' backyard and used his tablet to upload the HPG code to the crystal there. When stirring in the bushes made him nervous, Gary grabbed another stone and returned to the warehouse with the little blue man.

"There is some activity in the backyard at your place Colby," Gary said. "I think we should plant a crystal in the warehouse to relay from here through your yard and off to Stonehenge."

"Good idea," Jasper said.

Gary looked at Jasper sideways. It was unlike him to compliment or get along with Gary.

"What? It is." Jasper turned away. "Some people can't take a compliment."

After the final adjustments were completed, the newest crystal was planted in the center of the warehouse. It connected to the other in the Stevens' backyard. All that remained was for the first team to get to Stonehenge and plant the final bypass crystal so the entire group could follow and go on the offense.

Fizzlewink walked up to Colby, who stood alone in the corner, looking over his gathering of supporters, family, and friends.

"Quite the little army that you're starting my boy."

Colby glanced at Fizzlewink without much movement of his head. "Army? I don't know about that, but we can at least use the Nefsmari to distract and move us around as needed once we get there."

"They'll know what to do when the time comes. You just get that crystal in place, and I'll jump to let the others know it's done."

"I won't be planting the crystal. I'll need to keep the Druid busy."

"Then, who is going with you to plant the bypass?"

"I am," Shelly said. "I'll enter the in-between once we arrive and sneak in while Colby keeps the Druid distracted."

"And I'll be there to keep feeding Colby extra Emassa," Jasper said. "It's time to go."

Fizzlewink argued against taking a few more people, but Colby didn't want the risk. He knew he could reach the plains, but the more people he tried to transport, the more likely they would miss their mark as well as drain too much Emassa from him.

"Grab the crystal Shelly," Colby said. "Time to go. Is everything ready, Gary?"

Gary gave the thumbs-up and waved them off. "We'll be ready to go as soon as I know the relay working all the way to Stonehenge."

Colby nodded and pulled Shelly and Jasper close. "Shelly, remember as soon as we get there, jump into the in-between."

"The Druid can still see me somehow or at least sense me."

"I'm more concerned with Daphne, Rigel, and any seekers or other creatures the Druid has enlisted by now. I'll keep the Druid busy, Jasper, you keep our defense as best you can until the others arrive."

"Aye-aye captain. We are go for slipstream!"

"Geek," Shelly said. "Let's go."

The concentration Colby had to maintain was higher than any time previously. He was able to seek out his point of arrival, but remaining fixed upon the location was proving difficult. Twice he tried to set off but was pushed back by a lack of holding onto the destination.

Sensing the difficulties, Jasper pushed a massive amount of Emassa into Colby just as he made a third try. That did the trick.

Colby grabbed hold of his desire to travel through the lines and held fast. The push of energy from Jasper propelled him and his friends more quickly than expected through the magically charged conduits that crisscrossed the planet. When they arrived at Stonehenge, the trio was thrown from the lines in separate areas.

Colby landed closest to the henge, while Jasper exited farther northwest toward the museum building.

Shelly landed well past the heel stone, in a southwest position from the center where she wanted to place the crystal jump stone. It appeared that her arrival was unnoticed, however, being so far from the center of the henge. Shelly moved into the in-between where she could walk the dimension between life and death.

Being in this realm where spirits loomed and hovered too close for comfort, Shelly had to pay special attention to where she was walking. What existed in the corporeal world was present, along with things and creatures that roamed the gloom of the void. Most of the creatures in the real world could not see her, but everything in the in-between could, and they were attracted to her life force.

"Popularity sucks," Shelly said.

Navigating the path to the center of the henge was complicated, with the encumbering addition of dodging would-be passengers. The last thing Shelly wanted was to ferry back something out of this place or, worse, get dragged deeper in herself. When at last, she made it to the outer circle of stones, she found her way blocked.

The energy force used by the Druid to keep things out in the solid world was equally effective in the in-between. She couldn't place the crystal stone where planned. Looking around for any weaknesses or openings in the barrier also proved useless. She looked for Colby and Jasper to provide advice but found them busy with their own defense.

Colby wasted little time on preparations. He launched volley after the next at the Druid, though nothing penetrated the energy field encircling the uprights. Working their way around, Colby felt a tap on his shoulder at the same time Rigel and Daphne began attacking.

"I hope that's you, Shelly," Colby said. "Did you get inside this shield?"

"No, it exists on both sides of reality somehow. I can't place the stone."

Colby deflected an energy ball meant for his head. "Well, maybe it'll work anywhere along the lines. Just place it anywhere on an intersecting line but far enough away for safer arrival."

Colby charged away from Shelly to force Rigel and Daphne away from his sister.

Shelly turned, looking in circles for the lines as though they would be painted on the ground like lanes of a highway. Thinking back to her exit from the ley lines earlier, Shelly tried to recall what the trajectory would have started from. When she looked back at the heel stone, a glowing energy-being hovered and seemed to wave her forward.

The spectral form was the Shade, Shelly knew because the light it gave off was solid, unlike the undulating pulse of a Shizumu. Not knowing what the Shade wanted, Shelly couldn't wait for an explanation. Something felt comfortable and safe when she approached the wraith. It had a familiar presence.

The creature pointed toward the heel-stone and floated back several feet as if to make her more at ease with it being in such proximity.

Shelly waited only a few seconds before pulling the crystallized stone from her pocket and jamming it into the earth next to the broken heel stone.

Immediately, the crystal began to glow, and she was knocked back and out of the in-between by an invisible force of magical power.

CHAPTER 20

Colby felt the surge of Emassa before the wailing shriek of Nana as she arrived just after the magical bypass to the ley lines was activated. With that bypass also came a flood of magic for Colby to siphon for his own use. He had been having difficulty keeping up with the amount of energy he used versus what he could recharge with due to the open-source Hashtag Magic. Somehow the bypass in the ley lines was giving him a private supply of Emassa.

Not stopping his efforts toward the Druid, Colby put aside the concern of his newfound source of magic. It was enough for now that he had one. He needed that extra boost as he turned his attention away from the Druid to check on Darla.

Darla pulled herself into a tighter ball against an upright as Daphne approached with death in their eyes. She squinted and whimpered, awaiting the inevitable when she heard the yelling from Aria.

"Hey, you crazy bitch," Aria said. "Why not pick on someone your own size." She ran toward the magical clone and launched an attack as Nana signal her readiness.

Nana fumbled with the interlocking piece of the remaining enchantment from the Druid. It was tangled with her keys. When she wasn't moving quickly enough, Bellatrix took over and separated them. With a flick of the wrist and accompanying spell, Bellatrix sent the piece sailing toward its target.

The Daphne saw the device coming and managed a last-second deflection. Her energy ball hit the oncoming enchantment, sending it flying toward the Druid.

Afraid to attack her original sister, the Daphne screamed her rage and hatred into the air. As she turned toward anything that could serve as a target for her anger, she leveled her eyes on Darla.

"Today, you die, little girl."

Darla became defiant in the end. She reached to her lap and lifted the curled mass of fur, now showing its teeth.

"Sick 'er, fluffy," Darla said and threw the grimalt at Daphne.

The grimalt attacked without reserve to protect its new master. But while this temporarily distracted the Daphne, she had a free hand free to enact a final spell before succumbing to her fate.

The bolt of power that hit Darla in the chest caused an immediate reaction. Her skin began to dry and crack. Darla's final expression of shocked surprise fell away as her body returned to dust in a pile at the foot of a trilithon.

The grimalt became more enraged as it watched Darla fade away. Renewing an assault on the Daphne, the grimalt ripped at her flesh until it was thrown free and lay whimpering on the ground near Darla's remaining backpack.

Daphne, cast spells to close the gashes and bloody cuts along her body. She was in pain and struggling to build up an attack against Aria, who stood near, ready to strike. Knowing she would not last, Daphne made her way to the Druid, hoping he would protect her.

As Darla's remains drifted into an uplift of wind, her essence found its way back to Colby.

He felt the loss of his friend and golem while simultaneously gaining a grip on his chest that sent his soul into summersaults. The power of mental and emotional control reabsorbed into Colby's body as the piece of him that powered Darla as a sentient being, was reclaimed.

The emotional connection between himself and those around him increased tenfold. As he fumbled over the discomfort of mixed feelings, he felt a brush on his leg. The grimalt nuzzled Colby. Colby, in return, patted the grimalt on the head, now sharing Darla's attachment for the odd creature.

"I miss her already too, fluffy."

He was too late to save Darla but knew that her power—his power—was part of him again. Colby looked at the battle around him. He watched as Gary and Jasper maintained a steady attack to hold back the seekers that remained. Shelly was keeping the Shade distracted somehow, while Aria stalked toward her last cloned Daphne. When Colby sought out Nana and Fizzlewink, he found them standing aside, watching the center of the battle. When he turned in the direction of their stare, Colby found the Druid staring back.

The Druid smiled at Colby, his grin was the only thing visible under the shadow of his hooded form. As he bent forward to retrieve a shiny metallic object from the ground near his foot, the Druid failed to break eye contact with Colby.

"I have to admit, I am impressed with your solution to my barrier on the ley-gate," the Druid said. "Your ingenuity has never failed to show the growth and creativity we need."

As Colby approached the Druid, he did not notice the halt in fighting around him. "What do you want?" Colby asked.

"The same thing I always want," the Druid said. He stroked the watch that was secured to his wrist. "Which is to say, we want the same thing."

Colby saw his father's watch on the Druid's arm. "That does not belong to you."

"Doesn't it? Possession—it is said—is the primary requirement toward ownership."

Colby's reaction was an anger-fueled bolt of energy as he thrust his arms toward the Druid. The magic was powered by his tapping into the private supply of Emassa from the crystal stone. The assault broke through the Druid's energy barrier and hit him directly in the chest. Nothing happened.

"Again, you impress me." The Druid turned toward the heel stone and held out his hand. "This was particularly interesting and unexpected."

As the stone lifted from the ground, Colby watched the Shade wrap its arms around Shelly, preventing her from grabbing the rock in the air. He was powerless to stop the Druid from pulling the bypass to the ley lines into his outstretched hand.

"I must say, this private supply of Emassa your enchantment unexpectedly provides is serendipitous to my plans. I do hope you don't mind if I borrow the idea."

"Like you borrowed that watch?" Colby said. "I want it back. Now."

The Druid tittered. "In time, if you pardon my pun. The watch itself is inconsequential, so you may have it back when I have finished."

In a single thrust, the Druid threw the crystal stone into the ground at his feet. Purple energy rushed out of the rock and encircled the Druid. Lifting his arms to the air, exposing his rune-covered arms as his sleeves fell back, the Druid cast a spell.

"Ha'ashtagga Portocali."

The swirling Emassa collapsed into the Druid and burst outward in a blinding flash of white light and purple lightning. Each of the uprights in the henge was hit and absorbed the magic from his spell. The Druid's barrier around him fell as each of the stones opened doorways between one another. Gateways formed to various places on the planet.

Colby's level of energy plummeted as the magic he tapped from the crystal stone was redirected into maintaining the portals.

As the Druid finished weaving his spell, Rigel and the remaining Daphne scrambled toward him now that his barrier was down.

"What are you doing?" Rigel asked. "This was not part of the plan."

"Of course it was, though I've made some alterations as needed. I am always surprised each time I do this."

"What does that mean?" Said Daphne. When she saw the Druid was not inclined to respond, she crawled up to him. "What of your promise to me, to make me whole."

The Druid looked down at Daphne and pulled something from his pocket. "I fully intend to uphold that bargain." He grabbed Daphne by the hair and pulled her torso back, exposing her chest. His other hand slapped down on her, embedding the final piece of his enchanted rebinding charm into Daphne.

"What have you done?" Rigel said over Daphne's screams.

"She will be returned whole, into the body to which she belongs." The Druid looked at Nana and winked at the ancient witch hiding behind her eyes.

Rigel saw the exchange and grabbed Daphne. "Traitor," Rigel shouted and dragged Daphne toward a portal. "You will pay for breaking our agreement."

"I've broken nothing, skin-walker."

But the Druid's words went unheard by Rigel as he already disappeared through a portal with Daphne.

Colby tried to see where Rigel went, but the portals were shifting and changing. Locations across the globe continued to fade and change throughout the gateway. There was unfathomable magic at work, and he had no idea what to do. His first instinct was to retreat, but how. His stone was now being used for the Druid's spell. Attempts to jump the lines were being thwarted by the immense amount of Emassa flowing through Stonehenge.

As Colby's friends and family gathered around him, he waved them neared. He watched as the Shade released Shelly before it retreated toward the Druid.

"What was that about?" Colby asked Shelly.

"Not sure. Can we just get out of here?"

"My thoughts exactly," Colby said as he realized that wasn't 'exactly' his thoughts. An idea slipped into his train of thought from his subconscious. Before he knew what he was doing, Colby whispered a spell and focused his intent on the crystal bypass stone. "Hashtag Warehouse."

The spell took physical form as it grew of its own accord. Colby could feel the Emassa flowing from within his core and out through his phWatch. Still, there was an outside influence that Colby was unable to redirect.

Expanding outward from the center of Stonehenge, a force of will more than magic joined with Colby's spell and enveloped the entire inner henge within a bubble of power. The perimeter flashed and popped as images of the warehouse began to appear, then fade, first dim before becoming more opaque.

A final drain of magic from Colby and the spell became complete. On one side of Stonehenge was the warehouse. On the other side were the Stevens' backyard and house.

"This is new," The Druid said, his voice trailing off as he and his fellow druids pulled back and faded into a new barrier around the center stones.

Colby wasted no time to ponder the Druid's confused and annoyed tone. "Everybody go to the warehouse. Now."

CHAPTER 21

In the center of the warehouse now stood Stonehenge. As Colby and his companions examined the structure now filling the central space of their presumed safe haven, shock and disbelief filled the air with silence. Their only other option was to go back to the Stevens' home, but it too was connected to the henge in Salsbury Plains.

The spell connecting Stonehenge to the warehouse and Stevens' property appeared unbreakable. All attempts to destroy the crystal stone amounted to backlashes of energy and bruised bodies for anyone who attempted to touch, blast, or interrupt the flow of Emassa joining the magical bypass.

Colby and Jasper stepped into the henge circle to confirm a theory that they would move in an instant back to England. When they exited the opposite side of the spell, they were in the back yard at the Stevens' home. As they traversed the connected realms, they peered into the central barrier to see the Druid staring back at them, watching.

Colby felt a rippling coldness slither across his skin as he locked eyes with the Druid. He felt a moment pass between them. A single thought came to Colby's mind that was forced in by the Druid. Darla's face came into focus. She smiled at him and winked that knowing glance. His empathetic and telekinetic abilities were kicking in.

Though the loss was significant, Colby felt a touch less pain with Darla's destruction than he did with Rhea's. They were friends and would be missed, but they were primarily golem an extension of Colby. They were still with him, but he could not help but miss the physical presence. Colby was lost in hearing everyone's thoughts when a welcome hand rested on his shoulder.

"This is some crazy-ass portal magic," Jasper said. He pulled Colby back through the portal and into the warehouse.

"I've never seen anything like it," Bellatrix said. She fought for the use of Nana's body. It seemed more difficult than usual for her to assert her presence. "Each of these fluctuating portals seems to be blocked from entry by an energy force."

Colby confirmed the observation from Bellatrix when he touched the event horizon of the nearest portal. It appeared to be rotating between locations in the Middle East. When his hand touched the barrier, he was rewarded by a body shaking jolt of backlash energy.

"Cheese and crack-" Colby fell to the ground on his backside ten feet from the portal. "Ouch." He picked himself up after pushing away Gary's offered hand. "I don't think these shields exist on the henge side of this…construct."

"What makes you assume that?" Fizzlewink asked. "If we've never seen this kind of magic, how would you know more?"

"Perhaps it's the flying across the room after touching the barrier that you missed, Fizz. That's one thing." Colby pursed his lips and glared at his cat-man mentor. He made a blatant show of rubbing himself where he hit the ground. "For another thing, we saw Rigel and that last Daphne wack-job—no offense mom—escape through one from the henge side. Also, there is no energy field over the portals when Jasper and I went on a stroll through to the house."

"Ya," Jasper said. "It's like we can easily walk between the trilithons from here to the henge and on to the house and back again. These same forcefields covered the portals from the house side as well." Jasper turned to Aria. "By the way, Mrs. S, your back garden is kinda cool with a huge collection of monolithic stones."

Aria gasped. "What must the neighbors think?"

Shelly came back into the main room from outside. "I doubt the neighbors will be an issue. I was just outside, and where you would think this magic bubble would expand outside the building…well, it doesn't. And you can't see it until you're inside it."

Another quick trip cutting through the henge confirmed that once Colby left the yard, there was no visible sign of Stonehenge on the property. What he did notice was that it appeared much later in the day then he expected.

"The same thing back home," Colby said. "The house looks mundane from outside the bubble in our yard. Since it's in the back, there is little chance someone would inadvertently walk into it. I don't think a mundane would even notice if they had."

"Some sort of obscuring spell or effect, maybe?" Nana asked as Colby returned.

"I think it is much more than that," Colby said. "Shelly, did you notice how dark it is outside?"

"Ya, it was dark outside. So what?"

Colby lifted his phWatch toward Shelly. "These also tell the time you know. It's supposed to be 3:00 in the afternoon."

Time was moving at a different rate within the magic of the ley-gate-knot as Gary began calling the anomaly. It was the combined overlay of the three locations. He also pontificated on the possibilities of how it happened and practical applications of such magic.

Gary figured the Hashtag Private Gateway somehow contained a severing spell the Druid attempted. Somehow the spell got caught in the new magical stream and got mixed with the Hashtag Magic AI. The AI was capturing the runes and caught in a loop trying to decipher them.

"The Druid's is locked and rebounding between our crystals and the Ley-gate networks around the planet."

"That's all well and good, Gary," Aria said. "But can you do something to break it? We are exposed here."

"Beside shutting down all of Hashtag Magic," Gary started. "I really am at a loss."

"So let's just leave," Shelly said. "Isn't there some other place we can go?"

A disturbance in the connection back to Stonehenge signaled a visitor.

"You can't hide, but you are free to run." The voice was Bruce's with a dark edge. "Hello kitten," Bruce said to Shelly.

Shelly turned to the familiar pet name and angered by the person who spoke it. "Where did you hear that?" Shelly said. "Only my father ever called me kitten."

Bruce just smiled and winked at Shelly before turning his eyes on Colby. "You should run."

Colby sensed who was behind Bruce's skin. "Koyaanisqatsi," he said.

"Very good. Do you like how I adapted your little magic tool?"

Colby began backing away as Bruce moved closer. "What do you want?"

"What does anyone ever truly want, my boy?" The Shizumu using Bruce, continued to move closer toward Colby, awaiting a response. "No answer? It's quite simple, Colby. I want to belong. To be whole, to just be left to be free to live."

"So go be free somewhere else." Colby continued to back away from Bruce until he found himself within the henge. He took a moment to look toward the center of the henge and found the Druid and the Shade watching with interest. Bruce followed him into the henge.

"Now, this is some awe-inspiring magic." Bruce stopped just within the outer circle of stones and jerked his head to face the center. "What are you doing here?"

Colby assumed that Bruce was talking to the Druid, but saw agitation arise in the Shade.

Blue undulating energy began to flow across the translucent skin of the Shade. Its aggravation stirred as Koyaanisqatsi walked the perimeter of the circle.

Colby sensed the tension between the two entities and noticed the red glow begin to emanate from Bruce's body. The Shizumu was starting to separate from Bruce and was fighting to maintain its attachment to the borrowed body. Thinking there was a connection of some kind between the two spectral beings, Colby decided to act.

"Are you afraid of the Shade, Koyaanisqatsi? Does the specter spook you?"

Now the Druid began to move. He shook his head at Colby as though to tell him to stop antagonizing the Shizumu.

Colby had zero concern for the Druid expressing caution toward the situation. He continued his poking, hoping to break the Shizumu free of Bruce. "Come out and show the big bad ghost who's boss."

Not thinking about any danger, Colby continued to badger and prod the Shizumu without relenting. He moved closer and closer toward Bruce as the red glow grew from the Shizumu pulling away. Colby failed to notice that it was not his efforts that pulled the Shizumu from its host.

The Shade ignored the Druid, who shouted for it to remain within the inner circle. It passed freely from behind the energy barrier that encircled the center of Stonehenge. Though it did not go directly toward the Shizumu infested Bruce, it took a full circle around to come up behind Colby.

"Stop," the Shade whispered to Colby. "Father."

Colby stopped his taunting directed toward the Shizumu mid-insult. He turned to the Shade hovering behind him. Something gave Colby pause. In the split seconds of dimness between the flashing of blue that chased across the silhouette of the Shade, there was an image. Colby saw something in the Shade that was familiar and went beyond his own reflection.

As his eyes met the glowing orbs that stared back from the Shade, Colby could hear and feel what the Shade was saying. Before he could speak, a wild and groaning sheik sounded behind him.

Colby turned to see the Shizumu separate from Bruce's body, as the face of the thing shifted from that of Bruce, it took a form he had not seen for over a decade.

"Dad?"

Before Colby could make any sense of what was happening, the two forces began to battle. Red and blue energy began shooting off the tangled ball of entwined beings. Colby watched the two opposing forces, not knowing what to think. Only the hand grasping at the back of his leg took Colby's attention.

"Help me," Bruce said.

Colby grabbed Bruce under the arms and helped him to his feet. "Are you, you?"

"Who elth would I be?" Bruce stammered as he tried to keep his feet beneath himself. "Why ith my thunge not working?"

Colby tried not to laugh, but his anxiety and surroundings took control. Buckling over, Colby started laughing and blubbering hysterics.

Bruce looked at Colby than at his surroundings. As his eyes widened at the fighting spectral figures, he reached for and grabbed Colby by the shirt.

"Colby, what the hell ith going on, and where are we?"

Colby continued to laugh as he stood back straight and pulled Bruce toward the warehouse side of the ley-gate knot. "We need to get back to the others."

"What ith tho funny?"

"Nothing, Bruce," Colby laughed. "There is nothing funny about any of this."

Colby began to settle down as they approached the boundary between Stonehenge and the warehouse. As they stepped forward to pass through, Bruce was thrown free and into the warehouse while Colby was pulled back by Koyaanisqatsi.

"Not going anywhere," Koyaanisqatsi said. "You have something of mine."

Colby was shaking the dizziness from his head as he sat up. The

Shizumu hovered toward him, and his ghostly face pushed toward Colby's within an inch of touching noses. Startled, Colby recoiled after seeing his reflection in the glowing orbs the creature had for eyes.

"No," Colby said. "You can't be him."

"Can't I?" Koyaanisqatsi said.

"But you are Koyaanisqatsi, the demon of chaos."

Koyaanisqatsi pulled back a few inches. "A misnomer from an ancient language. More aptly, I am life unbalanced if you choose, but I've always preferred Jarrod."

Colby's face paled at the admission. He shuffled back on his hands, dragging his backside, trying to gain his feet. He found himself backed up against an upright, next to a shifting portal. His father's Shizumu half was closing the distance.

"Give me what is mine," Jarrod's Shizumu demanded.

"Looking for this?" The Druid said. He held up his wrist, exposing the wristwatch he took from Colby. "I'm afraid you can't have it. Not just yet, anyway."

Colby watched the Shizumu charge after the Druid and get thrown back by a protective barrier. Frozen by confusion and the horror of knowing that his father or at least half of him was an ancient demon, Colby stumbled to stand.

"Everything has two sides to balance itself," the Shade said from above Colby's head. "You must go."

Colby tried to form a question, but words would not come. Before he was able to resist, the Shade picked up Colby and pushed him through the henge perimeter nearby, which sent Colby home.

CHAPTER 22

Bruce was greeted with a throat punch from Shelly. He tried to crawl away, but shelly used a spell to lasso his foot and drag him back. Bruces, face hit the dusty cement floor with a crack. He lost part of a tooth, a little blood, and all his remaining dignity.

"What the hell are you doing here?" Shelly said and looked at Jasper. "Tie him up."

Choking and breathing with great difficulty, Bruce waved his hands to fend off further assaults from Shelly. He looked around for support, but nobody was interested in coming to his aid.

Fizzlewink stepped up to stop Shelly from an all-out attack. "He's just been through enough with Koyaanisqatsi vacating residence of his body. Who knows how long he was squatting in his head. That demon claimed responsibility for the altering of Hashtag Magic."

"How do you know?" Shelly asked.

Fizzlewink looked down at first but then rebelled against feeling ashamed. "I was eavesdropping."

Shelly seemed proud of Fizzlewink for a moment before her thoughts returned to Bruce. "So what. He's still a jackass." Shelly raised a fist toward Bruce. "Tie him up, or I will."

Bruce tried to argue, but was overpowered by Jasper and refused to oppose the overbearing glare of Nana who hovered nearby. He got up and shuffled to the chair. Gary pulled out for Jasper to bind him to and waited before speaking again.

Shelly wasn't through berating Bruce. She started with the list of things he did most recently but devolved into a tirade of grievances that dated back to when they were dating. The sound of Aria clearing her throat stopped Shelly's longwinded impeachment.

"I think that'll do for now, Shelly," Aria said. "Where is my son?"

Bruce stammered at first as his swollen tongue relaxed, and he regained proper speech. "He was pulling me toward this place when I got pushed. I don't know if Colby pushed me or what happened, honestly."

Shelly did not like the answer and slapped Bruce. "Wrong. Try again."

"I'm telling you the truth. I-"

Another slap. "I can do this all night."

"Shelly, stop," Colby said. He entered the warehouse from the main entrance. "He had nothing to do with this, directly."

Aria ran to Colby and smothered him with a tight hug while the others surrounded him.

Colby pushed back, only half-hearted. He allowed himself a bit of comfort for a change. With the recent deaths and more tragedy yet to come, Colby wanted to feel something other than pain and loss.

"What happened?" Aria said. She pushed Colby back to look into his eyes. She refused to take her hands off the sides of his arms.

"Besides a battle of wills between a Shade and Shizumu? Both of whom appear to be the split halves of dad's shi. Just another day in the life."

After the silence invoking statements from Colby set into the minds of those present, everyone began talking at once.

Aria dropped her grip on Colby and stumbled back three feet. She was the only one who stood silent.

"Hold on," Colby said. "First things first. Jasper, release Bruce from his bonds."

"NO," Shelly said. "He has a lot to answer for."

"He can answer for anything not related to his time as a host to Koyaanisqatsi. As for his possession, those acts he can try and recall, but should not take the blame." Colby gave Bruce a supportive nod.

Shelly huffed and glared at Bruce, giving him a watchful stare and two-finger gesture from her eyes, then pointed at him. She mouthed 'I'm watching you', and stepped back.

"I want to hear about your theory about your father first," Aria said to Colby. "What gives you such a firm belief that his split spirits are still with us?"

Fizzlewink agreed. There was no precedent for the existence of both Nefslama shi as a Shade and Shizumu at the same time. One always canceled the other out when encountering one another outside a body. This was the nature of their opposing forces.

Another voice came into the warehouse, Betelgeuse. "No two separated shi entities have ever existed untethered for so long., though it is possible for shorter periods. They have a natural attraction that creates a conflict and desire for domination. That is without a proper neutral force to contain them, they are in a constant battle of wills."

Colby rushed over to hug the old man. "Grandpa, where've you been?"

"Keeping myself busy with a long-planned task."

"Cryptic as usual," Bellatrix said. "You here to help or just take up room in this over-crowded place?"

"Bell, I wish I could say it was a pleasure to once again be subject to your caterwauling. I am here to help where I am able."

"Able or allowed?" Bellatrix said. "There is a distinction, you know." Bellatrix put Nana's hands on her hips as Betelgeuse waved her off and motioned Colby over. He turned back in Bellatrix's direction. "I can hear your eyes rolling you old pile of grimalt shit."

Shelly had to hold Nana back before Bellatrix used her body to attack Betelgeuse. "Easy old woman. Boy, you're a feisty thing."

"Get your hands off me." Bellatrix pulled free of Shelly's grasp and set off to the makeshift kitchen. "If anyone needs me, I'll be cooking in the kitchen."

"Cooking has a very different result when that woman is involved," Betelgeuse said. "Any incarnation of your grandmother has been a disaster in the kitchen." Patting the bench next to where he now sat, Betelgeuse invited Colby to tell him about what he discovered.

Colby explained what happened in the bubble encompassing Stonehenge. From the reflections of himself in the empty space between the energy of the beings to what they each said to him.

"I have to say I'm not at all surprised," Betelgeuse said. "Your father always had a way of going to the extreme, but this time I think he had help."

"What do you mean?" Colby said. "Are you saying that the Druid was involved?"

Betelgeuse revealed how difficult the forbidden magic is to split the shi. Add to this difficulty the fact that they have been kept from destroying one another for the last decade is a process unknown to the most knowledgable among the old counsel. Without knowing the full spell, Jarrod used to hobble Colby's magic in the first place, there was no way of knowing more.

"The Druid," Colby said. "Could he have been planning this ass part of whatever his game is here now?"

Bellatrix and Fizzlewink grumbled at the mention of the Druid. They also exchanged looks at Shelly and Aria. Colby caught the quick glances. He also saw that Betelgeuse noticed them as well.

"What is going on here?" Colby said as they all looked away. "Nana slash Bellatrix, what's the matter, Fizzlewink got your tongue?"

"Hey, I resent that. It's been ages since I've used my silencing ability on anyone."

"Wait…what? You can take someone's tongue?" Gary asked.

Fizzlewink waved Gary off. "Don't be absurd. One of my people's innate abilities is to mute a person, take their voice temporarily. It doesn't work on everyone."

Betelgeuse looked from Fizzlewink to Nana and smirked.

"No," Fizzlewink said. "I've tried, multiple times."

"Can we get back to my question about the Druid? I'm trying to figure out what is going on here?"

Nana was the first to admit she knew Bellatrix had past dealings with the Druid. It first happened in her own time a few thousand years prior. She made a long-ago bargain. What that deal was, Nana could not glean while sifting through what memories she had access to. But payment came due, and that involved using the enchanted device to reconstitute Aria.

"He gave me the means to enact a reversal of the magic that split and cloned Aria. I saw no downside."

"There has to be some reason," Colby said. "Someone this powerful needed you to do this? Why not just do it himself?"

Betelgeuse admitted that the Druid was an enigma. He began appearing in Nefslama settlements long ago, seeking knowledge and trading in new and unusual spells and enchantments. The Druid used odd words to invoke his magic that came from runes that covered his skin from head to toe. With each new spell he learned, he added to his collection of tattoos until one day, the man became so powerful that he created the ley-gates.

The Druid never asked for much until then. After the gates were constructed, the Druid began making bargains, and trading in spells the likes of which the Nefslama had never imagined. This is where the original spell to split the shi came from.

"The Druid was up to something for certain," Betelgeuse said. "but we never figured out what. By the time many of us knew there was a plan in action, he disappeared. I suppose we should have known sooner. He always seemed to know more about events to come than the best of our oracles."

"So, he left your time in the past to resurface here?" Colby said. "Then, he made some bargain with Rigel to help him come to the future?"

"I don't believe that is the case. The Druid is far more powerful than Rigel," Betelgeuse admitted. "The Druid popped up from time to time over the centuries. So I doubt he needed Rigel to come here. He may have been using the ley-gates back then to time-walk."

"What has any of this to do with dad," Shelly said. "Who cares about the history lesson. I saw dad's face in the Shade also. It felt like dad was there when the Shade grabbed me."

"I know I'll regret saying this, but Shelly's right," Colby said. "Once Darla, the golem was dispatched, her essence rejoined with me. I was able to feel an emotional bond to the Shade and the Shizumu. They are our dad. I don't think the Shiz-half of dad was working for the Druid, but the Shade seemed to be his slave."

"Not slave," Bruce said. "They are working together."

Bruce explained what he felt from the Shizumu that inhabited him. It wasn't malice, nor did he think the creature wanted to intentionally hurt anyone. It just wanted something, something it had been searching for nearly three thousand years to obtain. It searched over the centuries until it finally sensed what it wanted was near. The Shade, on the other hand, was working with the Druid, Bruce could sense this from the Shizumu.

"What is he after?" Colby said. "And why would a Shade be willingly working with someone who enslaved it?"

"Don't trust him," Shelly said. "Bruce is a liar and an anti-mage jackwagon."

"No," Bruce admitted. "Just jealous, I never inherited my father's magic ability. As for the Shizumu, I don't know what it's after, just that it feels close to getting it."

"And why do you think dad's Shade is working with the Druid?" Shelly said. "That makes no sense."

A build-up of static began to raise the hairs on everyone's arms.

Energy sparked along the border of the Stonehenge replica within the warehouse. As everyone turned to see what was happening, a seeker came through a portal, followed by Rigel.

"Thank you for the information. I think I know precisely what is going on here."

Without explaining or adding any insight, Rigel turned and stepped through the henge. He walked into the England side of the ley-gate-knot. His seeker blocked the path for anyone to interfere as Daphne followed Rigel.

Rigel turned back toward the warehouse and spoke to his seeker slave. "Kill my nephew first."

CHAPTER 23

Colby was directly in the path of the seeker as it charged forward from the portal. He readied himself with a spell previously stored in his phWatch. The magic began to form and was sent from Colby's phWatch, but someone else intervened. The blast missed its mark.

"Watch out," Bruce shouted and raised his arms toward the seeker. A burst of energy flew from his hands and knocked the seeker sideways. "Whoa."

"What the hell was that?" Shelly said. "I thought you didn't have magic?"

"I have my own phWatch," Bruce said. "I wasn't sure it would work. I mean, it worked while I was possessed, so why not now."

Colby fell to his knees from the drain Bruce's spell created. "Oh, it worked."

Bruce did not notice the effect his use of the Hashtag Magic app was having on Colby. His visible excitement with having the magic of his own blinded him to the cost. He began sending spell after another toward the seeker and its companions that began entering the warehouse from other portals.

The room broke out in a chaotic flashing of energy blasts and lightning as everyone began fighting off the seekers the Rigel instructed to kill Colby. Though they could see that Colby struggled, it was only Jasper who sensed the debilitating effect Hashtag Magic was having.

"Tap into the bypass," Jasper said.

"I'm trying, but I can't seem to focus on it." The excessive use of magic was causing Colby pain. "We need to drive these seekers away."

Bruce heard Colby and prepared a spell in his phWatch. Without waiting or checking with anyone, Bruce unleashed his construct on Stonehenge. **#ReversePortals**

The magic spread across the henge and seeped into the stones. A charge built up, and a red glow began to encircle the entire structure. As the power increased, so did the drain on Colby, who began to scream from the pain.

"Shit!" Bruce said. Bruce looked at what his magic was doing to Colby and tried to stop the spell. He only made matters worse. As Bruce tried to cancel his spells, he only added more power. He had not trained, and it became apparent as the warehouse filled with light.

The glowing peaked as did the power build-up. As a final groan escaped Colby's mouth. The shields that blocked entry to the portals from the warehouse side dropped. The backlash of power sent everyone backward with a pulse of magic that also began to destabilize the ley-gate-knot.

Stonehenge began to flicker. Seams of white light began to crack the bubble around the henge as the magic started to shatter. The crystal that was planted in the warehouse floor was breaking as well.

"Everybody out of the warehouse," Jasper said. "Now."

The seekers swirled around the henge, bumping into each other. The raw energy building was disrupting them in some fashion that provided the necessary distraction for escape. Everyone began to scatter, heading for the closest exit from the warehouse. They could not get the doors to open.

Nefsmari began grabbing people and supplies, then disappearing.

They rematerialized outside the warehouse just as the interior flashed with brilliant lights, and all the windows blew out.

Aside from minor cuts and bruises, most everyone made it out unscathed.

Colby was barely conscious but managed to whisper something to Jasper.

Jasper turned to a nearby Nefsmari, Conrad. "Conrad, take me to the house."

Conrad nodded, grabbed Jasper, and disappeared. They were gone for only a couple minutes and returned with a handful of crystalline dust.

"It's as you suspected, Colby. The same thing happened in your yard. The ley-gate-knot is gone."

Aria gasped. "The house?"

"Is fine, a little scorched. I can't say the same for the yard and garage." Jasper turned to Shelly. "You should call your car insurance company."

"Son-of-a-siren whore," Shelly said. "Why does my car always have to get ruined?" She looked at Colby. "Your Hashtag Magic is nothing but trouble for me, Cheese-Curd."

Colby moaned as he tried to sit up. His pained laughter caused him to grab his head. "Sure, your car is the most important thing here."

Shelly huffed and swung around to slap Bruce. "And you. What the hell were you thinking? You could have killed us all. Is there some medication your forgetting to take?"

"I'm sorry," Bruce said. "I'm new at this hocus-pocus stuff. The Shizumu was controlling me before. I'm on my own now."

"Speaking of," Gary said. "How do you have abilities now, and I noticed it was of a red hue."

"Strange things can happen to people who've been inhabited by a Shizumu," Betelgeuse said. "And this particular possession makes it more likely the Bruce would have blatant abilities that were awoken."

Betelgeuse postulated that it was likely a side effect of the Shizumu inhabiting Bruce's body. It must have awakened latent talent within Bruce that had not presented as a child. It was not unheard of for magic to require a kick-start in a developing mage. He advised Bruce to not use any more magic that was not practiced and asked

Fizzlewink to see to his instruction.

"I also don't think this explosion was Bruce's doing, at least not directly." Betelgeuse refused to elaborate. "I need to go see a man about a spell. Why don't you all go back to the house and regroup."

"Who are you going to see?" Colby asked.

"It's time we start putting this puzzle together from the outside in. Always best to frame things out to better fill in the whole picture. Go on to the house. I'll catch you up later." Betelgeuse said nothing more and pulled a Nefsmari close. "Take me to the academy if you please."

"Why are you using a Nefsmari?" Fizzlewink shouted as Betelgeuse disappeared. He looked around at the other humans. "You all need to learn to travel the lines yourself. We aren't your personal ride-share service."

"Cat-Cab," Shelly said. "I suppose the smell of a litter box while getting a ride is no worse than Pachouli and B.O. Perfume is not a replacement for a bath and deodorant."

Colby interrupted the banter. "Lessons on lei-line travel later Fizz, can we just get back to the house to check out the damage."

Fizzlewink sniffed himself before reaching out and grabbing Shelly. "I don't stink." He disappeared with her before Shelly could say anything.

***

The backyard was beyond a scorched as every tree, bush, plant, and patch of grass was ash and soot. The garage lay in a smoldering pile. Shelly's car had been flattened. Somehow the new spell that surrounded the Stevens' yard remained intact, so anyone outside the property did not see anything amiss.

"How do we explain this to the insurance company?" Nana asked.

Gary snorted. "Just tell them that a freak storm took out your she-shed."

"Really?" Shelly said and smacked Gary in the back of the head. "What about my car?"

"So tell them you lost control and drove into the she-shed."

Shelly rolled her eyes and began moving debris to get to her car. The noise from her efforts and verbal narration of said efforts threatened to disturb the neighbors.

"Shelly, do you think you could do that without running through your extensive dictionary of expletives?" Aria said.

Though Shelly's voice lowered to a mumble, the noise level of crashing debris made up for the difference.

Fizzlewink told her to step back and set the rest of the Nefsmari to work restoring the garage, car, and yard before they would return to the warehouse to begin those repairs.

"We may be limited in the extent of talent with Emassa, but we certainly know how to fix things." Fizzlewink then looked at Bruce, who sulked in the shadows. "You can start learning control by helping us. Come on late bloomer."

While Bruce and the Nefsmari got to work on restorations, Colby and the others went inside. Nana began unpacking what food they managed to bring back but was stopped from starting dinner by a universal cry for take-away. Nobody wanted to top barely surviving the night's events with a Nana cooked meal that might kill them all.

"What do you think your grandfather wants at the academy?" Gary asked. He plopped down in the end chair of the living room and threw his legs over the arm. "I mean, aside from the room in the basement, what else is there to learn?"

"Tiddle," Colby said. "He helped my father the night this all started. Maybe he knows more than he's told us."

"Why would he hold something back?" Jasper asked. "You think he lied or something?"

"I think there are too many secrets and half-truths surrounding that night." Colby looked at his Nana and sister, whispering in the dining room. "There are other secrets surrounding this Druid dude as well."

Colby lay on the couch, trying to rest and regain his strength. It wasn't easy, but with Jasper's help, he managed to replenish enough Emassa in his core to begin healing his aching body. Having Rhea's power back in his body allowed for self-healing, so long as he could maintain a flow of magic. Now having Darla's empathic and telepathic abilities allowed Colby to sense the duplicity coming from his sister and grandmother.

"Nana and Shelly," Colby said. "What are you whispering about over there?"

Nana shushed Shelly and walked into the living room. "Nothing important. How are you? Can I get you anything?"

Sitting upright, Colby leveled his stare at the old woman. "Need I remind you that with the demise of Darla, I now have here abilities? I can sense you are not telling me something."

Shelly looked away.

"Out with it, Shelly." Colby let the assertion of his voice accompany a slight taste of Darla's influence.

"I gave him dad's watch," Shelly said. "Oh, why did I just blurt that out." Shelly paused and then realized Colby made her say it and smacked him. "Why you little cheese turd."

Colby settled his immediate anger. "I see. And do you know why he wanted the watch?"

"No. He promised to help you and keep you safe."

Colby studied Shelly for a moment. His stare caused Shelly to look away, shame flowing over her features. Colby then turned to Nana.

"And your bargain, what was it you did for the Druid to get the magic to reconstitute mom?"

"I honestly do not know. Bellatrix already did something for the

Druid ages ago, and this was his payment." Nana looked into Colby's eyes. "I promise Fart-blossom. That's all the old bitch shared with me."

"Fine," Colby said after a few minutes. "So the Druid is helping us, previously planned something. All these actions: getting Rigel to bring him forward in time, eliminates the Daphnes, takes dad's watch, has dad's Shade working for him, and dad's Shiz happens to be the ancient Koyaanisqatsi demon and in town looking for something."

"Sounds pretty weird when you say it out loud," Gary said.

"I suppose not," Shelly said. "depending on how long this plan has been in motion. The Druid said something to me that I didn't really think about at the time."

Shelly told them of how the Druid said he performed a spell for a child centuries ago, but it was only a decade ago for Colby. Adding this to the puzzle began to make the connections.

"So it's all connected," Colby said. "We just don't know exactly how. If the Druid performed the spell with dad, that means he's been here before and came back through time, if he ever actually went back."

Colby knew that the only things that came back from the academy basement that night beside his mother were his dad's watch and the journal. And if the Druid was here the entire time, why would he allow Rigel to think that he was needed to bring the Druid through time. He needed to know what the connection to Rigel is as far as the Druid was concerned.

CHAPTER 24

Rigel stepped into the center of Stonehenge as the fluctuating barrier allowed. Wasting no time, he used a spell to attack the crystal stone joining the henge with two other locations. As his magic battered the crystal, cracks formed. Rigel looked up at the stoic Druid and glared.

No longer able to contain the Emassa flow, the crystal stone used to bypass the lei-line shattered. Any hope of repairing the connections to the warehouse and Stevens' home were gone with a flash of white light.

Rigel blocked the burning brilliance from his eyes with an arm while using the other to feel his way toward the Druid's position. When the light faded and the spots cleared from his vision, Rigel found himself only a foot away from the Druid. Rigel reached out to turn the Druid who faced away.

When the robed figure spun around, it was a faceless clay golem beneath the hood.

"What the hell?" Rigel said.

"You were expecting me to stand there, vulnerable to your attack?" The Druid said. "Have you learned nothing from your dealings with me?"

Rigel twisted his head to see the Druid standing ten feet to his left. "Hoping perhaps you were distracted enough to slip up." Rigel turned the rest of the way around and took a step toward the Druid, who lifted a halting hand. Rigel stopped. "I see you were not fooled."

"Quite the opposite actually. I expected you and watched your approach from the time you exited the portal into the warehouse."

"And yet, you failed to stop my breaking of the ley-gate connections."

The Druid laughed. "You fool yourself thinking that was your doing. I had already set those crystals to overload. I also saw the quickening of that tool Bruce, knowing his eagerness to spell-cast would trigger a reaction." The Druid stepped around an upright. "You have been playing my game of runic chess for centuries Rigel. You were simply too arrogant to recognize."

"I recognize you now, though I should have seen it from the beginning." Rigel leaned forward and squinted toward the Druid. "I suppose if you weren't always shrouded in those robes, it would have been more obvious."

Rigel raised his hand to the sky and looked at the back of his hand. "I've spent the last decade wondering why you chose this particular body when you offered to find me a host. My own brother. And somehow he just happened to be performing the correct mixture of magics to hide his forbidden-born son. The mixed magic child that might adulterate Emassa, I believe that was the warning of the elders.

"Magic certainly has changed in the last decade, but I think those changes started long before these modern times. And then there is all this urgency to kill my nephew's friends, but not Colby himself." Rigel turned toward the Druid and followed his path. "His family was marked as hands-off. Why was that?"

The Druid turned back toward Rigel. His patience was drawing thin as he began to pace. "If you have a destination in mind for your train of thought, please arrive at the station."

Rigel exhaled a heavy groan. "You can drop the façade along with your hood, I know who you are, and you have failed."

Now the Druid laughed. "Have I? I think you'll find I'm just getting started." The Druid raised his arms and threw back his hood, showing Rigel his identity. The runes that covered his body also marked his face and shaved head. With a whispered word, every rune on his body began to glow and swirl around on his skin. "Ha'ashtagga fragmente shi."

The magic charged from the lei-lines and rose around Rigel before he could react. He was restrained where he stood. "What are you doing to me?"

"The first step to completing what I started over ten years ago when I placed you within the skin of Jarrod Stevens. This body you inhabit is needed by another. I'm afraid you are going to have to find another host. Or you could just die. Your choice. A quick end may save you from the suffering you'll suffer if you remain in that body."

"But you bargained. You promised me a return to my flesh in exchange for bringing you here from the past."

The Druid nodded at Rigel. "Yes, and I always keep my word. But this flesh you are wearing is not yours and has been promised to another."

"If you intend on keeping your promise, where is the replacement?"

Without breaking from his spell-work, the Druid looked back at

Rigel. "I'm afraid we are not quite ready for that. One step at a time, Uncle."

As Rigel screamed with anger and pain from the tearing apart of his attachment to Jarrod's skin, Koyaanisqatsi emerged from behind a trilithon. He charged toward Rigel with inhabitation in his glowing eyes. The Shizumu jumped into Rigel's borrowed body but was immediately thrown free.

"It's not the time for you yet either," the Druid said and tapped the watch on his wrist. "You can not bond without the correct medium and partner."

His attention focused on Rigel; the Druid paid no attention to the shadow lurking along the edges of the henge.

Daphne, though greatly distressed after losing here sister clones, trained her thoughts on revenge. She moved from stone to stone, waiting for the perfect moment to strike. Only when the Druid was turned away, distracted by the Shizumu, did the demented clone of Aria act. Daphne was waiting for the perfect moment to strike.

The Druid was arguing with the Shizumu when Daphne attacked. She took the opportunity to blast him with a spell, disrupting his spells. When the Druid interrupted his chant and rune work, the Emassa dissipated, releasing Rigel from his trap. The moment of distraction did not last long.

Spinning around, the rage at himself by not accounting for Daphne was spread across the Druid's face. He lashed out toward the pair who began to attempt escape. Throwing one volley after another at Rigel and Daphne, the Druid failed to see the Shizumu expressing his own anger.

Koyaanisqatsi thrashed back and forth, trying to attack Rigel. Each time the spirit attempted to reach out, the Shade blocked his way. Because these two energy beings had opposing charges, they had both an attraction and a repelling effect on one another.

The Shade attempted to settle the Shizumu down, two sides of the same man's spirit fighting for dominance. The magical energy they expended spread out in waves that knocked everyone to the ground.

The Druid tumbled over and slammed into the fallen stones at the center of the henge. His arms ached from bracing his fall. Before he could stand, a jolt of energy knocked him back to the ground.

"Not so prepared after all are you, boy," Rigel said. Pain added an edge in his voice. He writhed as his spirit was separating from his body, but he would not relent. "Let's see how you handle this." Rigel charged the Druid, unleashing more blasts, and he told Daphne to retrieve something the Druid dropped.

While the Druid retreated under the constant bombardment, Daphne was able to grab the item Rigel wanted. She hid behind an upright and waited for Rigel to finish with the Druid.

The two halves of Jarrod's shi were entangled in a stalemate and paying no attention to their surroundings. They did not notice the removal of something vital to their rejoining.

Rigel was slowing his attack as he began to lose the ability to maintain form. Each step he took toward the Druid, he had to focus on pulling himself back within his borrowed skin. As he slowed, he waved Daphne over.

Daphne skirted the outer ring of uprights. As she stepped from behind one stone to the next, Daphne took a moment to look at the Druid. She noticed he was again paying her no attention and continued toward Rigel. Daphne did not pause to think about why the Druid was disregarding her yet again. He knew she was there, but she was of no consequence.

"You are having difficulties, Rigel," the Druid said. "Let me help you. You are losing allies and will soon have not a soul to stand with you against the inevitable."

"You've done quite enough already, boy." Rigel was fighting with his skin. He buckled over as Daphne reached him. "It's time I throw another wrench in your plans."

The Druid laughed at first, then he saw Rigel's convulsions stabilizing as he stood up straight. When Rigel turned, and his smile grew, the Druid's posture stiffened.

Rigel laughed louder. "No contingency for this," Rigel said. He raised his arm, showing the old watch now strapped to his wrist. When the Druid began to take aim, Rigel tittered and shook his arm. "You don't want to damage this now, do you?"

The Druid lowered his arm. His posture stiffened as he watched Rigel and Daphne.

"Thought not," Rigel said. "I do hope this doesn't cause you too much anguish. Then again, it should not matter for much longer."

"What are you talking about?" The Druid said. "I have no feelings one way or another as it concerns you."

"Well, it occurs to me that currently, that is to say here and now in your present incarnation, I am at a disadvantage. I haven't the power or experience to best you."

The Druid stepped forward. "Meaning what? I don't see how you might attain the strength to defeat me, Rigel."

"Since you, Druid, are here still, my seekers must have failed at the warehouse. So I will just have to jot off and kill the younger incarnation of you myself."

Daphne looked at Rigel and then at the Druid. "What are you two blubbering on about. Rigel, let's go."

"Just a moment, my sweet. Pay attention now, you might just enjoy this." Rigel turned back to the Druid. "If I kill you in your youth, how does that affect all your hard work? But then again, it might just have repercussions on myself. Yet if I am correct, this watch will provide some sort of temporal protection. Isn't that correct? Colby?"

The Druid lowered his guard and smiled. A conceding laugh escaped his lips. "Very good, Uncle. But you'll find it difficult to kill the other me in this timeline. The continuity of time and events have a way of looping back and correcting themselves. This isn't my first go at this, after all."

"But, I think it shall be you're last." Rigel turned to Daphne and grabbed her arm. "Time to go, my dear."

"Where are we going?" She asked.

"We're off to put an end to Hashtag Magic, and it's creator." Rigel stepped over the center of the henge, and both he and Daphne disappeared.

The Druid, Colby, pulled his hood back over his head and laughed as his sleeve slid down to his elbow, exposing an old watch still strapped to his wrist.

CHAPTER 25

Rigel was pleased to find that the Stevens and entourage had retreated to their home. Though he was required to travel a bit out of the way, Rigel managed a surprise appearance. The ley-gate in their backyard was blocked by a new crystal stone.

Bending down to inspect the stone, Rigel noticed the extra flow of Emassa. He took out a mobile phone and used it to connect the Hashtag Magic app to that additional flow of magic. After the app began siphoning Emassa from the ley lines, Rigel enacted a subrouting that started running through a series of spells on an infinite loop.

A crashing of dishes in the kitchen brought a satisfied smile to Rigel's face. He motioned Daphne to follow along as they sneaked past the door to look in through a window.

Colby was lying on the floor, his hands pulling at his midsection. Each loop of Rigel's magical interference was producing a backlash within Colby's magical core.

"What's the matter," Nana said. She tried helping Colby off the floor, but he balled up in the fetal position, screaming.

In between thrashing and gasps, Colby spat words out as he could. "Being drained," Colby said. "I can't keep up replacing what is being taken."

"Not me," Bruce said when everyone looked at him. "The app server wasn't designed for this. At least I don't think so."

"What do you mean, you don't think so?" Gary said. "Where is the server farm hosted? I need to shut this down."

"I'm not sure…I mean, I was being controlled. All that computer crap is foreign to me."

"Right up there with being a decent human being," Shelly said. "You have no clue."

Bruce had enough of Shelly. "Look, I can't change the past. All I can do is learn to be better. I could use your help instead of you constantly tearing me down, Shelly."

Shelly stood there looking at Bruce, her eyes blinking and mouth closed. She looked him over, seeing something new in her ex-boyfriend. "You're growing a spine. It's annoying."

Bruce let go of his hopeful smile and waved Shelly away. "You're going to be just like your grandmother when you get older. Don't let your control issues turn you into a bitter and lonely old hag."

Shelly had no words, but Nana did.

"Are you calling me a bitter old hag?"

Gary ran upstairs to get Colby's laptop and escape from the coming bloodbath. He gave Bruce a pitiful look as he passed. Running up to Colby's room, Gary retrieved the computer from Colby's desk. When Gary returned to the kitchen, Colby was sitting up, at least.

Bruce was still alive when Gary returned. He was, however, holding a frozen bag of peas to his cheek. Gary shook his head and sat next to Colby.

"I have to initiate the application to try and track it," Gary said. "Are you able to block or isolate the effects yet?"

"I don't know how to stop this drain," Colby said. "The only relief was that separate tap into Emassa. Since that is gone-"

"You need to close off your core," Fizzlewink said. "If you can't take any Emassa in, then the drain may stop."

Colby tried, but it was no use. "I just can't focus on my connection to Emassa. We need to find and shut down the app servers."

"I'm looking," Gary said. "It's not like there is a systems admin sett of tools for doing a traceroute on magical applications."

Gary used his abilities, not with magic, but with computers to trace the source of the Hashtag Magic main servers. However, once he found them, there was a problem.

"Um, we have a problem," Gary said. "I found and was able to break into the servers."

"And what's the problem," Jasper asked.

"As soon as I manage a shutdown command, they seem to be starting up somewhere else. If there is anything, you can remember, Bruce, that would be helpful."

Gary continued to track down and stop servers, but Hashtag Magic was nothing if not resilient.

Rigel planned it that way with help from Koyaanisqatsi. When Rigel saw Bruce in the house with the Stevens, he became agitated.

"That imbecile will ruin everything if he remembers anything about how we manipulated Hashtag Magic. Daphne, go around the front of the house while I draw the others outside. I suspect that the Connors boy will stay inside with Bruce. Kill them."

As Daphne slunk around the house, keeping close to the exterior walls, Rigel peppered the back of the house with bolts of energy. That got the attention he wanted. With the Nefsmari already busy at the warehouse with restoration, the Stevens' home presented a level battlefield.

"What do you want here, Rigel?" Colby said. He did his best to appear unaffected by the drain of Emassa.

Rigel laughed as he backed into the center of the yard. "I want what was promised to me, but for some reason, you have become an obstacle rather than an asset to my goals."

Colby did not need an explanation for what Rigel was insinuating. There was murder behind his eyes, and Colby felt the target on his chest.

Jasper walked up beside Colby. "I got this. I'll keep sending you Emassa-"

"That's not going to work, Jasper. No matter how much I take in, it just gets ripped right back out of me."

Jasper had no time to offer other options. Rigel attacked.

The backyard lit up with flashes of energy as Rigel sent one volley after the next toward Colby and his crew. Every return of offense from the Stevens met with a rebounding crack of power that sent their spells right back at them.

"He has some kind of shield," Shelly said. "Maybe I can sneak around in the in-between and hit him from behind."

Colby nodded for Shelly to try. For some reason, Rigel seemed much stronger than any previous encounter. He hoped Shelly would be successful.

Shelly disappeared around the house, so Rigel would not see her vanish in thin air. After entering the in-between, she emerged into the yard and began a slow and careful circle around the perimeter. If Rigel had a shield, Shelly didn't want to run into it and give herself away. When she focused her vision on the area around Rigel, she could see it.

A faint glow of energy produced a half-dome over Rigel's position. There was space along the back fence where she could squeeze past and beck behind him. She had her way in, but it would be tight.

Colby wanted to keep Rigel distracted, yet needed a break from the Emassa flowing through him. While Gary needed time to trace and shut down the Hashtag Magic servers, Shelly also required to get around and behind Rigel. Colby decided to get Rigel talking.

"What is it that has you so torqued up with me, Uncle?" Colby said.

Rigel stopped his assault. "It isn't personal, boy, and not really about you."

"Then what is it about? If I'm to die at your hand, I think I deserve to know why."

Rigel was not prepared for this kind of conflict. Talking instead of magical dueling was off-putting, but it didn't stop him from unloading on everyone in the yard.

His fight started with his brother, Jarrod. Jarrod was always the more significant brother. Better at everything in every way. Rigel blamed Jarrod for everything that went wrong in his first life. When he finally found a way to surpass his brother using the forbidden magics, Rigel was ultimately turned over to the council of elders. Jarrod was the one who was responsible.

Shelly listened to the conversation as she slinked closer to Rigel. She watched Rigel close as she made her approach. That's when she first noticed a change in her vision. A glow surrounded Rigel, his aura. He also had a pinpoint of white light at his center. As Shelly looked around, she saw that everyone in the yard had an aura around them and a white inner light.

Each aura was different, swirling with light. She had no understanding of what the individual colors and pulsing patterns meant. But one thing she was sure of was that each tiny white light at everyone's core was most likely their shi. They were all the same, except Colby's and Rigel's. Theirs were pulsing, in unison, with another light she saw at the edge of the yard in the ley-gate.

Shelly was right behind Rigel when Colby began to antagonize the man.

"So I'm wondering if it was jealousy of my father or disappointment in yourself that is to blame," Colby said. "I think it is the latter. Disappointment breeds bitterness, and you, Uncle Rigel, are a very bitter old mage."

Rigel's aura changed. Shelly began to hurry her pace, anticipating the backlash that Colby's words were provoking. Just before he had a chance to release his attack, Shelly launched an offensive spell.

#MagicBindings.

The snap of Shelly's magic activating, caused Rigel to pause and turn. His body became wrapped in Emassa-born ropes that sapped the magic from his hands. Rigel's attack was thwarted.

As the energy was taken from Rigel's spells, the barrier he erected fell away. Jasper descended upon the man, re-enforcing Shelly's spell with one of his own.

"Can't have you getting out of this," Jasper said.

Colby gasped and fell to his knees as Jasper's spell took hold. He tried to stand but was kept grounded by the crippling pull of Emassa through him.

"What is it?" Aria said. "What's happening to my boy?" She looked at Colby until something itching at her subconscious made her keep turning toward the house.

Colby tried to shake off the multiple sets of helping hands. He looked around, searching in vain for the source of his current drain.

Shelly faded into the in-between to confirm her suspicion. She looked now with new ability and vision, tracing the lines of energy that connected Colby to the ley-gate and crystal stone. Colby had many lines of power traveling off of him in all directions, and his new rune tattoos were glowing. Shelly traced the most significant draw of magic from Colby, heading toward the house.

"There is a problem," Shelly said. "I can see the Emassa while traversing the in-between."

"Since when?" Nana asked. Her tone was accusing, and her glare suspicious.

"Just recently," Shelly said. She continued before Nana had a chance to question more. "That's not important now, the fact that Emassa is piling into Colby and then going back out of him in all directions

…"

"So everyone playing that Hashtag Magic game Bruce created is draining my magic," Colby said. "We already knew this."

"No, Colby," Shelly said. "It isn't just that app doing this." Shelly looked around at everyone and grabbed Colby's hand to show him the in-between. "Can you see? There are lines from you to all of us here as well. And we aren't using that game."

When they returned from the in-between, Colby looked around. He could still see the energy flowing the same way it was in the in-between. Everything magical shone brightly in his eyes, and he traced their source of power back to himself.

"Crap on a cracker," Colby said.

"Gary better find a solution soon," Jasper said. "Where is he?"

Aria turned to the house again. Something didn't feel right. "We better go check on Gary and Bruce."

"They'll be fine," Shelly said.

Aria was not dissuaded by Shelly's reassurances. She felt another presence. "If Rigel is here, where is Daphne?"

A scream from the house rang out as an answer to Aria's question. As everyone began to run for the home, Jasper stopped and returned to Rigel.

"Someone has to stay here and keep watch on Uncle ass-hat here."

Shelly stopped and turned to Jasper before joining him. "I'll wait with Jasper."

Before they could get to the back door, Colby collapsed. "Gary. He's gone."

CHAPTER 26

Gary was dead. The golem that was Colby's best friend and critical-minded computer geek was reduced to a pile of clay powder on the floor. Colby's laptop remained open on the counter with the dusty remains of Gary's hands still on the keyboard.

Bruce was huddled under the table, shaking and muttering nonsense. His eyes were shut tight.

"What happened here?" Nana said.

"That crazy bitch killed him," Bruce said. "She just waltzed in here and without a word, bombarded him with balls of magic and lightning bolts. When that didn't work, she picked up a knife and stabbed him in the back of the head. He didn't even try to defend himself." Bruce returned to whimpering.

"Where'd she go?" Aria asked.

Bruce pointed toward the front of the house. Nobody realized that Bruce disappeared once they all turned away.

As Aria ran off—Nana trailing after—to hunt down Daphne, Colby turned his attention to the laptop. Gary's essence rejoined with Colby the moment his avatar disintegrated. In that brief instant of knowing, Colby gleaned what Gary's last thoughts were.

Gary thought of Colby and how best he could serve his friend. Gary managed to shut down all the Hashtag Magic servers out on the internet. His choice was between defending himself or running from Daphne, and giving his last moment of existence up to help Colby. Gary chose Colby.

Colby's eyes swole with tears while a lump formed in his throat. Though he knew that his friend always was and will forever be a part of himself, Colby felt loss deeper than he had prior. With each friend lost, each avatar of earth and fire destroyed, a piece of himself returned while another died.

His pain drove away the constant ache of Emassa being proxied through his body. Colby barely noticed the change. The flow of Emassa out of his body reduced to a trickle as Colby focused on his friends and their loss. He was shutting off the pain and at the same time, access to Emassa.

"What are you doing?" Fizzlewink said. He interrupted Colby's internalizing of his pain. "Something is happening to the Emassa."

The moment Colby opened his eyes, he lost the unexpected stranglehold he had taken on the power flowing out of him. The natural flow of magic returned, though it yet traveled from the leilines and through Colby.

Fizzlewink squinted at Colby's blank look. "Just then, you were doing something that was dampening the flow of magic."

"I don't know what you're talking about, Fizz. I was simply trying to ignore the pain I feel at all this loss."

Huffing and rolling his eyes, Fizzlewink jumped up on the counter next to Colby. "Get over it, boy. They were just tools, servants to your magic and-"

"They are…were my friends. I don't care if they were some creation of a twisted spell performed years ago. They were a part of me."

"That's kinda the point with a golem, Colby. Though I don't understand the circumstances of their creation, they were here for a purpose. And you still have one left."

With Fizzlewink's reminder that Jasper was his last surviving friend and avatar, Colby got up and ran for the back door. As he approached the kitchen, Colby felt a shift in the flow of Emassa in himself. It became much stronger as his rune tattoos began glowing and rippled to new positions on his body.

"We have company," Colby said. "My ink is changing again."

By now, Colby had linked the runes to the Druid, he just hadn't figured out the significance. In the yard, he saw the Druid standing near the portal ring of the small ley-gate.

Hooded and holding a toaster-sized device in his hands, the Druid stood motionless, waiting. His statuesque stance was short-lived as Daphne wailed and ran toward him.

The Druid set his burden down at his feet before lifting a hand, palm out, toward the charging woman. "Halt," he said.

Daphne stopped as though hitting a wall. After a failed attempt at gathering her dignity, Daphne looked around and spotted Rigel on the fringes of the yard. Before Daphne could say a word, she stopped at the motion of Rigel's hands, imploring her to keep his position quiet. She returned her dagger-filled glare to the Druid.

The Druid bent over and laid his device on the ground before opening the top and pressing a switch. As he stood back straight, the Druid allowed a low rumbling laugh to escape him.

Colby recognized the familiar tightening of his center. The core of his magic was being relieved by an interruption of the drain on his store of Emassa. He looked over and watched as the Druid turned on his Hashtag Magic dampening device. Though its appearance was different than that of Mr. Bodine's while possessed by Koyaanisqatsi, the mechanism was the same. It was a device to block Colby's AI program, which interpreted and converted hashtags into spells.

"He's blocking our magic," Colby said. "Where did he get that device?" Colby looked to Jasper for an answer.

"Mr. Bodine doesn't remember how he made the first one, let alone supply another to this douche."

Colby began to look between the device and the Druid and noticed the slight nod the Druid returned. In that instant, Colby realized the Druid was behind the first magic dampener and more. The Druid was orchestrating everything Colby had experienced in the last few years. Perhaps more.

"How much of what has been happening is your work?" Colby asked the Druid. "Where has your hand been pulling strings?"

"Everything and everywhere, my friend."

"You are not my friend."

The Druid snickered. "Who else but a friend would know you better than you know yourself?"

Colby did not answer. He stared at the Druid, who remained stone still. After the two remained in a silent mental debate for several moments, Colby staggered back.

The Druid laughed. "If you don't mind, I have a bit more tampering to attend."

With Hashtag Magic now blocked, Colby was unable to perform the spells he attempted to interfere with the Druid's magic. As he watched the robed figure draw out runes in the air, enacting an incantation, Colby shook his head at the familiar movements and stature of the man. Recognition settled upon his shocked expression as the realization hit him. He began to understand who the Druid is.

"This can't be," Colby mumbled. "How can-"

"Now you are beginning to understand," the Druid said. "You can't stop this, nor should you want to."

Aria watched the exchange with a split desire to understand her son's hesitation and the need to dispatch her last remaining Daphne. Her concentration refocused for her when Daphne began to charge.

"It's time for my reward," Daphne screamed. "I'll have my due."

As Daphne ran for Aria, the Druid's spell was complete, and the crazed woman's trajectory reversed. She hurtled through the air toward the Druid. The shrilling sound of her scream passing all in the yard had a Doppler effect that rattled their ears.

"You wanted a reward, dear Daphne," the Druid said as he held her fast in an invisible grip before him.

"You promised I could have her, to become whole. I want what you promised."

"And so you shall have it." The Druid pulled a gleaming metal object from his pocket. "Though you have misinterpreted our bargain. I said you shall be whole again, but you are a piece of another." He pushed the object into Daphne's chest.

Understanding flashed across Daphne's face as the last enchanted sigel of reconstitution burned into her body. As she dropped from the Druids release, Daphne began to convulse in unison with Aria.

As the eyes of those present shifted back and forth between Aria and Daphne, watching them stagger toward one another, only one noticed the disappearance of the Druid.

"Where did he go?" Colby asked. He saw the Hashtag Magic blocking device still there, still active, but there was no Druid.

Aria fought against the attraction pulling her toward Daphne, confused by the interference from the Druid. A reassuring whisper in her ear relaxed the struggle in her body.

"Don't fight this," Nana said. "Daphne has lost, and you will be whole again."

Aria turned her eyes to Nana and smiled in understanding before letting the enchantment have its way. She ran full speed toward Daphne. "It's time to say goodbye."

Daphne scrambled to gain purchase on the ground that seemed to fight her feet. The magic of rebinding was pulling her toward Aria as a magnet of opposing force, Daphne the negative to Aria's positive charge. In the final moment of her struggle, just before the two collided, Daphne let out a last phrase.

"You have no idea what's in store. The two shall never become one."

Aria heard but did not register the warning. She tilted her head back and spread her arms wide, allowing herself to consume the last vestige of her split shi.

Two figures blended together with accompanied flashes of power and light. Where four arms became two and likewise legs buckled and fell down as two, the fiery tones of red hair raised in the updraft. Two heads rattled in a semi-transparent final battle for dominance.

In the final moments of resistance, Nana implored Aria to take control, wringing her hands and wobbling back and forth with anticipation.

Shelly stood by smiling. "See-ya, Serina!"

"Who's Serina," Nana said.

"You know, that trouble-making sister on those old reruns of Bewitched you're always watching."

Nana laughed. "Oh, I get it, like a witch version of Bye Felicia." Nana made a bye-bye gesture to Daphne. "See-ya, Serina."

"This doesn't make us BFFs or anything," Shelly said.

Nana huffed and turned her attention back to Aria. She was recovering, so Nana made her way over.

As the magic of the enchantment faded and Aria took to her feet, her aura became visible while she settled back into herself. Aria looked around and smiled, relishing in the sensation of returning to full strength and embodiment. Her eyes scanned the yard, meeting the eyes of all present, seeing them for the first time in years with an actual constitution. When her gaze fell upon Rigel—who came of out the shadow of the bushes—Aria glared.

"There's my girl," Rigel said. "I've been expecting you."

CHAPTER 27

Aria snarled at Rigel. As she gathered and focused all her full magic abilities. Having all her split identities, rejoined caused a flood of Emassa to pour into her center. She raised a hand and thrust it toward Rigel. As the magic streamed from her charged fingertips, Aria smiled.

"It's good to be me again."

Rigel dodged the assault and took cover. Though he remained magically restrained, Rigel managed to keep his feet beneath himself as he attempted to find a suitable place of respite. Rigel wriggled in the bonds, allowing the residue from Aria's attack to lubricate his own attempt at breaking free. As he expected, the direct Emassa magic Aria used was dissolving the Hashtag Magic ropes that Shelly and Jasper restrained him with. The device the Druid used was working toward Rigel's own goals as he had hoped.

"Come now, my love," Rigel goaded Aria. "You have to admit we had chemistry before my brother came along and spoiled all our fun." He moved around the corner of the garage just enough to take another hit from Aria's anger-fueled magic.

The garage buffered the bulk of Aria's spell, allowing just enough magic to finish the job of breaking the last of his bonds. He retreated once again behind the side of the garage. Rigel rubbed the pain from his wrists, noticing Shelly just beyond the driveway.

Free to perform his own magic again, Rigel tapped into the Emassa and thrust a spell toward Shelly.

Shelly caught the gleam of magic in the corner of her eye in time to dodge the assault. Her new ability to see beyond the normal vision of the mundane, Shelly saw the glimmer of magic coming and slipped into the in-between.

Walking past Rigel—hidden in the space between the living and postmortem realms—Shelly fought the urge to reach out and throttle him. Instead, she continued past and headed toward her mother with squinted eyes.

The gleam of Aria's reconstituted shi was near blinding to Shelly's unique vision. She was unused to the sight of her mother in full embodiment of her soul. The added brightness was likely a result of her body's sudden ability to sustain an ample supply of Emassa. Pausing a moment to whisper in her mother's ear, she noticed the Druid behind Colby when turning her head.

"Rigel is free," Shelly whispered to Aria. "Gotta go see a Druid about a spell."

Shelly left her mother behind to retake Rigel and hurried her feet toward Colby.

Colby jumped at the sudden jerking of energy behind him. Turning to find its source, Colby immediately began to crawl with a strange feeling across the entirety of his body. A pulling and stretching tugged at him as deep as the bone. Colby felt as though each molecule of his being was fighting for release.

"Hashtagga shi impedus," the Druid said. "Mustn't allow that. Paradoxes are a messy business."

Colby felt himself again and looked at the face staring back at his own. Though the skin was fully etched with runes and worn with a few more years than his own, Colby was confident. He saw himself reflected in the eyes of the Druid.

"How is this possible? Are you Pace now…or then…or when are you in my timeline?"

"Future and past, depending on which point of view you choose. That is irrelevant at this point." The Druid reached beneath his cloak and retrieved a watch. "You need to get this swapped with

Rigel."

Colby took the wristwatch from his past and present self. "How am I supposed to switch this with the one Rigel has while that device is turned on?"

"Improvise. You have an innate ability to do things on instinct. Trust those instincts. You're going to need them."

"Why not just turn the damn thing off?"

The Druid tittered. "Sorry, not just yet. And who is Pace?"

"Pace is a rather old version of us. I don't know what his age is, but he spent a great deal of time in the past."

"Well the future has not happened for us yet, and the past can be… adjusted. If I ever met him, he never identified himself."

"Now I must attend my own business and you have help arriving." The Druid turned away and walked off.

Colby jerked around due to an unexpected tap on his shoulder. "What the hell, Shelly?"

"Sorry cheese-curd, I wanted a little chat with…where'd he go?"

"Oh, you mean, where did I go?"

Shelly lifted her right eyebrow. "So you know then."

"That the Druid is me from some other time? Yes, I am now. How long have you known?"

Shelly hesitated before saying anything, which seemed to give Colby all the answers he needed for the moment.

"Never mind now." Colby showed Shelly the wristwatch. "We need to find a way to get this swapped for the one Rigel has, though I'm unaware as to why."

"It shines in the center," Shelly said. "Is this one dad's?"

"No, I have dad's." Colby showed her the one on his wrist. "There are three of them. What's going on here. This version of me is far deeper into manipulating things than Pace, and this version didn't even know himself as Pace."

"The old man version of you? Why would he know him, the Druid is just shown up and is much younger than the old man version of you."

"Yes, but he has been futzing around since this all started, I think. Why wouldn't he have known about Pace?"

"I don't know, it makes my head hurt thinking about it all. Let's just do what he asked. The Druid seems to be on our side, he's helped mom after all."

Colby thought a moment. "I suppose, but how are we supposed to get this watch swapped?"

Shelly and Colby formulated a plan before slipping into the in-between. They made their way first to Aria, asking her to keep Rigel distracted. As they slid along the exterior of the garage toward Rigel's position, Shelly looked at the man and the watch he already wore. The same type of shine was emanating from the watch as the one they were to replace it with.

"Something is off here," Shelly whispered. "The watch he has shines just like this one." Shelly took a closer look. "It has a different rhythm in the way it pulses though."

"What does that mean?"

"I have no idea," Shelly said. "This ability to see auras and such is new. I'm still figuring it out."

"So, they are duplicates or something. Maybe the one Rigel has is spelled to fool him."

They agreed as they approached Rigel, to trust what the Druid wanted only because of who he was. When they were in position, Shelly kept her grip on Colby as he began to reach toward Rigel's wrist. They were unsure how being in the in-between would affect their plan, but there were few options.

Colby moved his hand toward Rigel's wrist with outstretched fingers. As his thumb and index finger reached to unbuckle the watch, Rigel looked down and locked eyes with Colby.

"What is this?" Rigel said and released a ball of plasma. The resulting blast—though buffered by the in-between—threw Colby and Shelly out into the living realm. "What are you two on about?"

Rigel looked at Colby and saw the watch in his hand. Lifting his own wrist to find, he still wore the watch he thought to belong to Jarrod, Rigel Snarled and readied another spell.

"Why do you have another watch, boy? Did you swap my watch for a fake."

Colby changed tactics immediately. "This isn't your watch. It belongs to my father." Careful to switch the watch to his right hand, Colby made sure Rigel would not see the third on Colby's left wrist. "You have no right to his belongings, watch, skin, or otherwise."

Rigel laughed and began removing the watch on his wrist. "Is that so. And who is to stop me? You? You have no magic at present."

Rage replaced the surprise on Colby's face. Without a formulated plan or spell, Colby lashed out with Emassa, he instinctively siphoned from the lei-lines.

The watch in Colby's hand was propelled toward Rigel and fixed itself on his wrist just as Rigel dropped the one he already unfastened.

Even as Rigel fell back from the resulting spell, he felt the change overtake his borrowed body and smiled. Raising his arm to examine the replacement timepiece, Rigel rose to his feet and turned toward Colby.

"Well, that was both surprising and disappointing." Rigel waved his wrist toward Colby. "A stroke of luck for me and well… disappointing for you to have lost your prize." Rigel stomped the displaced watch into the dirt.

The cracking of the crystal face sent a wave of magical residue outward as the magic in the old implement was extinguished.

"No!" Colby yelled as he dove forward, too late to stop the destruction of the other watch. "What have you done?"

Rigel laughed. "Don't place your blame on me, nephew. Your Druid has miscalculated in his game of shells. I can feel the power in this replacement watch. Now I have what I need to keep this body indefinitely." As he spoke the last word, Rigel's face contorted with shifting under his skin. He looked at the discarded watch, now broken, then tried to remove the replacement.

The new watch would not unbuckle.

CHAPTER 28

Rigel struggled to maintain form as rippling beneath his skin prevented the ability to concentrate. As he fought the pain and transformation trying to overtake his body, Rigel was unable to sense the arrival of Bruce.

Taking hold of Rigel from behind, Bruce wrapped his arms around the man and dropped him to the ground.

"Bruce?" Shelly said. "Where did you come from?"

Smirking his annoyance, Bruce turned to Shelly. "You never even noticed that I left, did you?" Seeing Shelly's blank expression, Bruce turned back to Rigel while still addressing Shelly and Colby. "Betelgeuse pulled me away to enlist my assistance with handling this guy." Bruce struggled to hold Rigel's thrashing body. "Something to do with an exchange that the Druid has planned."

Colby shot up and ran to assist Bruce. "What did my grandfather tell you?"

"Nothing really, other than told me to keep this guy still when he sent me back through the portal. That is after he took me to that smelly basement beneath your school."

Bruce told Colby and Shelly, how Betelgeuse and Tiddle were there, talking about some spell from a decade ago. They needed to retrieve something from a hidden room inside an altar. Tiddle took some small matchbox-sized item from the chamber and handed it to Betelgeuse. Betelgeuse then transferred something from the box to the inside of a watch, and the watch then disappeared. Then the three of them waited.

"Next thing I know, I'm being thrown into the magic lines with instructions to grab Professor stick-up-the-butt and hold him until the big guy shows up."

"Who is the big guy?" Colby asked. "You mean the Druid."

"I don't think so. They just said I would know when to let go."

A heartbeat after Bruce answered a guttural moan accompanied the blinding flash behind the foursome. Koyaanisqatsi was back, but he was shifting in his plasma skin. The same sort of rippling that was effecting Rigel was also happening to the Shizumu spirit of Colby's father.

Unsure of what was transpiring, Colby grabbed Shelly and pulled her back. Bruce was out of his reach, but Colby tried calling out to him for a retreat. When Colby thought Bruce might have time to get away and join them, he was pulled back by Rigel, who clung to Bruce like a safety blanket.

Bruce struggled to free himself from Rigel's grasp but was unable to physically pull away. When he tried a Hashtag Magic spell, it fizzled and dissolved.

"Hashtag Magic won't work," Colby said. Colby tried to repeat the blast he used on Rigel, but his instinctual magic would not obey. "We need to get Bruce free."

Shelly appeared torn between helping Bruce and abandoning him. Her emotions spun for what she once felt for him before his betrayal. But it was the memory of all he did even without the influence of a Shizumu possession that won.

"Leave him." Shelly pulled Colby into the in-between as a refuge. Pulling Colby to his feet, Shelly began to walk away when a glimmer on the ground caught her attention.

Where the crushed timepiece sat, she saw the remains of several minuscule—yet shining—particles of crystal. She tried to pick them up with her fingernails, but it was like trying to pinch fine tiny hairs from the skin. When she prepared to give up, her un-pinching of her fingers exposed her palm. The pulsing fragments rose from the ground.

The glowing points of light stuck to her palm with a static charge. Shelly did not think as Colby pulled her away. Clasping her hand closed, Shelly followed Colby's lead toward the house.

The duo reached the relative safety of the back porch, where they found Jasper, Fizz, Aria, and Nana, who all embraced the two before pulling them into a protective huddle.

"What's happening over there?" Jasper asked.

"I don't know, but whatever it is, you can be sure the Druid is behind it," Nana said with Bellatrix's Voice in control. "That manipulative puppet master-"

"Is me," Colby said. "Careful how you finish that thought, old witch."

The silence among the group at Colby's revelation allowed silenced the turmoil in the yard.

"Dude," Jasper said. "What the hell are you talking about?"

Colby did his best to explain that the Druid was some other version of himself from another timeline. His own grasp on the continuum was as yet fleeting. All he managed was to assure that the Druid was indeed Colby and had been working some master plan. This plan was, in a twisted way, working in their favor as well.

"He got mom put back together. I have to trust that he is also working on getting dad back and ridding us of Rigel."

"You don't sound convinced," Nana said with her own voice regaining control. "What has your other self revealed?"

"Nothing useful," Shelly said. "At least not more than we need to know in order to further whatever plans he's set in motion."

The struggle in the back yard reclaimed their attention.

While Rigel writhed in pain, the Shizumu—Jarrod—split in twain. Two red glowing specters swirled in a circle around Bruce and Rigel. As they encircled the two corporeal bodies, the Shizumu watched the struggle Rigel had maintaining form.

One of the Shiz dove for Rigel and entered his body. Bruce was thrown back and away as Rigel began thrashing in a seizure on the grass. Seconds later, the Shizumu that possessed Rigel was ejected. It could not take hold of the body.

Screeching from the displeasure of rejection, the displaced Shizumu went for the next available body, Bruce.

While Rigel's body thrashing began to abate, Bruce's began to glow, cracks of light appeared and spread across his skin.

"It'll kill the poor lad," Nana tittered. "He's already had a Shiz inside him."

"Not this one," Shelly said. "It had a different signature of an aura than Koyaanisqatsi. This…half that entered Bruce is not like what inhabited him previously. But if it'll help, I'll gladly go kick the Shiz outta him."

Shelly pointed to her eyes while Colby explained her new ability to see beyond the typical spectrum of human visibility.

As they watched, helpless to assist, Bruce's body began to relax, and the threat of spontaneous combustion receded. He lay still, save for his chest expanding and contracting with each labored breath. Bruce had been repossessed.

The other half of Koyaanisqatsi reeled with rage and swooped in to try and inhabit Rigel. Before it could attain more than a sliver of itself within Rigel's contorting form, a flash of blue light slammed into the invader, thrusting it away. The Shade of Jarrod hovered over Rigel.

"Another non-corporeal heard from," Aria said. "Now what?"

"It's Dad," Colby said. "They both are."

"Impossible," Aria said. "Your father was lost to us when he cast the spell to protect you more than ten years ago."

"Not lost," a new voice added. "He was obliged to my service." The Druid came around the corner of the back steps and nodded to Colby. "Both parts of father are here and ready to retake form."

"I hear some doubt in your voice," Nana said. "What are you not saying, Colby the Druid?"

The Druid smiled at Nana before lowering his hood. "All out in the open, I take it? No matter. The rest of the pieces are falling into place…mostly."

"What do you mean, mostly?" Colby asked. "Dad's shiz and Shade are here, as is his body…of sorts. Just get Rigel out of him so dad can come back to us."

Before the Druid could respond, their attention shifted back to Rigel and Bruce near the garage.

Bruce was now sitting up, watching the struggle taking place as the Shade of Jarrod Stevens began pushing itself into the body, still resembling Rigel. The body that initially belonged to Jarrod.

The Shade wriggled and flashed with desperation as it fought for purchase within the skin it remembered as home. The screaming of Rigel accompanied the Shade's own shrills in a chorus of tones that accosted the eardrums of those unfortunate to witness the battle of wills. Both Rigel and the Shade of Jarrod spun around inside the body that both beings wished to claim. Though Rigel had a foothold, it was Jarrod who dominated being the original owner of that corporeal form. Rigel's spirit, his own Shade, was ejected unceremoniously into the air above. But the body did not stop thrashing.

Unable to co-exist with the spirit that also claimed residence within his skin, Jarrod was forced to fight that specter as well. The struggle did not last long. As the shi spirit trying to remain was that of another, it would not be able to sustain a grip on its new home. Jarrod sent the demon away.

Bruce screamed his anguish at what transpired. The Shizumu within him began to slip away toward Jarrod, but paused and retreated back within Bruce before the boy scrambled away. He stood and headed toward the portal stones in the garden. Bruce did not get there.

The Druid appeared before him and branded the inhabited Bruce with an intricate rune on his chest. Bruce looked at the rune then back at the Druid before lashing out. His attempts at magic failed in succession. Helpless and trapped, Bruce took to the portal and disappeared. The other Shizumu following behind.

The Druid sneered and leveled a cold stare at Jasper before turning to Colby. "Go see to father. I have other things to attend before this is over."

CHAPTER 29

Everyone surrounded the body of Jarrod as it began transforming back into its natural form. They kept their distance from the Shade that now hovered aimlessly near Jarrod. As Jarrod's body morphed, Aria began to sniffle.

"I'm fine," Aria said. She got up and ran into the house. The Shade of Rigel followed her.

"I'll go after her," Nana said. "Not sure what all the fuss is about." Nana swatted away a pixie that flew into her face as she rose. "Can someone do something about these pests?"

Fizzlewink turned and swatted at the pixie. Forgetting himself, he began batting at the creature as it flitted around him, teasing and taunting the cat-man. "I'll get them out of the yard."

"Don't eat the pixies, Fizzlewink," Shelly said.

Fizzlewink smirked a pixie eating grin at Shelly before focusing on his prey.

Transforming into his cat form, Fizzlewink ran about the yard chasing away the swarms of pixies and clutches of grimalts that littered the yard lapping up magical residue. The sheer number of small creatures that spread around the yard feeding off the spent Emassa was proportionate to the vast amount of energy produced from all the magic. These creatures were considered vermin among most in the magical world. At the same time, some knew them for the clean-up purpose they actually served.

Several Nefsmari also transformed and began dispatching the creatures lingering in the yard. Shelly stepped back with Nana to watch the cats playing in the yard.

"This would go viral on the internet," Shelly said. "A bunch of cats going nuts around the back yard chasing pixies, someone really should video this."

Nana laughed. "We could win one of those funny video contests and get you a new car."

Shelly stopped laughing and frowned at Nana. "You know there is going to be pixie-filled cat shit all over your garden."

Now it was Nana who stopped laughing and left to get a shovel and bucket. "Fizzlewink, you need to clean up after you and your friends. My garden is not a litter-box."

Human attempts to assist the Nefsmari were mundane. They were unable to use their magic until Colby managed to disable the device that the Druid used to block Hashtag Magic. Having absorbed Gary's essence, Colby now had the knowledge necessary to turn the device off as Gary once did.

The thought of Gary made the pain resurface. Colby's heart ached. He missed his friends, all of them. Only Jasper remained, and Colby was uncertain if he would survive the Druid's plans.

"What next?" Colby said to no-one in particular. He did nothing to hide the frustration in his voice. "I don't think this is over."

"It isn't by far," Jarrod said, his voice cracking, yet familiar. "I'm still just half myself. I'd like to do something about that before this is all finished."

Colby was the first to arrive by Jarrod's side. Every emotion hit him at once. His journey to bring his father back was nearing its end. Colby had a physical version of his dad now to embrace. He did so and hugged with every ounce of his strength. His eyes—flooded with tears—squeezed tighter still against the memories of years lost and the fight he'd faced. Colby had his father back and refused to let him go.

"If you don't ease up a bit, you might squeeze me back out again, son."

Colby eased back his embrace but would still not let go. He grasped on the word son. Colby allowed himself to wash over with the joy of finally feeling that he was his father's son. His joy was short-lived as he felt the impact of more bodies.

Shelly, Jasper, Betelgeuse, and Fizzlewink all joined in the group hug.

"I feel a bit like a game of dogpile," Jarrod laughed. "I'm here and not leaving so easily." Jarrod pushed them all free. "Now, let me get a good look at you all with my own eyes for once in such a long time."

Jarrod looked at everyone in turn as they backed away—not too far—and smiled as he touched their hands and faces one-by-one. He started with Betelgeuse.

"Father-in-law," Jarrod said. "You haven't aged at all." This, he said with a laugh. Jarrod smiled at his wife's father and moved on to Shelly.

"My sweet girl, I'm not sure of this look you have going on, but I see that same little munchkin beneath all the face paint."

Shelly ignored the comment and stole another hug before Jarrod gently pushed her away.

"Colby, help me to my feet, please," Jarrod said. "We have much to discuss, but not until I've regained some strength."

"Nana will offer to cook you some dinner," Colby warned before turning up his own nose. He reached into a jar on the counter for licorice. "You can try some of this. Fizzlewink swears by it, but I've never proven it works."

Jarrod stopped walking toward the back door. He took the licorice and popped it in his mouth. "Unless the world has come to a close, I don't think your grandmother has improved enough to produce anything palatable that even a Dregg would eat."

"There are no more Dregg, at least none in the area." Colby pulled his father along toward the house.

"You have been busy." Jarrod smiled and pulled Colby closer as they walked toward the door. Next, he gave Fizzlewink a ruffle on the top of his head as the little man came closer.

"Hello, my old friend," Jarrod said to Fizzlewink. "I trust my son's guardianship wasn't too much of a burden."

Fizzlewink smiled back and began making a low gravely sound. "He had his moments."

"What is that noise," Nana said from the porch. She looked at Fizzlewink. "Fizz, is that some sad excuse for purring?"

"Shut your flappy old trap, hag."

Jarrod buckled over while shaking in his midsection. He was laughing.

Soon everyone was laughing as they entered the house, that is except Fizzlewink and Aria.

"You are all in good spirits," Aria said. "We aren't out of the preverbal woods yet. You all know this, right?"

Jarrod stopped just after passing the threshold. He gently pushed away from the hands of Colby and Shelly, who stood surprised at their mother's coldness.

"Way to be a Debbie-Downer mom," Shelly said. "Are you drinking again?"

Aria stepped forward and slapped Shelly. "I am not the same fractured woman I have been these past years. I will not tolerate your sass." Aria turned back and swatted at the Shade, who followed her. "And can someone do something about this incessant ghost?"

Jarrod patted Shelly on the hand as he stepped away from her and Colby. Touching Aria's warm, Jarrod turned her to face him. "He isn't going to leave your side for the present, my dear. You of all people should know the attraction he has to you, especially now that you are whole again."

Aria pulled away from Jarrod. "At least one of us is whole. You and your half-baked ideas and plans."

Jarrod laughed. "I see."

"You see nothing, Jarrod. You've never been able to see anything past your own schemes and plans. Like father like son, I suppose."

Jarrod hesitated before responding. "These are not my plans. They never were, and I think you know that. So who are you truly angered with here?"

"Shut up," Aria said. "You were the one who made the decisions that left me in pieces."

"No, Aria, you were the one who agreed. You were far too eager to save him. Let's not forget who was the true influence behind bad life decisions."

"Of course, I wanted to save Colby. But-"

"Not Colby, he is not the center of this argument." Jarrod grabbed Aria's hand. "You also wanted to save him." Jarrod looked from Aria to the apparition of Rigel's Shade.

Aria yanked her hand back and stepped away. She turned away from everyone in the room.

"Um, What's going on here?" Shelly asked.

Colby had been watching the interaction and looking between his parents and Rigel's spirit. He sidled up to Shelly and whispered. "I think he's talking about Rigel."

Jarrod heard Colby. "Yes I am speaking of your uncle. He always had a streak of trouble that left its mark on everything he touched."

Centuries ago, Rigel was found guilty of performing forbidden magics and several other crimes against both the magical and mundane. When traditional means of imprisonment did not work, a new and dangerous method was discovered when a researching mage was perusing the ancient scrolls. The result was a prison realm that would trap a mage's spirit, while their body remained in stasis.

In Rigel's case, however, he was too strong to be removed wholly from his corporeal form, so another element was required to bind him. This involved splitting his shi and anchoring the Shizumu half to another mage.

Aria was always opposed to that prison realm and the process it required. Though she was smitten with both brothers at the time, she only resisted Rigel because of his darker tendencies. Rigel reignited that feeling of being the second choice.

"We were a pair, my brother and I," Jarrod said. "We did get up to some questionable magic, but I always knew when to draw the line. Rigel on the other hand, well he always had to push boundaries. Ultimately it was one spell that got him caught." Jarrod looked at Aria.

"He should not have been punished so severe for something I agreed to," Aria said. "And then you had to go and get yourself bound to him through that Shizumu linking spell."

"It was the only way to weaken him enough to be bound. In the end, Rigel's use of that spell to split and clone you, it led to the spell to merge our Shizumu and imprison him."

"And yet, who turned out to be the wicked one?" Aria said. "It was your Shizumu half that broke free and spent decades playing mythic demon to half the globe's notice peoples."

"Koyaanisqatsi's manifestation was a complete surprise to all involved. We eventually caught the blended Shizumu and-"

"Locked him away in that…place."

"Yes," Jarrod said. "We locked him away, where you could no longer fawn over him. So you could concentrate on the brother who actually cared about you and not the family legacy he could hitch himself to."

Aria moved toward Jarrod as thought to disagree, bot lowered her eyes, and sat down. She refused to look at him.

Jarrod changed the subject and got back to telling his story. As it turned out, eventually, even that prison could not hold them. When the age of information dawned, and electronic and digital waves of energy began circling the planet, they inevitably interacted with the prison dimension. Koyaanisqatsi was able to break free, infest humanity, and then work out a plan of revenge.

"Ya, we know where the rest of that leads," Shelly said. "Mr. Bodine, the BSOD escapes, and so on. I'm more interested in hearing about this little love triable."

"Ancient history," Aria said. "I saw Rigel for who he was eventually, and then allowed myself to fall in love with your father. The rest is….well, its just the rest."

"I think you've left some important bits out," Colby said.

"How so?"

"You were still connected to this Koyaanisqatsi, while mom and the Daphnes were a thing…is that why my magic is the way it is?"

Jarrod took Colby's chin in his hand. "You are the way you are because that is how you are supposed to be. Don't let anyone ever convince you otherwise."

While Colby stared back into his father's eyes, his head began moving back and forth in rapid shakes. He realized it was his father's hand still holding his chin. It was jerking while Jarrod started to seize.

CHAPTER 30

"What's wrong with him?" Colby asked. "I thought dad was stabilized?"

Betelgeuse knelt down and took Jarrod's head into the crook of his arm. Closing his eyes and resting a palm on Jarrod's forehead, Betelgeuse chanted an inaudible spell. The effect was effective at calming the thrashing of Jarrod's body. Betelgeuse lifted Jarrod and carried him to the couch in the living room.

"He will rest a few minutes before waking. I'm afraid the reunion with his body is not entirely locked."

"What's that supposed to mean?" Colby asked.

Betelgeuse spoke of how the binding worked in the spell that banished Rigel's Shizumu to the prison. Too strong to be sent alone, the binding of Rigel to Jarrod's Shizumu was necessary to quell the strength of Rigel's spirit. To secure that binding, the enchantment had to be stored within an object. That object had to have been destroyed to unlock the spell that also created Koyaanisqatsi.

Now Jarrod's and Rigel's individual Shizumu were free and looking for their other half. Betelgeuse was not present for the ceremony that allowed Rigel to free his Shade and inadvertently Koyaanisqatsi. He was present when Rigel was imprisoned in the beginning.

Rigel was beyond what standard punishments the Nefslama used to deal with miscreants and criminals of the magical community. While most could be bound or stripped of power, Rigel was far too old and pure in his bloodline to be stripped of his abilities. All attempts at imprisonment failed until one day, a spell appeared among the stacks of ancient scrolls the Nefslama stored in their ancient library.

The scroll detailed a ceremony that involved splitting of the shi and binding of one Shizumu to another. It only summarized the part of how chaos might result. This chaotic state would render the being inert long enough to place in another realm where it would become trapped.

"So, this was where we were in that virtual world?" Jasper asked.

"Yes, but that plain became unstable as mankind progressed in technology, allowing the eventual escape when the ceremony was performed to hobble Colby's magic." Betelgeuse looked at Colby with sorrow. "A deed I wish had never been necessary."

"Why was it necessary," Colby asked.

"Don't interrupt," Bellatrix said and boxed Colby's ears.

Betelgeuse frowned at his wife and continued. He spoke of how a Shizumu of greater strength was needed to bind Rigel's, and that is where Jarrod came in. Jarrod allowed binding of Rigel to himself to weaken his brother enough for banishment. Though it was only a partial separation, it meant that Jarrod and Rigel were forever bound as one.

"That is until the hobbling of Colby broke that bond, allowing the creation of Koyaanisqatsi."

"All half-baked plans. We all know how that spell suddenly appeared in the archives." Aria gave Colby an unloving glare. "Perhaps you can fix that."

"Stop that, Aria," Nana said. "Move it." Nana took Aria to the kitchen to speak. "What really has you more bound up than my bowels after eating cheese?"

"This is what I was afraid of," Aria said. "Placing all this trust in the hands of another. I knew I should not get my hopes up."

Nana cornered Aria at the counter, but it was Bellatrix that spoke. "Listen you little shrew. You are back to being whole, are you not?" Bellatrix waited for a nod. "And your long-separated husband is on his way back to mending. You, better than anyone, will know how best to support him. He is your husband for better or worse. You've had quite your fill of worse, so look forward to the better getting started."

"I fear that this is a short win," Aria said. "I have a sinking feeling that something more devastating is on the horizon."

"What kind of feeling? Is it that surface irritation of too good to be true? Or is it that deep foreboding that comes from the core of your magic?"

"The latter."

"Do you feel this when you look at Jarrod?"

"No."

"So then go to him and be his partner. We can deal with the rest as it comes." Bellatrix gave way for Nana to resurface. "My sweet child, we will get through this. Now tell me who you have seen this tragedy surrounding?"

Aria began to speak but stopped herself. She patted Nana's hand in hers and began to walk toward the living room. "It is just all the excitement of current events. Perhaps it is nothing at all." Aria gave her mother another reassuring pat and left her behind.

Nana watched Aria enter the living room and avoid Colby. "Nothing, like my fat fanny, is nothing." She rejoined the others and squeezed herself between Colby and Betelgeuse. "So, what's the verdict?"

Betelgeuse looked at Nana, knowing the spirit that held court within the old woman's mind. Something was not right as both women living inside her had little use for him. "What are you up to?"

Nana acted as affronted as she possibly couldn't. "Shut your trap. I'm genuinely concerned for the welfare of my son-in-law."

"Sure, you are. I vaguely recall the day of their wedding and some old bat throwing herself on the ground when objections were solicited."

"Bygones and all that dribble. Can you just tell us all what the diagnosis might be?"

"Yes, please," Aria added. She scowled at her mother. "Stop badgering, daddy."

Nana mumbled under her breath but painted a forced smile that made her resemble a Shar-pei.

"That's really not helping," Colby said and laughed when Nana let go of her dog-faced grin. "Grandpa, what do you think is happening?"

"Hard to say as this is the first time I've been witness to the process. Only your father or the Druid has the knowledge to understand how this rebinding works."

"Rigel knows as well," Colby added. "But I hardly think he'd be a willing source of information."

"Nor do I think you'll find him to ask any time soon," Jarrod said as he settled and sat upright. "This is all perfectly normal and expected."

Aria began to cry and dove straight into an embrace with her husband. "I've missed you more than words can define."

"As I have missed you, missed you all."

After more embraces and reunions were shared, Jarrod eventually pushed everyone away. "This process is difficult to put simply. Retaking my form after Rigel rode around in me like a suit for so long, I have to remind myself who I am in a sense. It's akin to reforming a pair of gloves after someone else has put them on and stretched them out a bit."

"I think it's a bit more complicated than that," Colby said. "You are not whole, and the process Rigel used to trade your skin is different than you reclaiming it. It's like he still has squatter's rights or something."

"Who gets a gold star for today's lesson," Jarrod said. "Very much on the nose, my son."

"So, how do we fix it?" Aria asked.

"Time, patience, and well, then there is the problem of my Shizumu half being rather disagreeable."

"That's an understatement," Betelgeuse said.

Jarrod chided his father-in-law's statement, but could not dispute the facts he explained. It was never Rigel's Shizumu that controlled the joined spirit who became Koyaanisqatsi. It was Jarrod's. Being a strongly endowed magic user that maintained a strict balance of use meant that he was comprised of two extremes. One half was heavily fixated with the giving of one's self. At the same time, the other was darkly influenced by self-serving tendencies.

"Rigel was always selfish, so both halves of his shi were what you might consider dark or tainted. I always remained in a grey area. Each of my halves was on complete opposites of the spectrum as it pertains to magic service. Koyaanisqatsi is the manifestation of my half of that unholy binding taking the driver's seat."

"How is all this linked?" Shelly asked. "So at some point, Colby becomes this Druid guy and starts futzing with time…to what ends?"

"Only the Druid version of Colby has the full story," Jarrod admitted. "I came to trust him as I had no idea who he was until after the hobbling spell over a decade ago. That was when he made it possible for me to be a free spirit if you will. I was sent back in time to attend the Druid for centuries."

"Then maybe you can explain my hobbling, and why golem were created?"

Jarrod lowered his head before looking back at Colby. "I do not understand the full purpose of your golem. At first, I thought them friends or guides until I understood they were more a place to store your magic. The golem came into existence the moment your power was split."

"And now that all but one are dead…" Colby started. He looked at Jasper. "I still have Jasper. You are back. Mom is whole. Isn't it nearly at an end?"

Jarrod pulled Colby close. "Rigel is yet free inside others where he does not belong. I am not whole. You are not whole. I am afraid that whatever this other version of you has in store, Jasper will not persist."

The room remained silent for several minutes before Nana slapped her hands on her thighs and stood. "Right then. Anyone up for some dinner?"

"Not if you plan on cooking it," Shelly said.

"Shut-up Shelly," Nana said. "I am in no mood, nor is my kitchen stocked for a homemade meal. How about we all go to the diner?"

CHAPTER 31

Shelly walked into the diner first and grabbed menus. She led the entourage to a corner, selecting a round booth. Shelly reset the table from the previous occupants that inexplicably decided they wanted another table.

The diner was near empty, so seating themselves was not an issue. It also helped that Shelly held an on-again-off-again position as a waitress and hostess at the establishment. She worked when she wanted, and the owner was far too scared of her to disagree, even without magical influence.

"Order whatever you want, and we'll make it family-style," Shelly said. "It's on me."

Laughter and doubt mixed to meet Shelly's snarl. "I do have a job and my own money."

"When was the last time you actually came into work?" Colby said.

"And seating us tonight doesn't count."

"Says you. Maybe if you weren't always finding trouble, I could have a steady work schedule." Their argument went back and forth until Shelly had no footing left. "Never mind that, cheese-curd. Just order."

Shelly took everyone's orders and passed them on to the cook before returning with an unexpected guest. "Look who I found looking for us at the counter."

Tiddle smiled and shook hands with the older men among the group. "Good evening, all. I'm so glad for the invitation and happy to join you all."

"I'm sorry when were you-" Colby started.

"Jarrod!" Tiddle said. "So glad for your return. I must admit I was a bit tossed for a loop when I heard of your return. I'll say you look rather well, considering."

"Considering what?" Colby asked. His eyes narrowed at Tiddle. "Who exactly informed you of dad's resurrection of sorts?"

"Resurrection?" Tiddle laughed. "Funny way to put it, but not far from the mark, I suppose."

"Thank you, Tiddle. Please join us." Jarrod shook his head and frowned at Colby. The undertone of his look was meant to dissuade Colby's continued badgering.

Idle chit-chat dominated as Colby attempted to question Tiddle further. Even as Jarrod tried to steer the interruptions, Colby kept drilling the man for answers. Colby felt an odd tingling in his senses that warned him of something being off. He noticed his mother was also not looking upon Tiddle with welcoming eyes.

Colby watched Tiddle closely as he regaled the group with tales of old times when he and Jarrod were much younger mages. One story led to another, and Colby noticed at one point, even Jarrod stopped paying full attention. The only ones watching Tiddle were Colby, Aria, and Rigel's Shade. Colby caught the moment that Tiddle began to drift his conversation and shift his eyes between the Shade and Colby.

"I'm sorry, but who did you say told you of dad's return and invited you to dinner? I don't think you said."

Tiddle looked at Colby with an unreadable face. His unfeeling expression soon folded beneath the weight of his awaited response. "Why you did, my boy." Tiddle laid a hand on Colby's wrist. "Not to worry. We have everything well in hand."

Colby's next question was cut off when another plate of food arrived, delivered by an unexpected waiter.

"I hope everything is to your liking?" Bruce said. He dropped a plate of appetizers on the table. "Eat up while you can."

Shelly was the first to spit her food out. "What the hell? Where have you been?"

"Why the venomous tone, Shelly." Bruce leaned over to Shelly. "Oh, come now, my sweet. You still have feelings for this face, do you not?"

Shelly slapped Bruce. "Not as much feeling as my hand does."

"That's not Bruce," Colby said.

"Ya think?" Shelly pushed Colby to get out of the booth.

The table erupted from the surprise return of Bruce. Dishes, food, and cutlery spread through the air as Colby and Jasper led the charge, being seated on the outermost edges of the booth. The two boys sent hashtag spells attempting to bind Bruce but were unable. He was too strong.

Shelly saw to the few patrons and got them out of the diner, claiming there was a gas leak. It was a lame attempt, but the best she could manage. "It's always a gas leak in the movies and TV."

Colby and Jasper managed to get behind Bruce, allowing the others to help surround him. Together, they used Hashtag Magic to create a barrier that kept Bruce confined, but it wasn't going to last. Bruce began battering the inside of the enclosure with blasts of energy that were weakening the trap.

It was Tiddle who disrupted their efforts. He walked up to the barrier and raised a hand toward the perimeter. Before Tiddle could penetrate the shield, the Shade of Rigel flew into his body from the back. Tiddle shook for several seconds before adjusting to the invasion.

Colby shouted out to Tiddle, but the man turned toward him and smiled. Colby noticed the expression appeared to be one of satisfaction.

Tiddle looked like he was expecting this to happen. He nodded to Betelgeuse before turning his attention away.

"What's going on here?" Colby said. Then he noticed the watch on Tiddle's wrist, while his own was missing. "He took my watch," Colby said to Jasper.

Colby noticed that Tiddle appeared single-minded in how he approached the barrier. The man stood there and waited. Tiddle watched Bruce for a moment then would shift his head toward the center of the room.

A flash of light and static charge proceeded the arrival of another player. An image of Stonehenge began to appear in a widening portal. A robbed stepped through and now stood next to Bruce.

"Tiddle is working with the Druid," Jasper said and pointed to the center of their barrier next to Bruce. "The Druid is here."

Voices within the erected barrier did not carry over the noise and commotion outside. The Druid was speaking to Bruce, who seemed to be agreeing to something.

Colby and Jasper watched as the Druid created a spell then placed his hand on Bruce's chest. They could not hear over the noise of the others screams. What they could do was watch as the Druid's hand pulled back, and there remained a glowing rune branded on Bruce.

The Druid stepped over to where Tiddle stood expectantly. Reaching through the magical shield as though it were nothing, the Druid pulled Tiddle inside and returned to Bruce.

When the Druid turned, Colby caught his eyes looking back at him. There was a moment of acknowledgment that accompanied an unheard whisper. Stumbling back, Colby's mind raced again with visions shared from his future-past self.

There were repeating flashes of the basement underneath the school. In the hidden room where a pedestal rose from the dirty floor beneath a purple orb of light. The wheel of time flickered and formed at the center, spinning in a horizontal position. Three figures appeared, shadowy and indistinguishable from one another. Another flash of light and Colby now found himself walking from the room and into an open field.

Form Colby's vantage point in his new vision, he stood in the center of Stonehenge. Around him, the stones moved from their present-day positions. Restored to their original positions, all the trilithons and uprights were surrounding him. Colby found himself witnessing several repositioning of those stones and himself orchestrating the changes. Realignments, Colby realized. He was watching as the Druid incarnation of himself was performing multiple iterations of a spell. When he found his vision refocusing on the present day, Colby began to understand that this was the latest in numerous replays of events.

Colby signaled Jasper to stop his spell, and as the two boys dropped their magic, so did the others.

"Thank you for the distraction," the Druid said. "I'll take it from here, for now." The Druid disappeared with Bruce and Tiddle into his portal. The portal closed, leaving only the noise of broken lighting and ruined dining area.

"What the hell just happened out here?" The diner chef said. "Look at this place."

Shelly hurried to push the frazzled man and other staff into the kitchen. She began making up a story about guests at one of the tables getting into an altercation.

Colby began to pick up overturned tables. "If getting repeatedly inhabited by Shizumu doesn't kill Bruce, Shelly certainly will. What could they want with Bruce anyway?"

"I have to admit I am at a loss," Jarrod said. "I would have thought Rigel's Shizumu might have taken Bruce far from here."

"Did you know Bruce was taken?" Colby asked. "Why didn't you say anything before now?"

Betelgeuse stepped forward and cleared his throat. "That's not the issue here." Betelgeuse saved Jarrod from trying to find an awkward excuse. "Not with his Shade wandering free. If there is one thing Rigel has been craving above all things, it's his freedom and returning to power."

"So you knew this would happen? You were aware things would lead to this encounter?" Colby said. "Gramps, why not share with the rest of the group?"

"I did not think it would happen here. Koyaanisqatsi showing up inside Tiddle didn't help."

Betelgeuse explained that Tiddle was harboring the Shizumu of Jarrod. That was always part of the plan. Betelgeuse, Tiddle, and the Druid worked a spell to force the attraction of the phantasm to Tiddle, but once it was in residence, the specter had access to Tiddle's knowledge.

The Shizumu discovered that the spell was fake and that it required one thing to maintain a hold on him until it could rejoin its Shade.

"The watch," Colby said. "Tiddle stole my watch. What is significant about these watches?"

"They have something inside them that shines like a person's shi," Shelly said. "I could see it with my new ability. One of them shattered when Rigel broke that first watch."

"That would be the one that contained the binding spell holding

Koyaanisqatsi together," Betelgeuse explained. "When it broke, that led to Tiddle's ability to become a vessel for Rigel's Shade, but somehow the Shizumu got to him first."

"So, what about the remaining watches?" Colby asked. "What are they containing?"

"You'd have to ask the Druid that," Betelgeuse said. "But-"

"But nothing," Colby interrupted. "Come on, Fizz. Let's go," Colby grabbed Fizzlewink before Jasper grabbed Colby's shoulder.

"Where are we going?" Fizzlewink asked.

"Stonehenge," Colby said. "And I'm driving for a change, Fizz."

They disappeared.

CHAPTER 32

The atmosphere over Stonehenge roiled and flashed with magically conjured lightning. Colby immediately felt the spells that twisted and joined to produce whatever the Druid part of him was doing.

Ducking behind an upright, Colby pulled Jasper and Fizzlewink close. "Look over there, he's got both Bruce and Tiddle against that trilithon."

"What is he doing?" Jasper asked. "It looks like he's killing Tiddle. We have to do something."

"No." Fizzlewink stopped Jasper from getting up. "We have to trust that he has a plan to rid us of Rigel. Why else would he have orchestrated all of this?"

"Something is happening to Tiddle," Colby said before shushing his companions.

"You can come forward," the Druid said. "I've been expecting you."

Colby, Jasper, and Fizzlewink stepped from behind the trilithon and walked into the inner circle. They stopped fifteen feet from where the Druid stood, pulling his hand back from Tiddle's chest.

"You're just in time for the change."

Before Colby could inquire as to what the Druid incarnation of him meant, Tiddle began to squirm and scream.

Dropping to the ground, Tiddle appeared dead before the thrashing started. A ripple started at the top of his body. Rolling down the length of Tiddle's skin, the ripple ran along with accompanying groans. What little hair that sprouted from the man's scalp began to change from thin grey strands to thicker black hairs. More hair started to grow in quick succession.

As Tiddle's features were flattening on his face, the nose began to crack and reshape. Sagging skin started pulling taught, liver spots, and moles disappearing as age melted away. Rigel's face pushed up from what was Tiddle's head. The clothing this new body for Rigel wore became too small as legs stretched, shoulders broadened, and belly flattened. Tiddle was reformed into Rigel.

"Why would you do this?" Colby said. "Killing Tiddle so that Rigel could come back? What kind of bargain is worth another's life."

The Druid strolled around Rigel as he stepped away from the stone. As he encircled Rigel, the Druid slipped the watch off Rigel's wrist and tossed it to Colby. He never took his eyes off of Colby's.

"Killed Tiddle? Tiddle is not dead, just out of town, I suppose you could say. And he volunteered for this a long time ago. I am not here to kill anyone."

"Tell that to my friends. Oh, wait, you Can't because you killed them or had them killed."

"No people have been killed. Your friends, as lovely ass they were, well a golem may be a friend, but without a soul of their own, they are not a person. You can no more kill a rock than a golem."

"So then get Tiddle back," Jasper said. "Rigel is supposed to be in prison anyway. Bring our friends back too."

The Druid glared at Jasper then looked at Colby. "If you want your friends back, you'll have to do that yourself.

"If you won't help with the golem, at least send that bastard Rigel back to his prison," Fizzlewink added.

The Druid tittered. "Please keep your pets quiet Colby, I haven't the inclination to explain everything twice. Interruptions are a nuisance."

"Who's he calling a pet?" Jasper asked and looked at Fizzlewink.

"Don't you dare," Fizzlewink said.

Colby shushed Jasper and Fizzlewink before looking back at his Druid form. "Why give this watch back to me?"

"Because it contains what you will need to put Tiddle back together again. It is a portion of his shi crystal and will be necessary to draw out his spirit from the in-between as Shelly has named that realm. Its true name is purgatory."

Colby gasped at the thought of a piece of Tiddle's soul in his hand then thought back to his father's watch and the one that Rigel destroyed.

"So, the other watches?"

"Jarrod has his back." The Druid turned to Rigel and shook his head. "Unfortunately, this fool broke his when stomping on the timepiece during that kerfuffle in your back yard. But not to worry, we have a means of fixing that, eventually."

"How do you fix someone's broken soul?" Jasper asked.

The Druid smacked his lips and frowned when Jasper spoke. He addressed Colby and ignored Jasper. "When the time is right, you will know what to do. Let's not put the cart before the horse, as they say."

"As they say," Jasper repeated. "Who says that these days. Colby, your Druid self really needs to get woke."

As Colby put the watch, he held away with great care, he shushed Jasper. Colby then waved Jasper on as he moved closer to the Druid. When Fizzlewink hissed, Colby waved him off.

Sensing they needed help, even though Colby waved him off, Fizzlewink disappeared.

The Druid noticed Fizzlewink's departure and called out a spell that surrounded the henge with a new barrier of energy.

"Take care of that watch if you wish to get Tiddle back. The shi crystal is not easy to come by as it can only be attained by taking it by force, killing the owner, or splitting the soul."

"So what do we do to put Tiddle back and put Rigel down?" Jasper asked.

"Oh, just like the brute, the representation of our strength, to resort to forceful implementation. These things require much more finesse and planning, mud-boy. They also require the correct events to generate the necessary power."

"Did he just call me mud-boy?" Jasper readied a hashtag spell.

"Easy there golem, I gave you your power, I can, and will, take it away." The Druid, having avoided eye contact with Jasper this entire time, now leveled a cold stare. "I promised Rigel I would make him whole again. It was my bargain for his manipulated participation in my plans."

"I agreed to nothing of your plans, Druid. You tricked me into all this." Rigel began to find his voice and footing. "I have what I wanted and am done with you." Rigel leaped as though to enter the ley lines and fell to his face in the ground.

The Druid laughed. "You might find escape impossible, Rigel. I have blocked the way."

Rigel turned on the Druid and tried to attack with a spell, but not even a spark of magic left his fingertips.

"Oh, and I also stripped you of your abilities."

"How?" Rigel repeatedly tried to cast a spell. Each failed attempt left him more red-faced than the last.

"As amusing as this mime routine of yours is, I really must move things along."

The Druid began to walk a circle around Colby, Jasper, and now Rigel. The three stood within the perimeter of the Druid's pace as he completed the first turn. While the Druid chanted, a mist began to rise from the dirt as Emassa formed a ring of power around them.

"You see, the final act is approaching, and my part of this play nears an end, or should I say change. You see, all I have done has been due to Rigel. Dear old Uncle Rigel and his deeds got him in trouble so very long ago. And because dad was part of that ritual to banish the lousy mage, well let's just say it set off a chain of events for which I did not approve.

"Many events lead us to this point, and there are three magical acts that remain. They require the life of the past, death from the present, and a single mage from the future-past." The Druid laughed. "That last one, as you might guess, is us, Colby."

Colby had no words as he sifted through the revelations in his head. As the moments ticked past and the Druid continued another pass around the three, Colby's mind latched onto one statement.

"You've already had three deaths in the present. Does that spoil your plan?"

The Druid stopped his laps around his prisoners. "Most of my requirements do not need chronology, but in one thing, we have to be very precise." The Druid pulled Jasper from the circle, leaving Colby unable to do anything to stop what was to come. "The death here must be all your golem. They hold us back."

A glowing imprint of a hand burned through the front of Jasper's shirt. Flesh turned to mud and flowed along with the fingers that pushed through the back of Colby's last golem. Another inch of the Druid's hand pushed through and out of Jasper's chest, and he began to melt away.

Colby cried out as he pounded on the barrier that separated him from what unfolded before his stinging eyes. Tears flowed down his face in synchronized pace with every drip of mud puddled at the Druid's feet. The moment the last of Jasper was gone, Colby shuddered.

The shudder in Colby's heaving chest turned to a seizing thrash when the magic entered him. All that Jasper was, Colby's strength and will. It all hit him at once. Jasper's essence was once again part of the whole. That essence met with those of the other golem and combined to become all of Colby's power.

His body lifted into the air and burst with purple and white light.

Colby flipped upright while still hovering two feet off the ground. Without a word or conscious moment of acknowledgment, Colby flashed out of existence.

The Druid shook the clay dust from his hands and clothes as he walked toward Rigel. The barrier was gone the moment Colby disappeared. He dragged Rigel back to the upright next to Bruce and began to bind him when he stopped and looked into Rigel's eyes.

"Didn't expect I'd figure this out did you," Rigel said. He lifted his arm up toward the Druid, exposing the watch on his wrist. "You stored my power in this watch, but when the boy vanished, this was left behind."

The Druid attempted to grab the watch, but Rigel repealed him with a spell.

"I'll take my leave now, and save my gloating for another time."

Rigel disappeared into the ley lines.

"Well, that was awkward," the Druid said. "You know he really never knows when he's being played." Walking up to Bruce, the Druid flexed his fingers and let a few sparks fly. "Now, it's going to get tricky."

CHAPTER 33

Colby woke to lay face-first in the scorched grass of his backyard. He coughed out dirt and soot as he lifted his head and torso. As he sat up and began dusting himself, Colby realized that dust was the only thing he wore. What few burnt up strips of fabric that remained from his clothing, barely covered his body.

"What in the name of Mother Nature is going on out here?" Nana waddled out the back door and stopped at the top of the stairs. "Fart-blossom, where are the rest of your clothes? I hope you were wearing clean underwear."

Colby started to laugh but choked as his recollections snapped back into focus. Colby's friends were all gone, and the Druid version of himself was to blame. Colby buckled over as he heaved and wailed. With each gasp and moan, Colby drew on the lines of power deep beneath him. Emassa filled his core like no time before. Colby burst with force as he screamed.

The wave of magic that surged from Colby concussed throughout the neighborhood. As windows blew out and car alarms sounded,

Colby pulled again on the magic in all directions.

Emassa streamed back into him as it pulled away and broke every spell and enchantment it powered. Colby raised a fist in the air and shouted above the thundering winds. When his hand slammed into the ground, and a burst of light raised up from the crumbling dirt and wrapped itself around Colby's wrist. Colby stood and accepted the bond with the Emassa that ignited inside him.

The prickling burn started at his fingers and toes. Colby stretched out his digits. This stitching of his fingers and toes allowed every nerve ending was set afire, turning each fiber of his nervous system into a burning fuse. The sparks of power flowed in and across his entire body. Instead of the threads being rendered to ash as they burned, Colby's entire being transformed. He was a conduit for the Emassa and joined as one to the lei lines. He had unfettered access to all the power in the planet.

When the light faded and the last of any magic in the yard was stripped away, Colby stood in the yard, barely clothed. He blinked at the gathering of figures on his porch, and then the world went grey as he fell, nearly blacking out.

When he accepted the offered help to stand, Colby, regained his thoughts. "They're part of me now. My friends are all dead, but they are part of me. Everything is. I can feel the world within my fingertips."

Betelgeuse turned Colby around and looked down at Fizzlewink. "Go bring him a proper set of garments, please." Betelgeuse waved off everyone else. "Go on inside, I'd like a private word with my grandson."

Colby looked at his grandfather and waited for his eyes to focus. "What words of condolence are you about to wrap in a pearl of wisdom?"

"I'll have no smart comments from you. And I have no pearls of wisdom for this mess." Betelgeuse faced Colby and squeezed his shoulders. "You have to put this to rest, and you have to do it now. You can not sustain this power."

Colby stretched his hand and let out a burst of Emassa. The magic wrapped around a pixie that flitted about what remained of the garden. With a twist of his wrist and wiggle of his fingers, the pixie was turned into a butterfly. Colby tilted his head and wiggled his fingers again. The butterfly was turned back into the pixie.

The pixie squeaked out at Colby, cursing him in its unintelligible language.

Colby turned to his grandfather. "I think you'll find that with these runes, I'm quite capable of anything I wish."

"Not without thoughtful planning, control, and help from others."

"Well, then let's get going." Colby grabbed his grandfather's hand and pulled him toward the portal.

Betelgeuse pulled his hand free and stopped. "I'm afraid you are on your own. We can't help you without our magic."

"Then what's with the pep talk and claim I need help from others?"

Fizzlewink returned with a change of clothes for Colby and dropped them at his feet. "Get dressed. Nobody wants to see that."

"Come on, Fizz, you'll come, right?"

"I can't help you either, Colby. You've shut off magic again."

Grabbing the clothes Fizzlewink brought him, Colby dressed as his mother, Shelly, and Nana joined them outside. Though they remained on the porch, he could feel their worry as it dripped off their faces. He could also sense they were without a connection to the Emassa.

Colby felt it within him, though, the itching just beneath his skin that he couldn't scratch for relief. Emassa surging through him and exuding from every pore. He need only think of the need for its use, and the power poured forth from all around him. He felt invincible. He was enraged at the Druid and vowed then he would never become that person.

In the faces of his family present, Colby saw the fear in their averted stares and the distance they kept. They were afraid of him. Colby's feeling of invincibility was shifted aside by his heartbreaking. He had to put an end to this.

Without stepping to the portal ring, Colby grabbed his phone that also lay with the clothes. **#STONEHENGE**.

***

The Druid was waiting for Colby's return. "Welcome back. I imagine you created quite the commotion back at home."

"What do you know of it," Colby said. He conjured a spell from his phone. **#PLASMABALL**.

The magic gathered and formed before Colby even completed the typing. When it left his hand, however, the magic fizzled away before it got anywhere near the Druid.

The Druid laughed as he removed his cloak and discarded it over a fallen stone. "You're not going to be able to raise magic against me any longer, yourself that is." He pointed to Colby's skin and where he was scratching. "Ah, the etchings are beginning to surface already."

Colby moved his eyes to his own arm. The area he was scratching without realizing was beginning to form a rune. More were appearing all over his body as he began to look closer.

"What is this?"

"Evolution of sorts," the Druid said. "Time is a fickle mistress, you see. It is fluid yet sticky. Time is scattered and yet demands continuity. The two of us in one place and time pose a sort of knot. Have you never postulated why the symbol for infinity is a self crossing endless loop?"

The Druid explained to Colby his theory on the central crossing of the infinity symbol. He felt it meant the collision of a paradox. It is a point in the continuum that is not fixed and creates a causality that forces things to be repeated over and over.

"We, my as yet ignorant friend, are congestion in that flow of the infinite. Time has created a loop around us due to miscalculations I once made. I have swung around that single point in time repeatedly. I do hope this has been the last. If and When I am gone for good, you will know it. And you will know what you have to do to complete the cycle."

"Pace never said anything like that."

"I don't know who this Pace person is, but I imagine he might be a different incarnation of myself fumbling through the continuum. It doesn't matter in this critical moment." He disappeared and reappeared behind Colby. The Druid pushed a rune into Colby's back before stepping back. "And now, the transfer will finish."

Colby buckled over and collapsed to his hands and knees. "What have you done?"

The Druid looked at Colby and smiled weakly. He sat hard on the stone his cloak laid over. "I've begun the process of completing this particular loop. Once complete, we will have blended, and only one will go back."

"What is that supposed to mean? Go back in time? So what, I have to go back and become you?"

"No, you've already been me, from my point of view. Once we blend, you will have all my knowledge and experience. It was the only way I could ensure the desired outcome this time."

Colby watched as the runes continued to fill each inch of his skin.

For each new symbol that transferred from to him, the Druid slumped and faded. As much as he fought to not become the Druid, Colby had no choice. The transformation happened without his consent.

Time slowed before Colby's eyes. Then it reversed. Colby looked around him as the scenery changed around him. When the blurring of time cleared, Colby was back in the basement of his school. He watched the ceremony to hobble his magic, only it was a different version than the one he recalled. This version left Jarrod dead and Colby in the hands of Rigel.

Over and over, the scene changed, and Colby witnessed an entirely different version of the same ceremony. Each time the outcome was disastrous. Time kept circling back to that one event an having a retake. Colby Wass thrust back to the present where his body convulsed, and his lunch took its leave.

One last rune formed that burned the top of Colby's head. He did not have to see it to know the shape as it scorched the hair away. The wheel of time had moved and was now situated on his scalp. Colby looked over to watch the Druid fade into nothingness, leaving behind only a cloak and journal.

Colby stumbled over to the belongings and sat down where the Druid had faded away. He now wore the same appearance. Colby became the Druid.

History of his attempts at changing the past flashed before his mind as new memories took residence, muddling his train of thought.

Colby found his mind back at that ceremony, only this time, he was a participant. Colby now retained the final memory of that repeated point in time. It was the last one, the one that worked he now felt. Except there was one last thing to do to seal this final spin around the timeline.

Colby snapped back to the present. Colby felt the desire as though a final instruction was sent from his blended incarnation. He felt the looming presence lumbering toward him from the shadows that spread before him. Trilithons and uprights stretched their presence before him in the fading of the setting sun.

One thought made its way to the forefront of Colby's mind. He still needed to stop Rigel and save Tiddle. To do that, he needed his friends.

CHAPTER 34

Colby grabbed the journal that lay open at his feet. The pages he needed were already presented to him. He ran his finger over the intricate runes required to enact the spell. It was similar to the spell used for splitting the shi but centered on the focal point of one's magic.

As he began the incantation, there was a single doubt that crept into his thoughts when he saw the final rune. The wheel of time had many uses in spells. This one was the last part that split his magic among his friends, weakening himself. Colby left that piece out.

That's when he also saw the true meaning behind the wheel of time. It was there beneath him, etched in the grass. Colby at the center with two forces of magic swirling in concentric circles around him. From his place at the center, four sets of magical waves radiated toward his friends. The symbol was him and his connection to his powers all along. This was a symbol that represented Colby alone, his wheel in time. Colby was the center. His two magical forces encircling him. Four waves of magic flowed forth to the outer circle that represented the four friends who completed him.

The build-up of power released from Colby's center and extended out from his body, flowing into the robed golem that awaited. The Druid had these vessels prepared for his friends' return all along. There was a method to his madness, Colby could see that now. Only Colby refused to be a tool again, not even to himself. He would reform his friends, but this time they would be real. They just needed another spiritual force to be born from. Colby looked at the unconscious and still bound Bruce.

Reaching out with his right arm, Colby used his powers to pull the Shizumu of Rigel free from possessing Bruce. As he drew the spirit nearer, Colby began clenching his fist. He twisted his mouth in a satisfied and sneering smile.

"This will have us rid of half of you at least." Colby spread his fingers and spoke words that lingered in his mind from the blending with the Druid. "Ha'ashtagga Shizumu Dispersia."

The Shizumu screamed one final protest as its energy was divided into four. The release of spirit and magic spread to Colby's four golem friends. Once the clay bodies absorbed every spark of power required, Colby sealed the spell. His friends were back, but they were slightly different. This time they had their own souls.

The spell took a great deal of concentration, Colby was dizzy from the effort and unable to prepare for the embraces that followed.

Rhea, Darla, Gary, and Jasper all surrounded Colby and squeezed him in a group hug. Each, in turn, thanked and praised Colby for bringing them back. It was Darla who first noticed the difference in her being.

"Something is changed in me," Darla said. "I can't sense you the way I once did." She looked at Colby. "What did you do?"

Colby smiled and patted Darla's hand. "Nothing bad. You each now have independence from me you did not before because you shared my soul."

Darla looked at Colby and twisted her face in confusion. "And now, what you just created souls for us like you're a God or something?"

Colby laughed. "I am no God, not quite. But I did fashion you a soul of your own, from the remnants of a Shizumu that I destroyed."

"Ew," Rhea said. "You gave us a Shizumu soul?"

"Not exactly. I used its energy to reform four new shi from the one. Of course, I still had to put a little of myself in the mix, but we are no longer bound together. You are all your own person now."

"Sure sounds like a God to me," Gary said. "That's an awful lot of power, dude." Gary looked at Colby with a furrowed brow. His concern was evident.

"Not to worry, my friend. I'll try not to let it go to my head." Colby laughed without mirth. "We still have work to do." Colby waved his hands and released a spell. "Ha'ashtagga Emassa." The runes on his skin began to fade.

The flow of magic returned, and moments later, his family joined him and his friends at Stonehenge.

Aria ran to Colby. "Are you, how are you, are you…you?"

"I'm fine, mom."

"And not alone, I see," Jarrod said. "Welcome back, everyone."

Shelly hugged everyone in turn before she noticed Bruce was slumped over a few yards away. "You." She ran toward her ex-boyfriend. Before she could raise a hand to slap him, Colby stopped her.

"Shelly don't, he's been through enough. The wrath of Shelly can wait."

Shelly snarled at Colby and turned back to Bruce before lowering her hand. "Is he Bruce again then?"

"Yes, the Shizumu of Rigel has been removed and dispersed."

"Dispersed, where?" Fizzlewink asked. "How does one destroy a Shizumu?"

"You'd be surprised what the absorbed knowledge and power of the Druid allows me to accomplish. And I did not destroy the Shizumu, just repurposed its essence." Colby motioned his arm toward his friends and former golem. "They are their own persons now."

Betelgeuse let a low whistle escape his lips. "That is…well, it's-"

"Unheard-of," Jarrod said. "There is no precedent for such spellcraft."

Colby lifted his journal and tucked it under his arm. "You'd be shocked by the secrets now unlocked in this book." Colby tapped a finger to his forehead. "And up here."

Colby walked over to the center of Stonehenge and began an incantation. "The Druid that I became has dissolved into time, righting my course in the continuum, but the spells that brought him about are not yet complete."

"What is he talking about?" Gary asked Jasper.

"I think all the power is making him a bit loopy."

Colby laughed at hearing his friends chatter. "Not loopy, but there remains one knot in the timeline that is causing this loop to remain. As such, one must return to the past to sort out the present."

As he continued to chant and draw signals in the air around the center of Stonehenge, Colby explained the work of the Druid as he now understood it. When Colby was a child, the first iteration and where the time loop began, he was not bound with a spell. So much magic in one child was too much without proper restraint. A single temper tantrum allowed the child to create a temporal rift that resulted in his being pulled into the distant past. The Druid grew from that boy, out of necessity and desire to correct a mistake that repeated with each effort to stop it.

"Where do you think the order to not have a boy child came from? It was an effort of the Druid's to prevent your deaths. He, I tried preventing my own birth to save my family."

"It obviously didn't work," Fizzlewink said. "But it seems this last attempt did the trick."

"It's not over yet, but yes, that part of the endless trials and failures has worked. Now the loop must be closed, and we use the knowledge in my journal to go after Rigel once and for all."

Fizzlewink took a piece of paper from his pocket. "That's where this comes in, I suppose."

Colby nodded. "Yes, my friend. It's time for you to leave us."

"What?" Nana said. "I've just started to get used to the little annoyance."

Fizzlewink hissed. "Your outpouring of love is touching, witch."

Nana began to change her posture. Bellatrix emerged. "That message is for me, is it not?"

"Yes, in another time and place." Colby turned back to Fizzlewink. "You recall your Nefsmari peers swearing to a memory of you hiding away in that pyramid in the Yucatan? What they didn't realize is that they saw an older version of you being suspended in that spell. A spell created by Bellatrix under my instruction."

Colby's spell was complete, and a vortex opened, within the center was an image of a Mayan city in the distant past. Colby nodded to Fizzlewink.

"Not to worry, friend. We will see each other again." Colby motioned Fizzlewink to enter.

Fear began to grip the little blue man, but he grabbed onto one thought. He would be reunited with his family. It was inside that pyramid he would find his wife and children.

"Go to them Fizz, They are waiting for you along with a very important sarcophagus that requires your tending."

Fizzlewink made his rounds of goodbyes. Hugs and kisses, all of which the cat part of him always detested, were welcome for a change. When at last, he returned to the portal and standing next to Colby, he hugged his charge one last time.

"Things will be different when I step through?"

"Not so very different, I expect. Now go, my friend, time waits for no one." Colby guided Fizzlewink into the swirling mix of magic and time. As soon as his friend was entirely within the passage of time, Colby released the spell and closed the loop.

Colby turned to his family and friends. "Let's go home."

CHAPTER 35

Colby extended his extensive magic and pulled his entire entourage into the ley lines for the trip back home. As they traversed the lines, Colby wavered in his power. The light that usually flashed past in hues of white and pulsing purple magic flashed and winked in red tones. Something was not right.

The struggle to maintain his destination drained Colby faster than he could refill his core. At the moment they were thrown from the portal in the Stevens' backyard, Colby felt the paradox rebound within him.

Fizzlewink was in the yard waiting. He was accompanied by a female Nefsmari and two smaller demure versions of his wife, both female children.

"Fizzlewink?" Colby said as he pulled himself up. "I see you made it safely, and it's nice to see your family is well, but why are you here already?"

Fizzlewink lowered his head. "I'm afraid I failed to protect that thing your Druid self left behind in the pyramid. He got to it."

"Who got to what?" Nana asked. "What else was in the building?"

"I'm glad to find it was my body being held in a stasis enchantment," Rigel said, emerging from the shadows of the yard's perimeter. "I always wondered where it was being kept. After all, my spirit would not have been able to roam so freely if my body had been destroyed at the time of my imprisonment." He dragged a limp Tiddle's body forward and dropped it at his feet.

Before Colby could react, Rigel sent him flying across the yard, separating him from his friends and family. "Not this time, nephew. Now that the Druid is gone, we'll be doing things my way."

Colby began to get up, his head hanging low with his hair obscuring his face. When Rigel sent another blast of magic, it had less effect. Each consecutive attack bothered Colby less than the one before. He continued to rise, but the change was apparent.

The hair on Colby's head began to burn away as the wheel of time rune shone from the crown of his head. He stood straight, continuing to look down as he picked up the Druid's cloak without touching it. That same invisible force lifted and wrapped the cloak around Colby as the rest of his runes resurfaced.

"I'm afraid, in that you are mistaken, Uncle. The Druid has not gone, he is part of me now."

"And I have my body back, what's your point? I'll not be stopped now."

Colby laughed. "You have always failed to know when you are being used, Rigel. Dig deep. Look inside yourself."

Rigel snarled but began to fish around in his thoughts before focusing on his body. His expression shifted to concern.

"Ah, there it is," Colby said. He leaned over and whispered something to Fizzlewink, who stood by to help Colby.

Fizzlewink began to inch away as Colby kept Rigel's attention.

"You see that, deep within your core. There is something not quite right with your shi crystal."

"Impossible," Rigel said. The color drained from his face. "How? You've removed my shi and replaced it with something else."

"Not exactly Rigel," Colby said. He waited for Fizzlewink to be away from Tiddle. "It's a sliver of what it once was. It isn't just the shi spirit that can be split in twain."

Rigel realized what Colby was telling him in that instant. He could not become whole again, with only half of that part of his being required to hold the spirit together. "Give it to me."

"I'm afraid that is not possible, Rigel. You made that scenario void when you destroyed it."

The watch he destroyed, Rigel realized. At the moment that fact flooded his mind, the Shizumu that he harbored, Jarrod's, expelled itself from him and howled its anguish.

"Oh, did your plans to combine with the might of Jarrod's Shizumu just crumble?"

Koyaanisqatsi raged and swarmed Colby, but he was ready for it. With a flick of Colby's rune fueled wrist, Jarrod's Shizumu rebounded away and into Jarrod's physical being.

"Hold it tight," Colby said as he ran for his father. He grabbed the wristwatch his father wore and pushed it into Jarrod's chest. "Ha'ashtagga restorata."

The watch disintegrated as the crystal it held within was exposed. The rush of power that Colby called forth, push the crystal back to where it belonged, inside the person it belonged to. Jarrod was whole again.

The amount of Emassa Colby needed to force the rebinding of his father's spirit halves pulled his attention away from everything else. He pulled on the lei lines and everything around him, temporarily blocking out all magic to others again.

Unable to perform any magic, Rigel had to retreat. Though he was thwarted in keeping Jarrod's Shizumu, he used the distraction to take something else. While nobody was paying him attention. Rigel grabbed his prize and fled.

As the magic was set, and Jarrod's shi back where it belonged, Colby released his spell and fell with his father to the ground.

"Well, that was an interesting sensation," Jarrod laughed. "Can't say it didn't feel any better than when first it was removed."

"Yeah well, sorry for that, I wasn't myself when I gave you that spell."

Nana pushed her way over to Colby and Jarrod. "Are you properly full of yourself now? You still have all those tattoos. Though it looks like your hair might be salvageable."

Colby pushed Nana's fussing away. "I'll be fine, but I'll never again be the Colby I was yesterday. Nor do I plan on being the Druid I am supposed to be tomorrow."

"I'm afraid it isn't that simple, Colby." A shaky voice was added to the others. It was Pace. "I hadn't planned on jumping back here, but I have a warning."

"Pace, I thought you had limited ability to time jump left?" Colby said. "What could be so bad you chance coming back here?"

"I wish it not necessary, but if corrected, I will not have had the need. Now, look around. Do you notice something missing?"

Colby searched the yard. "Rigel is gone."

"Anything else?"

"Tiddle is still here, though we'll need to get him sorted out."

"Colby, Tiddle is not the issue, you can restore him easily enough if you still had your journal."

Colby renewed his search. It was gone. The journal he spent all this time unlocking and learning from was gone. "Rigel?"

"Yes, I am afraid so." Pace said as he began to fade from existence. "You must stop him while there is still-" Pace was gone before he could finish.

"Pace?" Colby said. "Wait, what were we talking about just then? Who is Pace?"

Everyone shook their heads, unable to recall the last few moments.

"What does it matter?" Nana said. "Let's all go inside, and I'll whip up a little late-night snack."

"Nobody wants that," Shelly said. "I'll order something."

As Colby joined his parents, walking arm in arm back to the house, a flash of memory knocked on the recesses of his consciousness. There was something wrong, but he couldn't remember.

"After dinner, we can talk about how to deal with Rigel, for now, we have much to catch up on." Jarrod was glad to be home.

***

Rigel huddled in the corner of what once served as Colby's warehouse of retreat and training. In his lap, he held the journal created by the Druid. Stolen from Colby, Rigel was perusing its pages, trying to decipher the spells it contained.

His magic was returning, but it was weak. He needed to get more and thought to brand himself in the way the Druid tattooed himself with runes.

Rigel screamed with agony, expounded by the stench of his burning flesh, as he used a heated rod to seal the wounds after each cut into his body. He was desperate to be randomly selecting runes he barely understood into his body. He maintained his task with only one thought to quell the pain.

"I am coming, nephew, and next time I am going to end you."

Thank you for reading. If you want to find more titles by J. Steven Young, check out my website or following me on social media.

website: www.jstevenyoung.com
Twitter: twitter.com/jstevenyoung
Facebook: fb.com/Author.JStevenYoung

Reviews help other readers make decisions one what to read. Please take a moment to leave a review of your experience reading this book on the retailer site or Goodreads.